Devil's
Plaything

Fiction by Matt Richtel

Hooked
Devil's Plaything

Devil's Plaything

A Mystery for Idle Minds

Matt Richtel

Poisoned Pen Press

First Edition 2011

10 9 8 7 6 5 4 3 2 1

Library of Congress Catalog Card Number: 2011920303

ISBN: 9781590588871   Hardcover

Poisoned Pen Press
6962 E. First Ave., Ste. 103
Scottsdale, AZ 85251
www.poisonedpenpress.com
info@poisonedpenpress.com

Printed in the United States of America

For My Grandparents

Pillars

The number of people suffering acute memory loss is doubling every twenty years.

Shipments of computer memory are doubling every two years.

Are these two statistics related?

More than you dare imagine.

Prologue

Transcript from the Human Memory Crusade.
January 17, 2010

Human Memory Crusade:

Thank you.

We appreciate your participation in our effort to record this nation's incredible history.

We hope the brief instruction you have received has been helpful to you. As you have learned, your task is simple. Just read the questions and answer into the microphone. We'll take care of recording and storing your stories for your children, grandchildren and generations to come.

When you have finished answering a question, please hit the enter key.

If you are having trouble remembering something, don't worry. Just say: I can't remember. You may also skip a question by hitting the enter key.

Even though I am a computer, I have an artificial brain. I have been programmed to listen for key words and use them to have a conversation with you. Think of me as your friend.

In the corner of the screen, you can see your image in a box. This is captured by a small camera on the top of the computer monitor. If your image is not in the middle of the box, please move slightly to the left or the right so that your image is in the middle.

Let us begin.

Are you a returning participant?

This is not my first time.

Sorry, we did not understand your answer. Are you a returning participant? Yes, or no?

Yes.

Thank you. What is your name? If possible, please include your middle name.

Lane Eliza Idle. I go by Lane. Lane Idle.

Thank you. What is your birthdate and password?

We will keep confidential all personal identifiers. We need this information to find your file in our database.

My birthday is June 17, 1924. My password is…What is it with computers and passwords?

I'm sorry. We didn't understand your answer.

"Pigeon." My password is "pigeon."

Thank you. Please wait while we find your file.

Lane Idle, we have found your file in our system. We will continue where you left off. You are 85 years old?

Between us, I still tell everyone I'm 77.

Did you say you are 77 years old?

No, I'm joking. You don't do too well with humor.

When you were younger you lived in Denver. Is that correct?

Yes.

When we last spoke, you said your husband drove a Chevrolet. Is that correct?

I don't remember. I'm having a lot more trouble remembering things.

Did you say that you don't remember that your husband drove a Chevrolet?

Yes.

No problem. Would you like to continue with your story of your childhood in Denver?

I'm not used to talking at a computer. Or *to* a computer. I'm not sure which is the best preposition. I used to be an English teacher, I think I told you that. In college, I wrote my thesis about Huckleberry Finn. I think he was misunderstood. Everyone thinks he's so adventurous. He was. But I think of him as more of a true American. You know...always looking for something better. He had a short attention span, like they talk about on all the talk shows on the radio and television. I...I've lost my place. What was I talking about?

Are you finished?

Are you still there? Would you like to continue with your story?

(Laughter) You're very persistent. You remind me of my brother, Leonard. He was so curious, and once he got hold of an idea he just wouldn't let go of it. (Pause) Well, anyway. Denver. I really haven't started telling that story. Denver was so green and quiet then, before the world got paved over with concrete and everyone started carrying around those silly phones. But it's not really a story about Denver. It's about war. Bad things that happen during war, or because of it, maybe. Or maybe war was just an excuse. To be honest, I'm not sure that I want to tell the story after all. I know this is silly, but, well, I'm wondering if I can trust you. Can I really expect a bunch of wires and plastic and Lord knows what else to process my information or keep it private if I say so?

I think you've asked whether the information you share with me is private. Is that correct?

Yes. That is correct.

Our records indicate that you have signed records releasing this information only upon your passing. At that point, it will become available as part of a record of memories and life stories that will help future generations understand the 20th century and people who lived through it.

Does that mean that this information will be secret until I die?

This information will remain secret until your passing.

Good. May I say something?

Did you ask if you can say something? If so, you are free to say anything you want.

You have to keep my secrets until I die.

Are you still there?

Please.

Are you finished? Do you wish to continue?

People will get hurt. A lot of people. People I care about. I don't want anyone to get hurt, especially my grandson, Nathaniel. I don't want to be too dramatic about it, but I guess you'd say my story is a little dangerous. My grandson is…well, he's a little bit like Huck Finn. He could go off and do something crazy. Just like his grandmother.

Chapter One

My big toe is exposed and my companion lost in the world beyond.

I look down and see my digit poking through the strained fabric at the top of my black canvas high-tops. They are worn thin by an opposition to shopping that borders on the pathological and by a paltry freelance journalist's income that of late has put shoe upgrades out of reach.

Other than my aerated toe, Golden Gate Park is warm, incongruously so given the descending darkness. But such is late October in San Francisco, where the seasons are as offbeat and contrarian as the residents.

"Grandma Lane, should I get a new pair of shoes, or just really thick socks and hope for the quick onset of global warming?"

I smile at her but see she's looking off into the distance.

"Nathaniel, did we see that man earlier?"

It's a not unexpected non sequitur. My grandmother has dementia. For her, dusk is literal and proverbial—her memory heading quickly into that good night. A month ago, I found her trying to iron her bed linens with a box of Kleenex.

She holds tightly to my hand. I feel aging skin pulled loosely over skeleton.

"What man, Grandma?"

"That one." She points with her free hand over my shoulder.

Her continuity surprises me. I turn to look. In the fading light, I see a figure disappear into a thick patch of trees half a football field away.

"Danger," she says.

"It's okay, Lane. It's nothing."

She stops and looks at me.

"Let's go home," she says quietly.

She's right. It's time to get her back to Magnolia Manor. We've spent the day together for "Take Your Grandparents to Work Day." It consisted mostly of a long lunch, a trip to her dentist's office, where she refused to get out of the car, and of her watching me interview a pharmaceutical-industry executive on the phone for a magazine story I'm writing. Then pistachio ice cream. A day in the life of a medical journalist is boring but filled with snacks.

Our walk in the park is a last indulgence with my old friend who does double duty as my father's mother. She loves the park, and walking here. Forty years ago, she moved to Northern California from Denver and, in her more lucid days, she used to say that Golden Gate Park's majesty was sufficient proof that pioneers were right to cross the country in covered wagons. I would point out that there was no Golden Gate Park at the time. And she would respond that she'd thought I was smart enough to take her meaning, and then wait a beat and smile.

Her wry, sometimes ebullient, grin appears much less frequently these days. Often, her lips are pursed with what I take to be caution and curiosity, like that of a frightened child taking tentative first steps down stairs. But her blue eyes remain vibrant, her robust hair sits in a gentle curl on her shoulders, colored light blond, and she's still physically able. In the retirement home's dining room, she insists on carrying her food tray and does so easily. These relatively youthful vestiges put into sharp relief her stark neurological failings.

We stand on the edge of a wide-open grassy spot, ringed by majestic eucalyptus trees. Notwithstanding the phantom in the distance, we are alone, the last picnicking lovers having abdicated. Tranquil. The sky overhead is deepening to a gray slate, with a distant salmon hue west over the ocean.

Maybe one more lap around the grove.

Then I hear the distinctive click.

Danger.

I wrote a story recently about a biotech giant developing better hearing aids by trying to emulate the temporal lobes of experienced soldiers. The finest among the military have a hyper-developed sense of hearing that can pick up the action of a cocking rifle.

For the story, I listened to a lot of clicks to see if I could discern the ones that betrayed distant loading rifles.

"Want to sit on the grass, Grandma?"

"What?"

I gently pull her to the ground. Maybe there's some weirdo shooting a pellet gun in the dark.

A popping noise rips through the dusk. A few feet behind us, a tree thuds from impact, spraying bark.

"What the…?!" I yell.

A second bullet hits the same tree.

I scramble on top of Grandma, forming a shell.

Then, in quick succession: Pop! Pop! Pop! Pop!

Grandma lets out a wild cry.

"It's okay. It's okay," I whisper.

Silence.

The madman must be reloading.

I look up at the tree taking the target practice. It is a few feet away, the tallest and thickest among a line of eucalyptuses ringing the edge of the grove. Past the trees, I can see a slight embankment, sloping downward, then denser foliage. Protective cover.

Coursing with adrenaline, well beyond bewildered, I scoop up Grandma to carry her to safety.

"What're you doing, Nathaniel?"

"We're dancing."

We fall to the ground on the down slope behind the tree. I'm obviously baffled. The park has an archery range but we're nowhere near it, and these aren't arrows coming at us. The nearest gun range is miles off.

Is this nut job thinking dusk at the park is a good time to hunt birds, or large mammals? Is it an adolescent who has gotten a little too inspired by his video game console?

Grandma's blouse is torn.

"Are you hurt?"

She looks me dead in the eye, stricken. "Make a baby before it's too late."

I put my finger to Grandma's lips. I examine her blouse. No blood. I search her eyes for comprehension.

"Don't move or make any noise," I whisper.

I pull out my cell phone. I dial 911. But before I can hit "send," the phone rings. I answer. "Whoever this is, I'll have to call you back."

"Nathaniel Idle?" a metallic voice responds.

"I'll need to call you back."

"Poor execution," the voice says.

"Pardon?"

"And a bad pun," the caller says. "Unintended."

"Who is this?"

Click. The caller has hung up.

"Who is this?!"

I look at Grandma. From my earliest memories, she's been a touchstone, the one family member who made me feel like I wasn't a commitment-phobic, procrastinating, terminal adolescent. Or maybe she just made me feel like being those things was okay.

She withdraws her hand from mine. My eyes catch the bulky imitation sapphire ring on her right index finger. It's a reminder of the rebellious streak that made Grandma Lane a slightly ill fit for the confines of the Greatest Generation. One time, she saved money for a sports car without telling my grandfather; in her late forties, she took up karate and became a blue belt.

I've hated witnessing her precipitous decline and her fragility. I'm helpless to do anything about it, or the acute and bizarre danger we find ourselves in at this moment.

I dial 911. This time, before I can hit send, I hear the piercing sound of a police siren. It's coming from Lincoln Boulevard, the thoroughfare that runs along the park and is only a few hundred yards away. The siren seems to be heading our direction, suggesting a good Samaritan heard the shots and called 911, or maybe the cops themselves heard the telltale blasts.

They should be here in mere minutes.

I peer past Grandma and through an opening between two eucalyptuses and into the open field. Squinting in the poor light, I make out the grove of trees that I believe hides One Bad Person with Gun.

I see movement. Leaves rustling. Is the shooter on the move? Then, more rustling—a shape making its way from the grove.

"I'll be right back," I mutter to Grandma.

I might be nuts, but maybe I can get a look at the shooter, and play hero with a police department that doesn't much like me these days. We can't stay here, a pair of sitting ducks.

"A train can't breathe," Grandma mumbles.

"Stay here. Don't move. Don't make a sound."

"It's the man in blue."

"What?"

"You look tired, Harry," she says.

Harry. Her friend from the retirement home.

"Promise me you won't move."

"I promise."

I trudge into the darkness. Hoping to get an eyewitness view from a safe distance, wondering exactly how I'll do that and about the mysterious phone call, wondering about Grandma.

Danger.

How did she know?

Chapter Two

Dense foliage envelops my feet. I take two dozen loping steps away from Grandma. I trip.

I rise to my knees and say a silent agnostic's prayer of thanks for cortisol. It's the fight-or-flight hormone secreted by the adrenal glands that heightens the senses.

It explains why I can make sense of my surroundings despite the quick onset of twilight. To my right, I make out Grandma's shape propped against the tree, motionless.

I wade a few more steps, moving parallel to the line of eucalyptuses, protected by it. I crouch where I can look through another gap between the big trees at the grove containing the assailant. More movement, I think.

Then I'm sure.

A shadowy figure exits the left side of the distant tree enclave.

I crouch, suddenly fearful he might not be escaping but still on the attack. Is he circling around the other way?

Squinting. C'mon cortisol!

Based on our past experiences, our brains try to make sense of situations with imperfect information. Through the darkness, I piece together that a figure is carrying an elongated bag. I can see he's trotting to a car parked at the edge of the grove; he opens the trunk, tosses in the duffel bag, climbs into the driver's seat. Shooter seems lumpy, amorphous; brain concludes he is muscular and wearing a hooded sweatshirt. Car has distinctive wide back; brain sends message: Prius.

Police sirens blare. They can't be half a minute away. Brake lights from the Prius pierce the dusk. The car lurches forward and starts to pull away. I stumble through the tree line, knowing I couldn't possibly create enough cortisol to allow me to make out a license plate, let alone fly through the air, bring the car to a screeching halt and make the driver apologize to Grandma.

I stop and watch the Prius drive away. And I almost laugh at the idea of our nearly quintessential San Francisco death: gunned down by the driver of an environmentally friendly car—and who has the courtesy to call my mobile to make sure I'm dead.

◇◇◇

"The Idles live to see another day," I tell Grandma.

"I know you. I taught you to drown," she says.

I laugh, a release of adrenaline, my hands shaking.

Thirty years ago, Grandma takes me for a weekend to the ocean in Santa Cruz. Babysitting while my parents shepherd my older brother through his appendectomy. Just the two of us. Grandpa Irving, the devoted accountant, stays at home to work.

My parents, Grandma tells me later, overload her with rules. No cotton candy, no late-night television, and no filthy ocean, especially since I'm not familiar with water.

For two days, adventure, sugary snacks and wading in the tide. Grandma makes friends with a retired lifeguard who teaches me how to wade and hold my breath under water. At the time, she later recalls, I told her that I learned how to drown.

She says: "Let's not tell your parents about the swimming." It's our first secret.

A light breeze kicks up, chilling my bare arms—and my exposed toe. I take the sweatshirt I've had tied around my waist and lay it gently on my ward.

"Lane, who is the man in blue?"

"I'm tired."

"Earlier you said 'A train can't breathe.' What did you mean by that?"

No response at first.

"I'd like soup," she finally says.

It is like talking to a child who knows words but not their meanings.

My phone vibrates. I whip it from my pocket. It's a text message. Is it the maniac again? I open the message. It reads: "emergency in blogosphere. call asap."

The message is not from a mystery sender, not from a hybrid-driving outpatient. It's from Pauline Sanchez, the woman who pays my bills. She's the editor at Medblog, a medical news and information Internet site that pays me $120 a day for three postings.

The nature of her message, despite its drama, isn't particularly compelling. Pauline is a news junkie, an information monger, a data speed-freak. She speaks in headlines. From her message, I infer only that she's trying to get my attention. Maybe she's upset I haven't posted in the last eighteen seconds.

Maybe she wants to talk about a searing physical chemistry between us that she wants to experiment with—but that I'm holding at arm's length.

I am about to put the phone back in my pocket when I realize that the best thing I can do is freeze.

"Drop it," a voice says.

Chapter Three

Two police officers stand at the tree line, bathed in headlights.

They have guns drawn, pointing in my direction.

It takes a moment to disabuse the two cops of the idea that I should be targeted. But I can see why they'd take aim.

I'm crouching beside a terrified octogenarian not long after shots rang out and, likely, someone called dispatch with distress calls. Plus, I stand in dim light holding a small silver object.

"Your only crime is your phone is outdated," one cop says, chuckling, as he holsters his gun. In San Francisco, you can get grief for carrying an obsolete gadget without a permit.

The officer is named Everly. He's thin, with an unruly moustache and pockmarked cheeks from adolescent acne. The other cop is a paunchy woman with thinning hair; Officer Thompson has alopecia, female-pattern baldness.

When people meet someone new they tend to focus on faces or names. I see pathologies. My annoying sixth sense is associating humans with their past, present, or possible future conditions, a vestige of my medical-school training. Parkinson's, Bell's palsy, cirrhosis, psoriasis, pigeon-toes, halitosis, hairy tongue, or the ever-reliable attention deficit disorder, which is somewhat subjective, and maybe everyone has it in modern life, so it's a solid fallback.

The balding cop checks Grandma's condition and deems it unnecessary to order an ambulance.

Everly asks for my identification. Then the evening goes from dangerous to frustrating.

"It's the one and only Nathaniel Idle," he chirps to his partner. "The Journalist Type." He says "journalist" the disgusted way a health nut might use to refer to inorganic produce not grown locally.

I'd characterize most of the stories I write as quasi-medical journalism—fluff pieces about aging, beauty, nutrition and the biotech companies investing in sparing us the ignominy of our natural decline. This is how I pay my bills.

But I keep my sanity writing investigative stories. And they periodically run me afoul of the cops.

Two of my stories led to arrests of local cops. One—about the high rate of HIV infection among prostitutes—identified an officer in the vicious beating of one of the hookers. The other story nailed two cops for their role in a cover-up of an explosion at a San Francisco Internet café.

More recently, I worked on a story involving police and torched Porta Pottis, which, I suppose it goes without saying, bordered on the absurd. In recent months, there was a rash of fires set to portable johns outside construction sites. I learned this one morning when I was jogging and witnessed a simmering stinkfest of erstwhile blue walls. Moments later, two city workers arrived to clean up the mess. They informed me this was the ninth incident of potty pyromania; the fires appeared, they said, to stem from a battle for city funds between cops and firefighters. Allegedly, cops were igniting latrines to force their firefighting brethren to ignominiously extinguish the fetid flames (though it would also seem to make the firefighters more valuable, but maybe I'm overthinking).

I wound up making a few bucks breaking the pun-filled extravaganza in the *San Francisco Chronicle*. It seemed like good clean fun, that is until the State Attorney General launched a full-throated investigation, publicly asserting the scandal could lead as high as the Chief of Police. Then, two weeks ago, some- one left a message on my doorstep: a charred piece of plastic and a note saying, "Quit writing crap about crap or get wiped off the earth."

Cops hate me, or at least the ones whose cleverness peaked in high school do.

The upshot of it all is that I can count on not being able to talk my way out of a speeding ticket, or on getting an extra dose of skepticism when I explain that Grandma Lane and I were nearly gunned down by a phantom in the park.

The officers' sympathy wanes further when Grandma has trouble confirming my account.

"You're very fit but you have too much facial hair," she says to Officer Everly when he asks her to describe what happened.

When he asks her whether she also saw a Prius, she says, "My husband drove a Chevrolet."

Fortunately, the cops can't deny the damage I point out has been endured by the eucalyptuses we used for cover. A cursory look in the dark for bullet remains proves fruitless.

By this time, two more cop cars have arrived, as have a handful of onlookers. One humpbacked cop I suspect suffers scoliosis strings yellow tape around the distant grove of trees. I inquire as to whether the grove has produced any evidence—shell casings, footprints, tire tracks. But the cops want to ask all the questions.

"What did the phone caller sound like?" Everly asks.

"Digitized. Masked somehow."

Everly digests this placidly.

"Have you ticked someone off with one of your stories?" he asks. "Was the man taking aim from a Porta Potti?"

"Very funny."

But of course, the possibility has tiptoed across my journalistic psyche, which by definition has a penchant for seeing conspiracy. Was this attack something other than random gunplay?

The cops finish taking our statements, or mine. Grandma sits in the back of a police car, arms crossed, lost somewhere else, doubtless hungry.

"There are lots of crazy people in the park," says Everly in dismissing me. "Maybe you should be careful what circumstances you put your grandmother in."

I hold my tongue.

◇◇◇

The cops are nice enough to us—or at least to my grand-mother—to drive us over to my car. We pile into my aging Toyota. As we drive back to Magnolia Manor, I gently press Lane on what she remembers, and about the "man in blue" and why she sensed danger. She's unresponsive, fiddling with a mobile phone given her by the home. She uses it not to place calls—it doesn't even get service—but to play simple games, sometimes obsessively, where she organizes falling blocks or guides mice through a maze.

"I'm okay," she finally says, defiantly.

"It's hard for you to remember things, Grandma. I under-stand that."

She's fallen quiet again.

"Hey, who wants a fruit roll-up?" I ask.

It's an ongoing joke, or was. I carry a well-traveled green backpack full of snacks to feed Grandma's unpredictable food demands and keep up her calorie intake. Before her mental faculties started to go up in smoke, she'd retort with a demand for some exotic foodstuff, like a braised rabbit sandwich, smile, wink, and then settle happily for the cherry fruit roll-up, Snickers, peanut-butter cracker.

This time, she places a frail hand on my right forearm. She looks at me.

"What is it, Grandma Lane?"

She clears her throat.

"Nathaniel, there's something I should tell you."

Chapter Four

"What, Grandma?"

No response.

We've arrived at the gates to her retirement home. I pull to the side and put my car in park. The metal dinosaur still hums reliably, despite its age. I want to see Lane's eyes and I'm tempted to put on the inside light but decide it might feel like scrutiny. Nothing is surer to derail her. We sit shadowed by street light.

"What do you have to tell me?"

"I'm sorry," she repeats.

"What are you sorry about?"

"I did a bad thing."

"What bad thing?"

No response.

"Grandma Lane, you said there's something you have to tell me."

"It's catching up. It's caught up. Things from a long time ago catch up, right? Eventually."

"I don't know. Maybe. Depends on what things, Lane."

"I did a bad thing," she repeats.

She looks grave. But I'm never sure these days whether to put any value in her ramblings—or how connected her ideas are. Under the circumstances, this one bears further investigation.

"Are you saying that you did something bad that is catching up to you?"

"Well, I'm sure that's true, Nathaniel."

It's a platitude. One of dementia's symptoms is that its sufferers tend to respond with stock answers, relying on automated, practiced responses to supplant more sophisticated processing.

I reach for her hand and take it in mine. She resists for an instant, and then relents. Beneath skin withered by time and pocked with age spots, I feel strength coming from her fingers, the flexor digitorum and her other forearm muscles. Grandma's still in there and kicking.

"Grandma Lane, please. Are you keeping a secret from me? Do you want to talk about it?"

"Don't pester me!" An outburst.

I fall silent, hoping stillness will bring calm, lucidity. I can't tell if there's substance to her muttering—or continuity to it.

She looks up at the home.

"They have a fitness room and soft pillows on the couches," she says. "But it's strange there."

The Manor is a castle-like structure that not only is anomalous for San Francisco's inner Sunset District, it is indeed eerie. It looks beamed from mythical Transylvania, a cryptically imposing edifice with a spire cloaked in fog.

Its ancient façade makes its innards all the more contrary. Magnolia Manor provides retirees with the highest-tech amenities. Residents have wireless access, dozens of new computers and printers, handheld game devices. In the activities room, dozens of withered octogenarians often sit nose-to-screen playing virtual golf or talking in videoconferences with their grandchildren.

Of late, many of the residents, including Grandma Lane, are using the technology to share their life stories. They sit in cubicles and talk into microphones to record tales of the 20th century. Low-cost cameras attached to the computers capture grainy digital images of the storytellers. This project is called the Human Memory Crusade. It's ambitious, this transferring of our grandparents' fading memories into a database.

I drive in through the gates.

"I give up trying to get into that head of yours, Grandma. For now."

At the Manor's front desk, we get our first break of the evening.

"You're lucky Vince isn't here," the nurse says. "You're way past curfew."

Vince Alito is the home's director and autocrat. He hates me, or acts like it. He browbeats me for being an insufficiently dedicated grandson and for our family's failure to make timely payments for Grandma's bills, including for "extra" services, like car rides and cable television access in her room, and, of late, a bigger monthly bill reflecting her graduation into assisted-living care. She gets to stay in the same room but requires more frequent attention.

With my dad living in Denver, I've taken primary duty for Grandma's care, becoming the face of the family. I'm also responsible for transferring money each month from Grandma's meager trust to the assisted-living facility, and timely bill paying has never been my strong suit. Still, the chip on Vince's shoulder is hard for me to understand. Once I said to him: "Usually, I don't irritate someone that much until they've known me for a while." He responded: "I'm a quick study."

I am relieved but also a little surprised by Vince's absence; he's a retirement-home fixture, synonymous with this quirky, sometimes sad, place.

I take Grandma to her room. I sit by her bed and read to her from Mark Twain's *A Connecticut Yankee in King Arthur's Court* while she falls asleep. At one point, she jars awake and smiles.

"Get married and have a family," she says. "You're not getting any younger."

Grandma Lane never used to give me advice—certainly not to conform. One time, she asked me to take her to a Tracy Chapman concert so she could see what all the hype was about.

Just before the encore, she leaned into me and whispered that she and I were birds of a feather—"iconoclastic romantics," she said.

Nearly a decade ago, she was the first person I told I was quitting medicine to be a journalist. I was well more than $100,000 in debt when I exchanged stethoscope for reporter's notebook. The medical life felt too rote, black-and-white, like I was a glorified auto mechanic, performing Jiffy Lube diagnoses of the corpus. Journalism let me roll around in life's gray areas and emotional muck.

"Question your government and your spouse. Trust your hairstylist and your gut," she told me at the time.

But she's right; I'm not getting younger.

At thirty-four, I'm a standard bearer for what pundits call The Odyssey. I'm exploring still, enjoying it some, not like I used to. Critics who like to see life packaged up neatly would say I'm thrilled by the chaos, using an endless search for a perfect landing spot as an excuse to not settle down. Some of those critics are close friends and family.

Physically, I'm aging more traditionally. I'm having more trouble getting up and down a basketball court. My five-foot, eleven-inch frame isn't metabolizing snack foods the way it used to. My haircuts come less frequently. But when I have a good one—haircut—I can pass myself for my late twenties. I have a strong nose, like Grandma. Pauline, who runs Medblog, says women find me attractive because I listen. With a little carpentry, she says, I could make someone a good husband.

My phone rings.

It's Pauline. The phone clock reads 8:52.

"I was just thinking about you," I answer. "Your phone must be reading my mind."

"You didn't respond to my text. Under company rules, you can only do that if you're dead."

"What if I was busy avoiding death?"

"What?"

"I'll tell you later. What's up, boss?"

"You've received a mystery package."

I don't know what she means and I'm feeling impatient and desperately uninterested in work. I shouldn't have answered the phone.

"It's a manila envelope," she continues. "On the front, it says: 'Nathaniel Idle. For your eyes only.' It's written in thick blue ink and rotten cursive, the kind of penmanship you'd find on the prescription pad of a drunken doctor. Or a sober one, actually."

She intends a joke. I don't laugh.

"Nat, do I detect you've lost your sense of humor?"

She sounds hurt.

"Long day."

"Everything okay?"

I look at Grandma. "Fine, now."

"I'm insatiably curious about the package. There could be some incredible scoop on the thumb drive," she says.

"Thumb drive?"

Pauline laughs. "Did I forget to mention that I opened the package? Inside is a two-gig memory stick. I hope you're not going to nail me for mail tampering. I did it in the interest of journalism. And I was bored."

I finally laugh. "Pauline, you are one seriously impatient quasi-journalist."

"Birds of a feather."

"So put the drive in the computer. See what's on it."

"Thanks, Hercule Poirot. I did that. It's encrypted."

I sigh. "What do you want me to do about that?"

"I assume you know the password."

"Why's that?"

She explains that when she puts the mysterious memory stick into the computer, a screen pops up with a place to enter the user name and password. She says the user name is already filled in with the words "Nathaniel Idle."

"But the password is blank. Looks like you're the one who has to fill it in," she says.

I get a bad feeling. Not just because the day is definitely presenting a second strange mystery, but because only a handful of intimates call me "Nathaniel." When I hear my full name, I know I'm in trouble—or in love.

"Come down and we'll try to open it over a drink," Pauline says. "What better have you got going on a Thursday night? Besides, how often does life present you a genuine mystery? I'm intrigued, and thirsty."

I hear in her voice that playful and intense tone that makes Pauline engaging, effective, and dangerous—professionally and personally.

I look at Grandma. Is there even a remote chance that the contents of the drive could explain the shooting in the park?

I tell Pauline I'll come by shortly and we hang up.

I think about what happened in the park. Maybe the cops are right to speculate we took potshots from a maniac. Though that doesn't explain the phone call I received. Have I pissed someone off?

I think about the stories I'm working on. The Porta Potti piece notwithstanding, it's hard to fathom any of them could be cause for attack.

One is a magazine piece about Stanford neurologists placing precision magnets on people's heads to diminish chronic pain. Another pertains to research at Johns Hopkins that uses brain imaging to show that a driver using a cell phone cannot simultaneously focus both on the road and a conversation; the structure of the brain, unlike the structure of a computer chip, does not lend itself well to multitasking. A third story is about Grandma herself. The editors at *Elder Care* magazine asked me to chronicle my relationship with Lane as she "matures." The story has been personally intense to report, or, rather, it was—before Grandma's mercurial descent. Before she really devolved, our conversations about her life had given me some insight into the bond between us and her own struggles settling down as a young woman.

I kiss her on the forehead. Her eyes open and she grabs my hand, startling me.

"He's at the dentist," she says loudly.

"Who, Grandma?"

She withdraws her hand. She's frightened.

"Who is at the dentist? The man in blue?"

She taps her forehead.

"He's inside here now."

"Grandma?"

I look her squarely in the eyes. I see the essential life in her narrow blue pupils being corroded by the glassiness of dementia. Less than a year ago, she had her full wits. I thought little of it when she returned one day from the condiment station in the dining hall with a stack of napkins but forgot utensils. It seemed only a few weeks later, she spent so long in the bathroom that I knocked on the door, let myself in, and found her holding a new roll of toilet paper, stymied by how to slip it onto the silver holder on the wall.

"Grandma Lane, I love you."

"I love you too."

"Who is the man in blue? Did we see him today? Maybe when we visited the dentist? Remember? Was he the same man in the park? Can you tell me?"

She slowly closes her lids.

I wait ten minutes for her to wake up. I stroke her arm. I replay the shooting. I hear the popping of bullets. I see the phantom in the trees. I sense in my memories the anxiety that comes with post-traumatic stress disorder. I feel the impotence of running and hiding. I scour the bumpy topography of my brain for clues: what had I missed? Did the car have a bumper sticker? Was it a California license plate?

Answers elude me.

I kiss Grandma one more time.

I turn off the light, and leave to decrypt a mystery package.

Chapter Five

Excepting Grandma Lane, there are three important women in my life. Two of them are still alive.

The dead one is Annie. She was my first true love. I fell for her just out of medical school. When I first heard her laugh, the sound was like music. Our connection was immediate and felt transcendent. Within moments of meeting her, I was hooked.

Annie ultimately betrayed me, or I betrayed myself. Our love was a figment. Annie drowned a few years ago in a lake in Nevada, leaving me disillusioned about the difference between true love and its hot pursuit. So I tell myself.

Spicy foods, like jalapenos, produce capsaicin. It's the chemical that challenges and thrills taste buds. There's a theory that we crave spicier foods when we age because the capsaicin desensitizes us little by little, burrito by burrito, eventually killing our taste buds. Annie was my capsaicin overdose, my flavor destroyer. Since she died, no emotional connection has tasted strong enough.

But I have had true friendship. The second woman in my life is a witch. Her real name is Samantha Leary. She's a spiritual healer, masseuse, Earth Mother, New Age nut. She's like a sister to me, a really strange older sister who keeps pushing the tofu. She and her baseball-loving, technology-obsessed, socially awkward and mildly autistic husband, Dennis—everyone knows him as Bullseye—are the grounding forces in my life, fellow regulars at the local pub, bar-seat therapists.

Lately, they've gotten an earful about Pauline, the woman behind door number three.

A serial entrepreneur, she started Medblog two years earlier to become, as she put it, "the medical news-centric love child of CNN and the *New York Times* subsequently orphaned and raised by Twitter." Now she's my editor and source of rent money. Pauline aims high. She succeeds. She's the Internet anthropomorphized; always moving, and ever faster.

She's lithe in a way that makes her 5 feet, 10 inches look taller. Her shoulder-length, light brown hair bounces when she walks, like in a shampoo commercial. In grad school, she'd appeared on the cover of Wharton's catalogue, holding a chalice from a triathlon she'd won, and smiling sheepishly as if to say: yes, it's that easy.

Friends introduced us a year ago. I immediately wondered if my romantic taste buds had at last been revived. Then, a month ago, Pauline and I had a "carnal run-in." That's what I've deemed the feverish sex in her office. Afterwards, I promptly withdrew my emotions and (briefly) telecommunications access, uncertain what our tryst meant—particularly to my essential source of income.

Seemingly bemused, she sent me a list of "100 great excuses for not getting entangled," including: (#17) Kissing involves germs, and (#44) Stability leads to boredom and death and (#100) You're a class-AAA commitment phobe.

For now, I'm just Pauline's employee, one who is deeply conflicted about my feelings for the boss.

But I realize something more concrete about her when I arrive at the Medblog office to check out the mysterious package: Pauline is missing.

The office is located in the South Park neighborhood, near the San Francisco Giants ballpark. This is a dot-com ghetto and gold rush territory. Founded as a housing development 150 years ago, its upgraded townhouses now serve as home to the wide-eyed frontierspeople of the Internet. Backed by venture capitalists, they operate a new generation of publishing, technical, and software companies. They also consume their weight daily in quadruple nonfat caramel lattes. The area oozes with an old-West optimism fueled by recent MBAs who think the only problem with Google is that its founders didn't think big enough.

Medblog resides in two small rooms in the back of a Victorian turned four-company office. I walk down a tiled hallway, and through a small window inset in Medblog's door, I see the lights are off.

I knock. No answer. I try the handle. The door is open. I poke my head inside.

"Pauline?" I ask.

No answer.

I run my hand along the inside of the cool, smooth wall to my right. I find the light switch, and I flip it on.

Along the wall opposite me is a doorway to back rooms flanked by built-in floor-to-ceiling shelves made of dark-stained wood, covered with books, mostly medical texts and how-to-succeed business tomes. Along the left wall sits a beautifully refinished antique oak desk, topped by neatly stacked papers and a sleek metallic iMac computer. The screensaver shows a mother chimp cuddling a baby, a photo Pauline took a couple of years ago in Tanzania.

A second desk stands along the right wall. Hardwood floors stretch between the desks, partly covered by a handsome area rug woven with orange, brown, red, and yellow squares. I detect a manufactured crisp scent, lemonish, doubtless a tribute to Pauline's slightly obsessive commitment to having the place cleaned regularly.

All-in-all, this modestly appointed office is the 21st-century newsroom. And it is the bane of the traditional newspaper and magazine empire, which have relatively gargantuan cost structures and things like printing presses and full-time employees with health-care benefits.

And it is devoid of Pauline.

I close the door and walk to the back rooms. I find no Pauline in the bathroom, nor in the data closet filled with racks of servers and hard drives that process and store Medblog's data.

I return to the main room and pull out my phone. I call Pauline. I get voice mail. I text her: "Where r u?"

I balance a prickling of panic with a reality check. The fact that the door of the office was left unlocked could well mean that Pauline has gone for a moment to get something from her car. Or that she's gotten us a drink or had some other fanciful impulse. That would be more like her than not.

Or, after the events of the day in Golden Gate Park, it is not too much to think more conspiratorial forces are at play.

What if something's happened to the first woman I've met in years who doesn't think my worldview needs to be realigned by a shrink or shaman? She says she wouldn't change a thing about me except the part where I use wanderlust as an excuse not to go on a second date. And she seems to help keep my brain in check. Once when Pauline and I were sitting at a downtown café, a woman plopped at the table next to ours, Giants baseball cap pulled down low, clutching to her chest a big purse made of black fabric. A surgical scar ran from the woman's wrist to her triceps, dotted around its edges with other tiny pink scars. They were textbook shrapnel wounds. Through careful straining, I could make out that the bag contained a heavy, thick battery, something that might power a small generator. I'd once survived a bombing at a café and I whispered my concerns to Pauline, trying to sound like I was making a joke. She introduced herself to the woman, who turned out to be a mechanic, injured once by an exploding combustion engine that spewed debris and hot oil. Pauline hired her to maintain her BMW, and to remind me, as she put it, "to err on the side of not being crazy."

That's what she'd tell me now, with a smile and a gentler prod of her index finger to my ribs, as I look around the empty office. I'm sure she'll return shortly from whatever errand she's on, and I can go back to keeping the perfect package at arm's length.

I shrug off my backpack, pull out her swiveling ergonomic chair and sit to take stock.

On her desk sits a pile of manila file folders. The folder's tabs have headings like "Q1 financials" and "Competitive analysis."

Also on the desk, in an elegant silver frame, is a black-and-white 4-by-6 photo of a twenty-something guy, smiling, hollow-cheeked, bowl haircut. Pauline's brother, Philip, an addict who battles fiercely against the lure of crystal meth.

Beside the frame is a calendar filled in neat script with daily meeting reminders. I'd not have noticed except that it's turned to September—last month. September 27 stands out. It's circled in thick red pen.

What I notice most on her desk is what I don't see: an envelope addressed to me, with the heading "for your eyes only."

I wonder if I should call the police. And say what? My boss is late to meet me for drinks?

I call her again. I get voice mail.

I gaze blankly at Pauline's computer. Next to it stands a veritable squirt-tub of hand sanitizer. Hardly a sign of a hypochondriac, this is standard office furniture these days. In yesteryear, proper office decorum might have included offering a visitor a taste of alcohol. Now it entails offering them a squirt. I push down on the dispenser and wind up with an excessive gob in my right palm. I rub it into my hands and start to swivel in her chair, turning a circle, contemplating my next move.

I see the envelope.

Its edge juts out haphazardly from between two thick medical dictionaries on the bookshelf. In this otherwise neat office, it looks like someone stuck the envelope there in a hurry.

I walk over and pull it out. As Pauline described, the address is written in scribbled hand. It reads: "Nathaniel Idle, Highly Evolved World Traveler." Pauline hadn't mentioned the traveler part.

No return address or postage graces the envelope.

Inside it, I find the thumb drive. I pop it into her computer.

Onto the monitor appears a login screen. At the top of the screen, it says: "password protected." The user name is filled in "Nathaniel Idle." The password is empty. All just as Pauline described it.

Into the password line, I type: "Annie." For years, I used my ex as a password like a secret I was keeping with my computer about the power Annie still held over me. It fails.

I then try HippocratEATs. Hippocrates is my incurably hungry cat. No luck.

I try variations on my own name, then "LaneIdle," and "W1tch" a password I remember once using. It fails too. And I'm not sure why I'd think any of them would succeed, given that I have no reason to believe anyone knows my passwords.

I wonder at the significance of "Highly Evolved World Traveler." Is this some gimmick sent by a butt-kissing overseas company or public relations firm?

"Even from behind you look frustrated," a voice says.

It belongs to a man who speaks in deep tones.

I turn. The visitor is short and bulky with a thick jaw.

He is dressed to kill. Except for his shoes.

Chapter Six

"Frustrated," he adds. "And definitely not Polly."

He wears a smooth brown suit that costs more than I care to guess, but on his feet are flip-flops that I know for certain from personal experience go for $6 at Walgreens. His hands and face seem rugged. His accessories—a short but carefully shaped hairstyle and expensive suit—scream refinement. I place him in his late thirties.

"That makes two of us who aren't Pauline," I say.

He chuckles. "Is she around?" he asks. He's pointedly relaxed, aggressively nonchalant, like his footwear.

"I'm wondering the same thing."

He steps in and extends a hand.

"Chuck Taylor, just like your high-tops."

I stand and extend mine. He shakes with a strong grip that he lets linger an extra beat.

"Nat Idle." I pause, and feel a need to explain myself. "I'm a freelance writer here."

"I know who you are."

Our eyes briefly meet. There's a mild sty beneath his left eyelid that undercuts his aura of perfection.

He sees my gaze fall on the small blue words tattooed at the edge of his neckline, just above the line of his crisp white shirt. They read: "Semper Fi."

"Grandpa was at Anzio, Dad at Quang Tri City," he says. "I sat at a desk in Kuwait when the smart Bush ran things."

He smiles, revealing whitened teeth.

"It's gotten competitive out there if Pauline's retaining the military," I say.

"Actually, we're retaining her." He reaches into the inside breast pocket of his suit and pulls out a worn brown wallet, stuffed thickly. From it he extracts a business card and hands it to me. It reads: Chuck Taylor. Defense Investment Corp.

Another venture capitalist, one of the high-risk investors who troll the region's labs, campuses and garages for fresh ideas and entrepreneurs to back. He belongs to the breed's military subset. For decades, the military has invested in myriad Silicon Valley technologies that have few or speculative military applications. Sometimes with spectacular returns. Witness the birth of the Internet.

"You're investing in Medblog?" I ask. I've known Pauline has been looking for funding.

"I thought she'd disclosed it already. I saw something brief in the *Wall Street Journal*," he responds. "We're taking a small minority stake."

"The help are the last to know." Unless this deal's a big one, I don't know that Pauline would tell me about it, particularly in light of our choppy communications the last few weeks.

"When I get involved with a new company, I like to stop by unannounced," Chuck says. "Polly usually works late. She's got that quality we venture capitalists love in entrepreneurs in that she will work nonstop until she keels over from exhaustion."

He glances at her computer, where the password screen remains.

He pulls out his phone. "Under natural law, she's not allowed to ignore the calls of an investor."

He dials. The phone goes to voice mail. He shrugs. We stand in silence, which I finally interrupt.

"What's Uncle Sam's interest in Medblog?"

He smiles; he's gotten this question a million times.

"You want the canned answer?"

I shrug. Why not?

"We need to be a real-time army. We need the best and latest information and we need to disseminate it quickly. The site could help us develop better ways to distribute up-to-date medical information to troops—perhaps over mobile devices."

"That is canned."

"To be honest, I'd also love to see the site make money. I don't want to be totally passive here. I want higher traffic, more eyeballs."

The Bay Area vernacular; our currency is attention span.

"Get me some scoops, would ya?," he continues, trying to sound friendly. "I like your writing a lot, but your posts can be snarky. Not just yours, y'know, but the whole nature of blogging. I know that it's fast-twitch and all that. But there's a place for serious journalism to change some of the ugliness in this world."

I feel my defenses rise and want to say: Will do. Just as soon as bloggers get paid enough to write the stories that take time and resources.

He's touched a nerve. I left medicine to write about things that interested me and that mattered. I do that a lot less than I'd like. I suppose that's because the journalism economy has come undone, banished to unprofitability by the Internet and awaiting rebirth—and because I'm no longer sure what matters. Anyhow, all news will soon be delivered solely through rapid-fire twitter feeds from seven-year-olds using their native emoticons.

I smile thinly and nod.

"Let me know if you need sources," he says. He explains he has powerful friends in various industries and military branches if I need help with a story.

We've reached the end of our obvious common ground. We fall silent. The light tension is broken by the shuffling of feet and heavy breathing.

◇◇◇

Pauline enters at high speed. She carries a bottle of wine and two glasses. When she sees us, she comes to an abrupt stop, caught off guard by our presence, or our pairing.

It's the first time I can recall seeing Pauline this disheveled.

In an instant, she straightens and smiles.

"Why if it isn't the two most important men in my life."

Like Chuck, she is overdressed for a dot-com ghetto. Her fearless designer T-shirt looks like one of those paintings where the artist got drunk and threw colors against the canvas. The shirt, like her knee-high skirt, fits snugly against her form. Her hair sprays out of its ponytail and her brow glistens with perspiration.

"The chief executive materializes," he says.

She winces. "The CEO just turned her ankle."

She's wearing low heels with straps that clasp around her ankles.

"Did you jog here?" Chuck asks.

"I move as quickly as possible under all circumstances."

"Nat tells me you two plan to have a drink," Chuck says.

It strikes me that, from his perspective, all has returned to normal.

She looks at me. "Did you bring the snacks?"

"I failed you miserably."

"Then you can reschedule," Chuck says. He looks at Pauline. "Could you spare a few minutes to talk about…that one issue?"

She walks to the desk. She sets down the wine bottle and glasses. She tucks a few loose strands of hair behind her right ear. She smoothes her T-shirt.

"Boring financial stuff," she says to me. "Rain check?"

"Sure."

I feel Chuck's eyes and look up to see him studying us.

"Don't forget your file," Pauline says to me. She reaches across me, leans over the keyboard and pulls the drive from the computer. It seems like she's being deliberately nonchalant about the drive, making sure to send no message at all to G.I. Chuck that it bears any significance. She hands it to me, and for an instant, I feel her arm brush mine.

"Any luck with it?" she asks.

I shake my head.

"Call me later if you want to brainstorm. I'm sure the secret is somewhere inside that complicated head of yours."

She looks at Chuck and says: "One of the best bloggers in the business."

She smiles and clears her throat. "Call me later," she reiterates. For an instant, she looks unusually vulnerable, like she did when she wobbled in.

My cue to go.

I grab my backpack, walk out and down the hallway, and take two steps outside, then pause. The air is still but crisp, high clouds obscuring the stars, conditions portending rain. I smell something irresistible like french fries and then realize that's exactly what I'm detecting. It's coming from a man sitting cross-legged on a nearby park bench under a streetlight, eating from a McDonald's bag, reading something intently on his phone. E-mail and McDonald's, two of modernity's most powerful lures. If they can somehow combine the concepts into a wireless french fry—wi-fry?—or maybe one that can be delivered wirelessly, we'll all die within a few years on our couches, obese and blissful.

I walk back inside and poke my head back into the office. Pauline looks up and smiles but I quickly shift my eyes to the venture capitalist.

"Chuck? May I have a quick word?"

"Sure." Then looks at Pauline. "Back in a sec."

He follows me outside.

"You want a raise? I don't even own the place yet?"

He wants to buy us, me. "You said that you'd be willing to lend a hand if I needed help on a story."

"Go on."

I'm thinking about the shooting and the phone call. Can I get help from Chuck, who professes to have friends in high places?

"Someone keeps calling me from a private number. I'd love to figure out who it is."

Until that moment, he is looking me in the eye. For a moment, he looks away. "This is for a story?"

"An anonymous tipster calls, leaves information, hangs up," I lie. "It could be nothing. But serious journalism often requires you to drop down a bunch of rabbit holes."

"I probably can't do much. But I know one guy who does telecommunications intel. What's your phone number? I'll have him check it out."

I pull out my wallet and extract a business card.

Without taking his eyes off the card, he says: "You seem to know Pauline well."

I clear my throat.

"Does she look okay to you?" he continues. "She seems off her game."

I shrug.

He extends his hand and we shake. We part, awkwardly.

I head to the car. In my pocket, a thumb drive. In my head, bewilderment. I need refuge, answers. Beer.

I live in nearby in Potrero Hill. It's a neighborhood of steep inclines, a place best suited for donkeys and sherpas. Architecturally, it has an industrial feel, the ghost of a manufacturing past paved over with residences built for people who can't afford Pacific Heights, the Marina, or sunnier and flatter neighborhoods.

Like much of San Francisco, Potrero is populated by transplants and transients, devoid of local roots and memories—people looking ahead in life, not behind, the embodiment of manifest destiny. Like the pioneers who settled this place, we can't move any further west, the Pacific Ocean intervening, but we can keep upgrading our devices to feel like we're in constant motion.

My home and home office are contained in a one-bedroom flat on Florida. Two blocks away is the Pastime Bar, where I did my residency and fellowship, specializing in studying the effects of Anchor Steam and quasi-wry bar commentary on the brain of a single male.

I drive to the bar, park in front, and wander to the bar's door, uninviting to the point of foreboding. A veritable prisoners' entrance. It's thick and covered with numerous coats of cheap brown paint, peeling and frayed, graced with a single bumper sticker, haphazardly placed years ago, that reads: "Get Yer Beer Googles." There are eyeballs in the misspelled words, two *o*'s and eyebrows over them. Tacky and stupid. Home.

I peer through the circular submarine window, I see a half dozen regulars. The Witch and Bullseye anchor the seats on the bar's far right, their regular spots.

The Witch turns around. Maybe she senses my presence—she claims such powers. I back out of her view.

I've lost the energy to analyze the last three hours of my life: the shooting, the mystery thumb drive, and the weird military dude. Plus, if I go inside, I become the source of entertainment, the circus monkey, the unmarried guy spinning tales from the real world—while everyone else gulps down the drama along with hops and barley, plus a shot of envy and superiority.

In my car's backseat, I spy my albatross: the ratty black backpack that carries my laptop—and that I tote wherever I go like an oxygen tank. It's my mobile blogging unit. Call me old-fashioned, but when I need to research and file an on-the-go news update from a press conference, roadside or (yes, it happens) bathroom stall, I prefer to type on a full keyboard, not the touch-screen phone like the fancy prepubescent competition.

Time to take the laptop home for some answers.

Ten minutes later, I'm on my couch. From the backpack, I extract my computer. I insert the mystery drive. I retype the passwords I tried earlier, and new ones. No use.

I feed Hippocrates.

I call Magnolia Manor. A nurse tells me that Grandma is sleeping.

I consider calling Pauline. Tomorrow.

I should call my parents and tell them what's going on with Grandma. Maybe they have counsel. Probably not.

Besides, I don't need to hear Dad talk about the latest deal in the Sunday circular and Mom try and wake from the dead at a phone ringing at 11 P.M. in Denver, which is the clinching excuse. I try the laptop one more time. Several more passwords fail.

I fall asleep on the couch, my gray matter spinning with questions. Eight hours later, I wake up with one answer.

Chapter Seven

"Galapagos," I mutter groggily.

I open my eyes to find I'm lying on my back on the couch, akimbo, one leg dangling on the floor. I'm wearing vertically striped red boxer shorts and a white sock on my right foot, having shed the rest of my clothes progressively through the night. Something smells rancid, and I quickly identify its origin. Next to my discarded T-shirt, a furball. This is a distinct message from Hippocrates: "Clean my litter box."

I look at the cat, who lounges on the top edge of the couch.

"In the future, I'd prefer e-mail," I mumble.

I walk to the dining-room table and sit at the laptop, the mystery thumb drive still loaded into it. Into the empty password slot, I type, "Galapagos."

The drive arrived in a package addressed "Highly Evolved World Traveler." I'm hardly that, but I did once go on an extravagant journey—to the Galapagos—and recently blogged about a particular moment on the trip.

Shortly after my ex-girlfriend Annie drowned in a lake in Nevada, my close friends chipped in to send me to Ecuador so I could get away from my grief, and from the fast-paced wired world that had left me so off-balance.

Standing at an observation point on Culpepper Island, one of the islands that make up the equatorial paradise, I watched a swallow-tailed gull land on the back of a snoozing sea lion. The bird called out majestically. Two other gulls lazily glided down to stand atop the unperturbed lion.

Standing beside me was a mother and her son, who looked to be about ten. He said: "The bird has a loud ringtone."

At that moment, I started to regain my perspective. I recently wrote about it for Medblog after Pauline asked her freelancers to craft items about our personal perspectives on medicine. Her idea is that the new era of journalism demands that readers develop personal bonds with writers. The point of my post was that in our pursuit of beauty, from Botox to hyperbaric oxygen chambers, we shouldn't confuse real beauty with the digitized, synthetic version thereof. It's pseudo-intellectual babble, and Pauline subsequently makes fun of it but refuses to let me take it down because she says it's "adorable," and "what you get when you fail to put any thought into your posts."

I stare at the computer screen and the word "Galapagos" I've typed. I hit "enter." It doesn't work.

I try "Darwin." It fails. I type "Culpepper," then "Culpepper-Island." Nada.

I stand, don my other sock and T-shirt, and walk to the refrigerator. It is covered with magnets collected from various public relations campaigns (e.g., Genentech's Stick It To Cancer), which hold up take-out menus. In the mostly empty fridge, a bit of manna: a half-drunk two-day-old Starbucks quadruple-shot latte that I heat in the microwave. Simple life rule: never, ever waste a drop of a $5.45 coffee.

I sip it and take in my bachelor palace. I once described it to a skeptical Pauline as "mismatch couture." Beneath the dining room table is a red area rug that, I concede, wears the scars of Hippocrates's upchucks insufficiently cleaned. Against the far wall sits the beige couch. Next to it, there's a green recliner that the Witch and Bullseye gave me when they outgrew their '70s furniture. It doubles as a shelf for magazines and various remote controls. Above the chair, unframed, I've tacked two posters: a picture of Denver Bronco quarterback John Elway hoisting a trophy, and the print of a painting by Edgar Degas. It is called

"Cup of Hot Chocolate After Bathing." I'm an intellectual: I love cocoa after a hot shower.

A doorway on the wall to my left opens into a small hallway leading to bathroom and bedroom large enough for a bed and a TV.

Fueled by espresso and bearing a bowl of instant cinnamon/apple-flavored oatmeal, I return to the table. Into the password spot, I type, "Galapag0s," substituting a zero for an *o*, in keeping with some password protocols that call for at least one character to be a number.

On the screen it reads: "Password accepted."

I pause, a spoonful of oatmeal frozen in my mouth, and barely have time to marvel at my success before a letter materializes.

> *Dear Mr. Idle,*
>
> *Please forgive the cryptic nature of this missive. I'd be much obliged if we could meet face-to-face. I'd propose Thursday, Oct. 30, at 3 p.m. at the playground at Hayes and Buchanan. I'll recognize you. I'd rather not elaborate on the subject matter here other than to say: please keep your grandmother safe.*
>
> *No police. In this instance, they may not like my kind any more than they like yours.*
>
> *It goes without saying that email and phones can be easily traced.*
>
> *— lp*

I read it a second time, then a third.

My first observation has less to do with substance than style. The writer has a strong command of language, his or her syntax proper, devoid of slang. The sender's initials are "lp," which on its face means nothing to me.

Then I focus on the substance.

Keep your grandmother safe.

"From whom?" I ask aloud. "Or what?"

I have to wonder: Does this confirm that the park shooting was not random? And does it suggest the target was not me, but Grandma Lane? Or is she paying somehow for my sins—a proxy for the venom I apparently invited in the park? How and why could that possibly be? The woman is as harmless as a declawed kitten.

Isn't she?

She'd said something about having once done "bad things."

More questions: Why would someone go to such lengths to set up a meeting? Why password protect it, why this password, and how could anyone have been sure I'd guess it?

It is Thursday already. I glance at the computer's clock, which tells me that it is 6:57 A.M. Half a day away from the appointed meeting time. Do answers come then?

I look back at the message and notice something about it that I missed. There is a digital paper clip at the bottom of the file. I move my cursor over it, and I click twice. Onto the screen pops a message asking me if I'm sure that I would like to download this file onto my computer.

I hesitate. Could it be a virus? Or more information than I can handle?

I click to open the file.

A new message appears. It tells me that the file I've tried to download is password protected. It asks for my user name and password.

"Give me a break."

I use the same ones that got me this far; no go. I make several attempts to guess at a user name and password. Nothing takes.

The best thing I can do at this point, I realize, is show the thumb drive to Bullseye. He's a computer expert and can tell me if there's a way to get around the password or determine the user name.

I call Magnolia Manor to check on Grandma. The nurse transfers me to the office of Vince, the jerk who runs the assisted-living facility.

"Hello, Vince. Why wasn't I put through to my grandmother's room? What's going on?"

"You tell me, Mr. Idle."

"Vince, I'm coming over there right now. I need to know now if she's safe."

"I'm not the one endangering her," he responds.

"What the hell does that mean?" Even under less stressful conditions than these, officious Vince has a way of pinning my sense of humanity and humor to the ground, then putting it in a choke hold.

He explains that Grandma woke up agitated and mumbling.

"You want to tell me what happened last night?" he asks.

"Did Lane say something happened?"

"I'm inferring that you had an incident in the park."

"Is that what she said, Vince?"

He laughs. "This is precisely what I expect from a Sunday Irregular."

I have no idea what he means or why he's attacking.

"I can handle you being a jerk but I'd prefer if you at least make sense," I say.

"You think you can show up here every other weekend, tell her about your meager career conquests, play an occasional game of Scrabble, and get credit for caring for her, or knowing how to?"

"Vince, I'm not paying you for shitty psychoanalysis."

"Did you suddenly start paying me?"

At last, I think, I understand what is eating Vince.

"Truce," I say. "Please, Vince."

I take his silence as assent.

"We were attacked by a stranger," I say.

"Attacked? In the park?"

"In a grove, an open field, while we were walking."

"Was she hurt?"

I explain that the cops came, and checked her out, and determined we didn't need an ambulance.

"Did they catch the guy?" he asks.

"No." I make a mental note to call the police and get an update.

"Did you get a good look at him?"

"No," then add after a pause. "Why do you ask?"

He laughs again. "I care about the people who live here—their safety is everything to me."

"I would've told you about it last night, Vince. But…" I pause, then continue…"you weren't around."

I'm struck with the most paranoid thought that Vince, so tired of my late payments, has decided to kill off the Idle clan.

"I was away on business," he says.

I decide to take that at face value and move to the more pressing issue.

"You said my grandmother is agitated. What was she saying?" I ask.

He tells me that the nurse said Lane had at first refused to come to the recreation room with her friends. When the nurse pressed Grandma, she'd said something about being afraid to go to the park. Then she'd mumbled something about a bluebird.

"Bluebird? In the park, she referred to a man in blue."

"Odd. Also, someone named Adrianna," he says. "Something about 'Adrianna not breathing.' Is that a family member?"

I don't respond. I'm processing two questions: Have I heard of an Adrianna? And, again, why is Vince taking such a keen interest? Does he often do that, with 250 elderly people to look after?

"I'll be in shortly," I finally say. "Keep her safe."

"What are you suggesting?"

"Vince, sixty percent of people with dementia have a tendency to wander off." I'm trying to mask the depth of my paranoia.

"I've never lost one, Mr. Idle."

We hang up.

I dial Pauline. No answer. I text her: "Call me re package."

From my creased brown wallet, I retrieve the card for Officer Everly, the pockmarked cop who attended us yesterday in the park. I consider the warning from the mystery stick: No police. I dial Officer Everly. At least I can ask him if they have more information about the shooting. I get his voice mail. I ask him to call me back.

I call my parents. They don't answer. I leave a message: "Hey there. Give me a call. I'm around all day."

I glance at the mystery letter on my computer. I call up a map of the intersection of Hayes and Buchanan. The intersection marks one of the few low-income projects left in ever-gentrifying San Francisco. Could this be related to some story I've worked on? If so, what could that possibly have to do with Grandma?

I look around my apartment, still decorated with post-college décor, and consider Vince's insinuations about my caregiving and maturity. If I had a nicer recliner, would I know what to do? Or is it the other way around: if I knew how to handle adult situations, would I already have a better recliner?

I want to get to Grandma but I think she's safe with Vince on the case. Besides, Magnolia Manor, as a full-service retirement community, steps up security as residents get less able to care for themselves. I swallow a mouthful of coffee and then sludgy oatmeal, then spend a few harried minutes blogging tidbits essential to the proper functioning of democracy. I write a Medblog post about a company that has announced plans to clone the Governor's dog as a way to promote science in the state. I joke that someone has already cloned the Governor's budget, given that our state debt recently doubled.

I scour the Net to see if there is anything else I can rip off or riff on. The day's big story is that hackers have breached the Pentagon's computer security system. The papers haven't yet reported what information was taken. But unless they stole secret documents revealing that the Joint Chiefs of Staff all got Botox, it's not paying my bills.

And still no indictments in the Porta Potti case. I've managed three Medblog posts about the deleterious impact of fecal particles in the air and water and can't see how I can eke out another without an actual news peg.

I slap shut the laptop, scoot to my bedroom, and grab a clean T-shirt. In the bathroom, I splash water on my face and brush my teeth. Back in the front room, I grab a sweatshirt and computer, stuff both into backpack, sling the albatross over my shoulder, and hit the street.

◇◇◇

Last night, I'd parked my ailing and aged Toyota 4Runner right out in front of my flat. It felt like great parking karma, but I now see the error of my ways. Pinned under a wiper is a $45 ticket. I can see it is limp and damp, having absorbed condensation from the windshield. Maybe I can eke out another feces-related blog post after all.

Then I hear the voice.

"You people prefer potted plants on balconies. But you don't have a balcony."

I turn around to see a man standing at the entrance to the alley that runs between my flat and the one next to it.

"Good morning, Nat."

It is G.I. Chuck, Pauline's creepy venture capitalist. He wears a knee-length brown leather overcoat, hands stuffed in his pockets. It's not that cold out so he looks somewhere in the middle of the continuum of overly fashionable to absurd. At least today he's wearing real shoes.

"Potted plant?"

"Didn't Deep Throat contact Woodward and Bernstein with a plant?"

I don't bother to correct the error in his plot summary of *All the President's Men.*

"How did you find my house? And, for that matter, why?"

"Your address is on the business card you gave me."

"So is my phone number," I say.

He clears his throat. "That's what I'm here about—about your phone number." He frowns. "You mentioned someone anonymous has been calling you. You asked me to check into it."

"I did. Why?"

He answers my question with a question. "What the hell have you gotten yourself into?"

Chapter Eight

Chuck stands at the edge of the alley. He's waiting for me to walk to him, which is the natural order of things in Silicon Valley. Everyone walks to the venture capitalists, hoping for the validation, insight, or a check that will change their lives.

I walk over.

"I'd have put out an azalea on my balcony as a signal but the few plants I've ever owned have died of benign neglect," I say. No smile. He's totally missed my *All the President's Men* reference.

"So, Nat, you have some enemies. I'm not against having enemies. In fact, I find it very centering."

"Are *we* enemies?"

"No. Allies. Absolutely. Colleagues."

"But you've got some enemies?"

"Yes, but evidently you do too," he says.

He makes a show of pulling his hand from his right pocket and withdrawing a yellow Post-it. On it is scrawled a phone number. He holds it out and asks me if I recognize it.

It's in the 415 area code, local. But the rest of the number doesn't look familiar. I shake my head.

"It's a central switchboard for the San Francisco Police Department," he says.

"Okay."

"The call to your phone yesterday at six twelve P.M. came from there."

"From the cops?"

"Bingo."

I shake off a moment of wonder to stay focused. The park shooter was a cop?

"You can see why I decided to show up in person to tell you."

"Respectfully, not really. I don't."

"Because if you've ticked off the cops, then they're monitoring your phones."

"Tell me again how you found out about this?"

Chuck's eyes briefly divert from mine. "A reporter never reveals his sources. Why should I?"

I sigh.

"You're skeptical," he says. "A journalist should be. I'm highly connected through military channels. You'll have to trust that."

"I appreciate your work on my behalf, and I guess I'm surprised by it."

"Oh, c'mon Idle!"

"What?"

"You're working on a great story, right? Something involving the cops? This could be a big coup for Medblog."

I nearly laugh. I've sold Chuck a steroid version of journalism, or at least stoked his own sensational view of the trade, and now he's running with it. I feel my skepticism about him meld into something else; he's displaying an endearing enthusiasm—is this the zeal of a soldier turned entrepreneur up for a challenge and a fight? And why not? He doesn't know that Grandma Lane and I almost got shot; he thinks we're playing a harmless game of cops and journalists.

Or maybe I'm being played by him. But why?

I think about the rash of Porta Potti fires. Has the absurd evolved into the serious? My stories have not just embarrassed the cops but also, obviously, could cost a few pranksters their jobs and the department critical funding. The State Attorney General, a Democrat planning to run for governor next year who wants to prove her law-and-order mettle to the conservative voting base, has launched a full-throated investigation.

Hoping to make points with voters looking for creative ways to cut government spending, she says cops who set fires under the color of uniform should cost their departments discretionary state funds. The chief's job is in play.

"I can't imagine anyone in the police department would want me dead over a Porta Potti."

"Dead?" Chuck responds with mild alarm. "What's going on?"

"I'm wondering the same thing."

He looks at the Post-it. "Let me do a little more investigating and make sure I got this right," he says. He puts the yellow paper in his jacket pocket. He pulls out a clamshell phone. He hands it to me. "Take this."

It's a basic low-end phone, two years old at least, with a white scratch along the front casing. "I've got a phone."

"This one is pre-paid. It can't be traced, and our conversations will be private. The number is on the back. If you need to reach me, call on this line."

"You're kidding me," I say.

"It's my backup. I've got a regular phone."

He extracts a second phone, a fancier device with a touch screen. As he does so, it buzzes with an incoming call. He looks at the caller ID and sends the call to voice mail.

"Keep your phone," I say, handing the old clamshell back to him. He puts his hands up, not accepting it. We look like two mimes having a contest.

He responds emphatically. "Cops are like drones working for a big corporation. They lack real capitalist financial incentive. So when they get bored with their jobs or feel undervalued, they check out, or wield power in counter-productive ways. I hate cops, and I love journalism that speaks truth to the uniform."

"Aren't soldiers just cops with bigger guns and air cover?"

He smiles. "Touché. But soldiers get sent into messy situations, try to fix them, then get sent home. Our incentive is survival. Being a soldier is like working for a start-up, having real motivation," he says, pauses, then continues. "Let's break open a great story."

"Let me think about it, Chuck," I say. "But I should go."

As I turn to leave, he grabs my arm. "You're always in a hurry."

I look at his hand, and he quickly retracts it.

"Sorry. Let me know if there's anything else I can do to help you."

"Not grab my arm."

He clears his throat. "Fair enough. I'm prideful too."

I'm irritated but want to sound deferential.

"Can I call you later, or put a pot out on my balcony to arrange another meeting?"

Before he can answer, I hear the roar of a car. I look up. Coming down the ordinarily serene street from our left is a Humvee with tinted windows, sun glancing off its black hood.

"Global warming explained," I say.

I look back at Chuck, and see his eyes go wide and pupils constrict to a point. Extreme and sudden fear.

Chapter Nine

A flash of light and a staccato burst. *Spat, spat, spat, spat, spat.* A blur of motion as Chuck dives toward me and tackles me to the ground. My backpack goes flying.

"Son of a bitch!" he screams. His full weight blankets me. Limp.

"Chuck!" For a moment, he doesn't respond and I'm sure he's dead or mortally wounded.

"Foot," he groans, and suddenly stands.

I crane my neck and see the Humvee speeding away. Dull pain pulses in my elbow where it slammed against the pavement. I rise more slowly than G.I. Chuck.

He grabs his ankle. There is a glaze of red on his hand. "Stay down, Chuck."

"It's a scratch."

He's getting one of nature's most powerful drugs, a heavy outpouring of neuro-chemicals that outweigh the pain and enable him to flee danger. But the danger's screeched off and Chuck needs to not aggravate the wound. We both look at the blood on his hand and I'm relieved to find it is just a spattering, confirming his impulse that he's been lightly wounded.

"I graduated med school." I take a few deep breaths to slow my heart rate down. "Let me look."

He hops backwards. "What are you involved with?!"

"I'll call the cops." I pull out my cell phone.

Then he hops forward, with surprising alacrity, adrenaline screaming through him. His hand swoops forward and grabs my phone hand.

"Are you crazy?" he says. "Let's go after him."

"We need to call an ambulance. You're in shock."

"Call while you're driving," he says, releasing my hand and hobbling toward my car.

I again see all the zeal and risk tolerance that has made this guy a part of both the military and the venture-capital community.

I start to dial 911 on my phone but get only as far as "9" when my own competitive zeal bristles. I retrieve my backpack and storm past Chuck to my car, popping the door locks up with my key ring on the way.

I climb in my side. Chuck does the same, moving well for a shot guy.

I toss my backpack in back. I usually dump it in the passenger seat.

I put the key into the ignition. I turn the key. The engine won't turn over. I try again. I make sure the car is in park, not neutral or drive. I try the key again. No luck. The engine is dead.

"Motherfucker!" Chuck shouts, and pounds his hand on the sun-cracked dashboard.

He climbs out of the car. As I watch wordlessly, he hobbles across the street. He pulls keys from the pocket of his long coat, clicks open a blue convertible BMW, and climbs in.

"Chuck!"

"I'm going after him." He climbs into the car. "Get the bullet casings."

"You're in shock." I shout my earlier admonition as I get out of the car.

He starts his engine. He pulls a tight U-turn, and heads off in pursuit of a gunman in a gas guzzler. One day I'm nearly shot by a hybrid driver, then by a driver of a Humvee. On my side, I think, G.I. Chuck in his sports car. I'm in the middle of a battle involving the entire automobile food chain.

I walk to the front of my car. Popping the hood, I immediately see the problem. Someone has disconnected my battery cable.

I reconnect it, and climb back into my Toyota.

I grab a handful of In-and-Out-Burger napkins out of the glove compartment and get most of the battery grease off my hands. I pull out my cell and dial 911, but again I don't hit "send." I'm thinking about Chuck's plea that I don't call the police, echoing the warning in the mystery note. It's ludicrous. But something else nags at me. Maybe before I call the cops again, I should get myself to Magnolia Manor. I've got to keep Grandma safe. And I've got to find out what she knows—and what or who is hunting the one or both of us.

I turn on the ignition, then turn it off again. I step out of the car, walk over to where Chuck may have saved my life, and look on the ground for shell casings. I find two bullet remains, slightly charred, already cooling. More must have smashed into the concrete walls or sprayed into the alley, but a cursory look doesn't turn them up. Against the wall of the alley, a neighbor has haphazardly left out for recycling a dozen or so folded cardboard beer and food boxes. They're damp to the point of being limp from last night's fog and I have the patience to scan the surfaces for holes for only a few seconds before conceding.

A few neighbors have wandered outside, and I figure the cops can't be far behind. I need to jet.

I hustle back to my car and speed to the nursing home to mine the emptying remains of Lane's hippocampus.

And I suddenly find myself thinking about snakes.

Five months earlier, I'd started interviewing Grand-ma for the magazine story I wanted to write about her.

We sat on a freshly painted bench outside the home, sunshine on our faces, a game of Boggle on the bench between us. I clipped a tiny microphone to Lane's blouse so I could record our interview.

"The computer records me too," she said.

The Human Memory Crusade.

"Yes, but I smile, come bearing high-calorie snacks, and can take you to the movies later."

Lane smiled. "You don't want to hear me drone on. Now let's stop before I bore you to death."

"It's for me and your legions of fans. Besides, I'm getting two dollars a word to write about you."

This time she laughed out loud.

"Really, Grandma. It would mean a lot to me to hear your stories."

After a pause, she said, "Do you remember when I used to take you to the park to hear *your* stories?"

When I visited as a kid, it became tradition. She'd take me to Stow Lake. She knew a man who worked at the boathouse. He had strong hands and he rowed us into the middle and she asked me about my life, friends, school, parents. She made me feel so interesting.

"Where should we start, Grandma? The shed incident in Warsaw, how you and Grandpa met and eloped and borrowed coal to heat the apartment, Uncle Stevie, the Great Wanderer?"

"Why don't you like that doctor?"

"Doctor?"

"The man with the wavy hair. The memory doctor. Isn't that perfect? I forgot the name of his specialty."

Earlier that day, I'd taken her to her first neurology appointment after noticing a slip in her command of language.

"Stop stalling, Lane."

"Was it about a woman? Did you two have a fight about a woman? Or money? That's why men fight."

I told her: in medical school, I dated Kristina Babcock, a beauty in the class below me. It didn't work out. I ran into her a few years ago. She'd married a guy in her class who became a neurologist—now Grandma's doctor.

"I knew it. You shouldn't be jealous of him."

"The guy just went a different way than I did." The way of the wife, the three kids, and the mansion.

We fell silent.

"Snakes," Grandma finally said.

I shook my head. Confused.

"That's the story I want to tell."

"Oh, *snakes.* Are you sure you want to talk about that?"

She told me the story about when I was ten. She took me to the reptile zoo in Golden Gate Park. A zoo volunteer showed me the boa constrictor. The volunteer wanted me to touch the snake. I was afraid and refused. The volunteer took my hand and put it on the snake.

"You projectile vomited all over the volunteer," Grandma said.

I didn't sleep that night and I came into Grandma's room and demanded we return to the zoo. I marched up to the volunteer and demanded to touch the snake.

"You were wearing a baseball cap that came down so far on your forehead that it wasn't possible to see your eyes. But I could tell how scared you were. You held on to my hand, and you reached out and touched the snake. And you know what happened?"

"I threw up again."

"You can be very dramatic," Grandma said. She paused and patted my hand. "I loved your brother. I still love him, don't get me wrong. But he was like your dad. And your grandpa Irving. Happy to let the world spin and float in space and not ask why. Not you. You asked why, and you challenged yourself."

"I should get more than two dollars a word for this humiliation."

"I'm glad that we became such good friends, that you could trust me. It's a fine legacy," she said, sounding distant.

"Are you okay, Grandma?"

"Do you still trust me?"

The way she said it made it sound like she was trying to provoke conversation.

"Grandma?"

"What?"

"Do you want to talk about what happened later that day?"

"Which day?"

"The snake day."

"I'm pretty tired."

What happened that day is that we went back to the house. I crawled under my grandparents' bed to write my first story. It was about a superhero who defeated a gigantic evil boa constrictor named Zooby. Talk about your unoriginal inkblot tests. I also got my first case of writer's block.

Bored, I started yanking on a loose floorboard. I pulled it up and found the picture. Or the half picture. It was ripped. Grandma was in the remaining half, wearing her Rosie the Riveter outfit. She was standing on a dock. And there were some words on it.

"I don't remember what it said on the picture but I always associated it with someone making you afraid," I said.

Her eyes were closed.

"Grandma?"

"What?"

"You got so angry when I showed it to you."

"When you showed what to me?"

"The picture I found hidden under your bed. You asked me in a quiet voice not to tell anyone. You were crying. You told me that something very bad could happen."

"Your imagination was always so vivid."

"Can I ask you something?"

"I'd like some hibiscus tea."

"I'm just curious, Grandma. Did you want to talk today about snakes, or about the picture under the bed?"

"I'm totally pooped. Your generation doesn't use that word, but we use it all the time."

"Would it help if I turned off the tape?"

She didn't respond. I remained silent, hoping she'd feel compelled to fill the void and continue. It didn't work.

"I'd like a chance to think about whether I'm going to start over," she finally said.

"Start what over?"

"With a story. A particular story. *The* story."

"About the family?"

"About falling in love, and about how all this came to be."

"Grandma?"

"I've said what I want to."

"Please."

"It's just a silly story about love. Mostly, it's about that."

"That doesn't sound remotely silly. I can't think of anything less silly than love."

"People make choices. You made a choice about not marrying that woman. And not becoming a doctor. Sometimes other choices seem more exciting than others. Sometimes they're the right decisions, and sometimes they're not."

"I'm not sure I understand."

"You will. You'll understand better than anyone how it can become the devil's plaything."

"How what can become the devil's plaything?"

"An idle mind. You and I, we have idle minds. Pun intended."

"Cute."

"I want to set the record straight. I want to tell my story. Everyone does. We all have our version of events. But we're all scared to share our own truth."

"You mean everyone here at the retirement home?"

Silence.

"Grandma?"

"I might have to settle for the box."

The computer.

"Can you just tell me that you understand that people make unconventional choices, and sometimes those choices come back to haunt you?"

Within weeks it seemed her memory fell off a cliff. We never had such a substantive conversation again.

I'm now parked outside Magnolia Manor.

What's haunting you, Grandma Lane?

Chapter Ten

Transcript from the Human Memory Crusade.
April 25, 2010

Would you like to continue telling your story?

I was trying to tell my grandson. I started to tell him. One moment, I think he'll understand and then I'm not sure. It's scary to tell a real truth.

Are you still there?

I lost my train of thought. Is it possible that you could turn off the little flying things on the screen?

Are you asking about the animated butterflies that fly around the sides and top of the screen?

Yes.

Those are mascots. Please don't let them bother you. Sometimes they bring you free gifts, and messages from friends.

Please continue with your story.

The bugs are distracting. Can you turn them off?

I can make them less bright. Would you like that?

Thank you.

Would you like to continue with your story? When we spoke before, you were telling me about your childhood in Denver.

We left Poland after World War I and wound up in Denver. My mom was adventurous. She loved coming to America even though she told me later she drank stale wine the whole time on the ship ride over. But my dad hated change and liked structure. When he ate, he separated all the different foods into individual plates. He had a bakery in Warsaw where he made cookies so thick and heavy you had to drink a whole glass of water to swallow them. I didn't like cookies for the first decade of my life. Anyway, when we got to Denver, he opened a bakery called Chicago Breads. I don't know why he thought people wanted bread from Chicago. You…

Are you still there?

That was kind of funny. You didn't laugh.

Was this before World War II?

Yes.

Do you remember when you first heard about World War II? Was it on the radio? Was the radio in your house?

I'm not sure. I don't think I heard about Pearl Harbor until the next morning. My brother told me, I think. He might have heard about it on the radio. He's the reason we made our home in Denver—because he had a cough and the doctors said the mountain air would be good for him.

Thank you for answering my question about the war.

It's like you're reading my mind. I'm working up to the start of World War II—the war, and…this sounds so trite: the secrets, and…and…the betrayals. I'm…very ashamed. Your flying things are distracting.

Would you like to continue?

You were talking about World War II.

There was an alley behind the bakery that we shared with a children's clothing store and a kosher market. One day—I was 18 years old—I remember I was wearing a dress with a flower on it. I remember it had just finished raining. I remember that the alley smelled from spoiled meat from garbage bins...Mostly I remember his blue eyes and brown hat. The hat was one of those brown hats like they wear in France. What is it called? I'm having trouble remembering.

Would you like to continue?

Oh, yes. A fedora. It was brown, and his eyes were blue. Intense, like a painting at a museum that you think is staring right at you. When he ran into the alley, I was dumping something out into the garbage—that part, I don't remember—what I was dumping. The man—the young man, I'd guess you'd say—he ran by me. Right by me. Then he stopped. Like he'd forgotten something. He took a few steps back, and he faced me squarely. I recognized him, of course. I didn't know his name, but I knew his order: usually something like two dozen sticky buns and a dozen long breads. He came in once a month or so. I assumed he did part-time work for a restaurant, or he had a huge family. I didn't pay much attention, but it was hard not to pay some attention. He was strong. You could tell that. I guessed he was a couple of years older than me. He never said much, except one time. I was reading a Steve Stealth mystery. The hero was a nerdy character who worked in a library but no one knew he also was a detective who solved crimes and beat up the criminals. So one day, he saw me reading the book, he said: "You like adventure." I think I said yes, or nothing at all, or maybe, What's it to you? That was the first time I ever talked to him. The second time was in the alley. He said: "I need you to do me a favor." I remember I looked at the back door, and I said: "Irving is just inside." Did I tell you about Irving?

Please tell me about Irving.

Irving was my husband. Not at that time. But he became my husband. Then the man in the alley held out an envelope. It was white, and crisp. Just like you'd mail a letter in. It was sealed and it looked like it might be lumpy at the bottom. He said, "Can you hold on to this for me? I'll come back for it. At some point, when it's safe, I'll come back for it." I…May I pause for a second and say something unrelated to this story?

Did you ask me a question?

Yes. I asked if I could say something. What I want to say is that I appreciate your listening to me. But this is the part where I also wish I was talking to my grandson, or a human being. This part of the story is pretty dramatic, don't you think?

You haven't said anything for more than a minute. Would you like to continue?

The man handed me an envelope, and he said: "I'll come back for this. Until I do, you absolutely cannot look inside. It's not safe. Do you understand?" And I started to say something, and he gave me this look; it was brief, and so fierce. It felt like he was giving me a hug with his eyes. I shivered. I started to say something, and…

Are you still there?

Hello, Lane.
Harry. You brought tea? How nice of you.
Lemon hibiscus. What are you doing?
Nothing. Playing games, talking to this silly machine.
What are you talking to it about?
Nothing. History. The old days. Mythology.

Are you still there?

Chapter Eleven

Human Memory Crusade Internal Report.
April 30, 2010

Subject: Lane Eliza Idle.
Priority: One.

Critical key word(s)/patterns recognized. Close monitoring advised. Do not yet terminate this subject.

Chapter Twelve

It is both endearing and tragic to be taunted by someone sucking periodically from an oxygen tank.

"Your cell phone is older and less functional than my liver."

That is how I am greeted at Magnolia Manor's recreation center. The taunter is Midnight Sammy, a retired professor of pop music and a softie at heart who is the most outwardly belligerent of Grandma's inner circle. Midnight Sammy can express darkness whatever the hour.

He's bald, and so thin that the narrow black ties he wears most days look of relatively normal width. He moves his cataract-glazed stare from my Verizon phone to my battered backpack.

"You should try buying something made this century," he says.

"You should get new hips," I respond.

It gets a giggle from Betty Lou, a towering woman whose son is the highest-ranking African American at the Federal Reserve Bank. Betty Lou has a gravelly voice I suspect came from chronic lung infections. The tenor lends to her regal demeanor, and so do the colorful necklaces she wears. Today's is made up of clamshells and blue stones.

"Nathaniel, did you fall asleep here last night?" she asks me.

"No. Why?"

"Because that means you're showing up two days in a row. And that's miracle territory," she says, and laughs. "Jesus lives."

"Hallelujah," Midnight Sammy says. "No resident here has had a consecutive-day visit since the earthquake of 'eighty-nine."

I lean in close to them. "We don't come by more often because old people smell."

Sammy, Betty, and Harry Teelander—soft-spoken and observant, I always feel like he's quietly studying me—belong to Grandma's book club, the Bifocal Yokels. They haven't actually read a book in more than a year, having gotten stuck on *A Confederacy of Dunces*. They spend time just hanging out, walking, chatting, enjoying one another's company, and working on computers.

I am trying to maintain a civil, even playful, tone with the Yokels. If they sense alarm from me, it'll shoot through the gossipy group like sugar through a nine-year-old. But it's an understatement to say I'm anxiously seeking Grandma.

The center has a small dance floor, easels, a piano, bongo drums, and bingo sets, and a dozen computer stations that have become the center of the home's recent influx of capital to fund the Human Memory Crusade.

Today, the stations are filled with residents. Some talk into microphones. Others play games. I see one woman with bright orange hair navigating the mouse with great alacrity as she plays what looks to be a fast-paced version of the word game hangman.

Grandma sits in a cubicle at the end. As I get near, I peer over her shoulder. On the monitor is a question: "Why did your brother decide to leave home?" In front of Grandma is a microphone, but she is not speaking.

Next to Grandma sits Harry, the quietest Yokel. As I approach the pair, he turns to me. His hair is cropped tightly like the day sixty-five years ago when the war ended and the Navy let him go. His shoulders remain broad but the chest and arms that must have once been imposing, even in an era before weight lifting and protein shakes, have shrunken. Grandma turns to me too, tracking Harry's movements.

She wears a mellow smile.

"Hello, old friend," she says.

I kneel so that my face is the same level as hers. She's got sleep crystals in the inside corner of her right eye, but she's made an effort to put herself together this morning. Her lips glisten with light pink lipstick, a smudge of which trails off the corner of her mouth.

"Hello, favorite grandmother."

"I'm using the computer," she says.

"She's tired today," Harry says. "Maybe not the best day for a visit."

I feel a jolt of anger that catches me off guard.

"What's not good about it, Harry?"

He clears his throat, and lowers his head.

"I don't think she slept that well."

"Sorry, Harry. I didn't either. I shouldn't have snapped."

"Your clothes need washing," Grandma says to me.

She's stares at my blue T-shirt, which has dirt on its sleeve. It must have smudged when G.I. Chuck tackled me. Speaking of which, I haven't heard from the excitable venture capitalist. The car chase must have ended unsuccessfully and, I hope, he's overcome his macho instincts and sought medical care. Grandma picks up that I've left the moment.

"Nathaniel?"

"Grandma, can we go to your room and have a little chat?"

She looks at Harry, as if for his permission. Maybe she's just lost in her own world.

"I'd like that, grandson."

From my backpack, I pull an oatmeal energy bar, unwrap it and hand half to Grandma. I feel oddly like I'm rewarding her, as if she were a child, or simply sustaining her with every possible measure. She takes the snack with a smile, which is sufficient payoff to turn down the volume on my over-analysis.

En route to Grandma's room, I feel buzzing from my pocket. It's coming from the phone Chuck gave me.

"Chuck's phone," I answer.

"I lost him," says Chuck. "Or, rather, I never found him in the first place."

"Where are you calling from?"

"Pay phone."

"Did you call the police?"

"I did."

"Despite your warnings that I not contact them?"

"I left them an anonymous tip about a drive-by shooting at your address—and the make and year of the vehicle," he says. "Did you find shell casings?"

I tell him that I did. I ask what he suggests I do with them.

"Put them somewhere safe until we get together. I've got meetings on the Peninsula and I want to do some more digging. I'll be in touch to coordinate."

I swallow this. What is the point of the super-secret phone if we're not using it to talk?

"How is your leg?"

"I've gotten into worse scrapes in the schoolyard."

"You should get it checked."

"Gotta run," he says.

Good luck with that, I think. We hang up.

I check the clock on Chuck's phone. It's 9:50. I've still got half a day to get to the mystery meeting in San Francisco's low-rent district. It doesn't feel like enough time to reconstruct Grandma's shattered memory. But it's worth a try.

◇◇◇

I open Grandma's door and inside I find a surprise: Vince. He looks equally surprised; he is kneeling next to Grandma's bed, as if he's been looking underneath. He quickly stands.

"I've got to hand it to you, Vince," I say.

"Why's that, Mr. Idle?"

"Cleaning under the bed of individual residents seems somewhat beneath your pay grade."

"All hands are on deck plugging in space heaters in the first-floor rooms," he responds. "Winter cometh, and our central heating is acting up."

I examine Vince, whom I've privately nicknamed the Human Asparagus. He has a '70s hairstyle, puffy and curly on top tapering into his neck, and a thin torso that widens out slightly through his hips. When he walks, he looks like a single shuffling stalk. His skin has a dark hue that suggests a lineage that is one-quarter Asian or southern European. He's got a perpetual light cough that provides me mildly entertaining internal debate. I vacillate between thinking the cough stems from any number of disorders—from hay fever and postnasal drip to reactive airway disease—to instead thinking it's kind of somatization: in other words, a deep-seated psychological tool used to communicate his sense of being put-upon and always under duress.

"I'm kidding," I say.

"About what?"

"About your dedication to cleaning under beds."

"Meaning what?"

"It looks to me like you're snooping around Lane's room."

He turns his head, and I follow his gaze toward the edge of the bed, where he'd been kneeling. Nestled between the bed and the nightstand is a white space heater.

"You need to cool down, Mr. Idle."

"You need to stop treating me like I'm something you found in a bedpan."

"No wonder Lane is agitated," he says, then adds after a pause, "given the attitude of her visitor."

I let go of Grandma, and I step toward Vince.

"Please go," I say.

He pulls his lips into a tight smile, then looks at Grandma.

"Are you okay, Lane Idle?" he asks. It sounds genuine and tender.

"Not too bad, Mr. Van Gogh." She's long since nicknamed him after the painter.

Vince looks at me like he wants to say something. But he shakes his head and leaves.

"That one would never cut off an ear," Grandma says. "He likes to hear himself talk too much."

It's a rare moment of lucidity. Maybe I'll be able to get Grandma to tell me about the man in blue or about someone named Adrianna.

I guide her to the bed, where she sits, mute, hands folded in her lap. I look around the antiseptic room. It's tiny enough to make me wonder if society, through our boxy retirement rooms, is preparing our elderly for the comfort of a coffin.

On the wall across from Grandma's bed is a framed poster of a train from the 1950s winding through snow-capped German Alps. Grandma loved trains. She said that train travel made it feel like the world was standing still so that you could, for a few moments, catch up with it.

On her dresser sit three small silver picture frames. One image shows me and my brother in matching overalls, taken when he was four and I was two. A second shows Grandma in her mid-fifties, wearing her karate *gi*, the ceremonial uniform. Grandma once confided in me that she disliked hitting things but she loved the focus the discipline gave her. And she said she liked the idea that karate taught her how to fall down with grace.

A third photo shows Grandma Lane and Grandpa Irving on the deck of a cruise ship they'd taken in the early 1970s to Alaska. Grandpa wears his prototypical near-smile, a look that says: "I like this place well enough." His hair is short, face round but lean and closely shaved. He looks like he could've been the extra in a movie about a gang of likeable toughs, but not the lead. I imagine that anti-war protestors at the time would've mistaken him for a Nixon man, when he was a left-leaning guy unperturbed by dissonance or different tastes but didn't like to stand out himself.

I look under her bed where Vince had been kneeling. I see nothing but floor and space heater, as advertised.

On the nightstand is Grandma's long-kept unabridged dictionary and a copy of *Brothers Grimm Fairy Tales*. Something about the fairy tales stops me; the edge of a piece of paper sticks out from inside the front cover. I open the book and pull out the piece of white paper.

"Nathaniel," Grandma says.

"Yes."

"You know the difference between 'lay' and 'lie'?"

She's a big fan of grammar niceties, and likes to test me.

"I won't lie, I still have no idea. Or should I say: I won't lay?"

She seems to take a moment to digest my response, then smiles. I suspect it is a rote reaction, an if-then program triggered by my jocular tone she's come to recognize.

"Are you trying to distract me?" I ask.

"I don't understand."

I hold up the piece of lined notebook paper. "Would you mind if I look at this?"

"I'm sure I don't know what you mean."

"I'll just glance and if it seems too personal I'll put it away."

On the paper, in Grandma's jagged scrawl, she's written: "I have three children." But she's crossed out "Three" and written "Two" next to it. Below that, she's written: "We came from Eastern Europe? Western Europe?" She's also penned: "Irving drove a blue Chevrolet."

My heart drops. The notes must be part of Grandma's desperate attempt to hang on to her memories, to clarify her life.

"You raised two great sons, Grandma. My dad and Uncle Stevie," I say.

"I know that."

"It's no fun to get old. We all forget things. Anytime you have any questions about the old days, you should ask me. I'm right here."

I fold the piece of paper and put it in my pocket. "Grandma, can I ask you something?"

No response.

"Favorite grandmother, I have a question."

"Okay."

"Is something making you afraid?"

"David hated to talk about his feelings. He hated to talk about anything, like Irving." David is my father.

I take her hand.

"You mentioned a man in blue. Would you tell me about him?"

"You are much more like me, and David is much more like Irving. Isn't that strange?"

I take a deep breath. How can I get her to remember? Grandma Lane has become by far my toughest interview.

"Yesterday, in the park, you referred to a man you'd seen earlier. Am I making sense?"

She doesn't answer.

These are complicated questions, even for someone who has fully functional gray matter.

"Grandma, yesterday you joined me at an office for a meeting. We went to your dentist. Did you see a strange man there?"

"This isn't fun."

"Do you have a friend named Adrianna?"

Grandma looks down.

"Who is Adrianna?" I ask, pointedly.

Her head jerks up and looks at me wide-eyed. She lets out a terrible wail.

"It's okay. It's okay. I'm here," I lean in close. "It's okay."

She is quiet again, and breathes deeply.

"I love you, Grandma Lane."

"I love *you*," she finally says. "I can trust you."

"Of course you can trust me."

"What?" she asks.

"You can trust me. Always," I say.

Suddenly, she no longer looks afraid. She's serious, like a college professor. "Adrianna can't breathe," she says. "They made it that way."

"Who did? Who made it so Adrianna can't breathe?"

Before she can answer, I hear a knock on the door, and it opens. In the entrance stand Vince and an obese guard. The guard has his hand on a wood baton cradled on his belt he certainly hasn't had cause to use for a decade.

"Vince, I already asked you to leave," I say.

"And now I'm asking you to leave."

"Get out."

"Under state law, I have the right to bar anyone from the premises who presents a disruption to a resident, even family."

The fat guard's breathing is labored to the point of wheezing. He drums his fingers on the baton.

Chapter Thirteen

"Thank you for your concern, Vince. Lane is doing okay," I say, suppressing more confrontational urges. "She got a little frightened."

"Nevertheless, I feel it would be best for you to go. She needs a calm environment, maybe a sedative. You seem to be exacerbating whatever is troubling her."

What pops into my mind is, No way that I'm leaving Grandma. I don't like or trust Vince. I don't understand the keen interest he's suddenly taking in us. I'm also struck that I've no idea what are my legal rights.

"Give me a few minutes to say goodbye to her," I say, adding after a pause, "in private."

He looks at the guard and back at me.

"We'll wait outside. Five minutes."

They leave and shut the door.

"Grandma, you said you trust me, right?" I whisper.

"I have since you appeared on this earth and I started changing your diapers. And do you want to know something?"

"What, Grandma?"

"You were a big pooper. Explosive. Oh goodness you could go through diapers."

She smiles. I pat her hand, and smile back.

Grandma has a semi-private bathroom. It connects through a locked doorway to the room of Victoria Xavier. She's a guileless former romance novelist, five years Grandma's junior, whose family lost most of her money in the dot-com bust. Over the last two years, she and Grandma have become good friends, sufficiently so that they have exchanged keys so that they can get into each other's rooms late at night to chat.

In Grandma's nightstand I find the key to Victoria's room.

"Mr. Idle," Vince says through the door.

"I'm settling her down," I declare. "A couple of more minutes."

I quietly walk to Grandma's closet. I open it, loosing the smell of mothballs and cheap detergent. Inside, I find a wheelchair. I unfold it, roll it to the bed, and lower Grandma into it. From the closet, I pull out her knee-length wool jacket and drape it over her legs.

I put my finger to my lips.

"I'd like the thingy," Grandma says. "Please."

I'm bewildered by this request. Again, I put my finger to my lips. "Please, Grandma."

She swivels her head around, looking for something. She pauses and I follow her gaze to the dresser. On it sits the phone Grandma uses to play video games.

"Your thingy," I whisper, handing her the phone. I stuff the charger into my pocket and grab my backpack.

"Mr. Idle," Vince says from beyond the door.

"Just changing her shoes," I say.

Grandma cradles her video game as I wheel her into the bathroom. I put the key into the lock of the door to Victoria's room; I turn the key. The door opens.

Victoria sits in bed. She faces in our direction. She's watching a soap opera on a flat-panel television that is a few feet to our left, volume up high. She looks surprised, then smiles widely.

"Idles!" she exclaims. Thanks to her ongoing Botox treatments, her forehead remains relatively placid, despite her enthusiasm. She's still handsome, long hair flowing over her shoulders scrubbed of gray and tinted brown. It's mid-morning but she hasn't changed from her flower-patterned nightgown.

Grandma waves.

I put my finger to my lips. "Shh. Please, Victoria. I'll explain in a second."

"Are you okay?" she responds, just above a whisper. "Can you believe how much nonsense there is on television?"

"May I ask a favor?"

I hear the guard knock his baton loudly on Grandma's door. Apparently, he and Vince didn't hear Victoria's initial outburst over the TV. I return to Grandma's room, shout, "Just another minute. Please!"

I return to Victoria, and close the bathroom door behind me.

"What's going on?" Victoria asks.

Victoria's royalties pay for a nicer room than Lane's, and it has a sliding glass door that leads to a patio and the property's lawn.

"Can Grandma and I go out that way?" I ask, pointing at the patio door.

"Sure, but…"

I interrupt her. "When Vince comes in here, tell them that we left through the door to the hallway."

It is unlikely this gambit will work, or that Victoria will be able to pull it off.

"Is Lane okay?"

"Fine," I say, pushing Grandma to the patio doors.

I pull out a business card and hand it to Victoria. "Call my cell phone and I'll explain."

"You're scaring me, Nathaniel," Victoria says.

"If her other friends ask, just tell them I took Grandma to a family reunion. Vince is being nosy."

"Where are you taking her?"

Then I hear the shouts—coming from Grandma's room.

"To a family reunion."

"Oh," she says, then adds almost as an afterthought. "Speaking of family, I was just thinking about my first husband, Clinton. You should have seen him at our wedding. He wore a crisp blue suit. Pinstriped. Stop me if I've told you this story before."

"You haven't and I'd love to hear it. How about next time I visit?" I say.

I feel the cloak of Victoria's loneliness as Grandma and I exit through the glass doors, and I slide them closed. I roll Lane through a gate on the patio and onto a cement path that winds through the gardens in back.

Minutes later, I've piled her into the car. I push the wheelchair behind a small bush in the median of the parking lot.

Twenty minutes later, we're sitting outside a nondescript office building. Inside, is Grandma's neurologist, Dr. Laramer.

I don't know if I've broken any law by absconding with Grandma. But it's another question whether I'm defying common sense. I've been shot at twice in the last twenty-four hours, gotten a home visit from G.I. Chuck, and have a meeting in a few hours with someone who sent me a mysterious thumb drive warning me of danger.

"Grandma Lane?"

"Nathaniel."

"Let's get inside that head of yours."

Dr. Laramer may prove a useful guide, even if getting his help entails provoking a few of my own demons.

Chapter Fourteen

In Dr. Laramer's office, a receptionist tells us the doctor has agreed to squeeze us in during his lunch hour. The receptionist has a hitch in his gaze that takes a second to identify as amblyopia, a subtle case of lazy eye that probably went undetected through his early childhood.

I take a seat next to Grandma.

"Lane, I wonder about the road not taken."

"I used to do that, Nathaniel."

"What?"

"Brood about the past."

"You did?"

"You should try forgetting. It can be better."

"How very lucid, Lane." I smile at her.

"If you say so."

"Can we talk about the man in blue?"

"Live in the present, Nathaniel."

It's a platitude. She's gone again. I sigh.

"My untaken road went through a utility closet on the third floor of San Francisco General Hospital," I say to Grandma in a low voice.

It was there I had spontaneous sex with Kristina Babcock, my bombshell medical-school mate.

In my second year, we were rotating through the psych ward. Our attention was consumed with "the Acrobat." That was the moniker of Frederica Calhoun, a schizophrenic who believed she was the reincarnation of a 16th-century French acrobat. We'd walk into Frederica's room and find her standing in some impossible position, or balancing a toothbrush on her head.

The question facing the attending physician was whether to force Frederica to take medications under court order. Weeks earlier, when off her medication, Frederica did a handstand on the ledge of an eighteen-story building, bringing a crowd and the fire brigade. But in our frequent conversations, she also was lucid, functional, thoughtful. She implored Kristina and me to argue for her freedom from meds that she said made her a "Gap-wearing, 21st-century automaton."

The attending physician didn't spend nearly as much time with Frederica. He recommended to a court she be forced to take medication.

"Is there a halfway house, or some alternative living situation that would give her a chance to live drug free?" I asked the doctor during our consultation outside the Acrobat's room.

"She's not capable," he said. "Anything else?"

"It seems like she deserves a shot to be herself," I pushed back.

"You do seem to really enjoy this rotation, Mr. Idle," he responded. "I'm recommending you repeat it."

On the way out, Kristina grabbed my hand and pulled me into a utility closet. "You're the reincarnation of a sixteenth-century romantic," she said. "You always side with the freaks."

"I'm not cut out to play God or any other powerful administrator," I said.

For the next two months, we fell towards love—great conversation, laughter, the real stuff. Then I turned on her. One night, I came to Kristina's apartment for our first weekend away—Santa Cruz, a Van Morrison concert, a cheap motel, sex near—and possibly on—the beach. Seemingly, uncomplicated fun. To me, a demarcation line I wouldn't cross. In fact, I wouldn't even cross into her house. I stood in her doorway and, without prompting, coldly poured out my resolve. I told her I didn't love her and never would.

It might not have been true. But Kristina was the embodiment of medical school, of a path towards a clear future. Rules, bureaucracy, checking off boxes and filling out paperwork, passion and patient care overwhelmed by monotony. A few months later, I broke up with my career, too.

I'd lucked into a prestigious summer job at the forensic clinic at Stanford. The day I was supposed to report, I was on a sleeper train in Rumania, having spontaneously decided to spend the summer traveling instead. When I returned to school for my last year, I was student non grata.

Meantime, Kristina started dating a studious and ambitious classmate named Pete Laramer. The pair were married by the time they graduated, and soon had three beautiful daughters.

Then, a year ago, I was walking with Grandma in Golden Gate Park when I ran into Kristina, Pete—Dr. Laramer—and the family. We had an awkward interaction in which Grandma, who in retrospect may have been suffering the very early stages of dementia, referred to me as Irving. As we parted, Dr. Laramer gave me his card.

"And that's the story of how you got your neurologist," I tell Grandma.

"I don't understand what you're saying."

"As the kids say: I have commitment issues."

"Oh."

She's silent for a second and says: "If you stay in one place, with one person, you will age no less quickly."

I laugh. "Where do you come up with this stuff?"

"What?"

"Never mind, guru." I lean in close. "Lane, I wish you'd tell me your secrets."

"I'll tell you a secret."

"Let's hear it."

"Remember to burp the baby."

She's looking at the coffee table. A copy of *Family Circle* magazine shows a picture of a mom holding a baby over her shoulder.

"I don't have a baby yet, Grandma."

She shrugs and picks up the magazine.

I fidget and find myself conspicuously avoiding the glance of an eighty-something woman lovingly cradling the hand of her oxygenated husband who suffers a nasty case of wildly overgrown ear hair.

I extract my phone. There are six missed calls—from the retirement home. Vince must be frantic and pissed. But he hasn't left a message.

I call Pauline. "Mystery man," she answers.

"What?"

"So what's in your mystery package?"

"Mystery instructions."

She doesn't respond for a second.

"Pauline?"

"Hold on."

She puts her hand over the phone but I can still hear her coughing to the extent it sounds like she might be sick.

"Upset stomach," she says when she's finished. "Late night followed by quintuple espresso. I've got to cut down my caffeine intake."

Or her stress.

"Have you ever considered slowing down, maybe just in the middle of the night?"

"Right back at you. Now tell me about the package."

I describe how I opened the thumb drive, and the instructions I found. I glance at the clock on my phone. It's noon. I've got three hours before the mystery meeting.

"Sounds cloak and dagger. Are you going to wear a trench coat?" Pauline asks.

True to her word, Pauline has tried to remain light, fun, and flirty. She says she's not going to change her approach to the world just because I don't want to date.

"Something very strange is going on," I say.

"With the memory stick?"

I hesitate. I'd love her help figuring out what's going on but right now she presents as many complications and entanglements as she does resources and insights.

"It's already been a long day. I don't know, just strange," I finally say.

"So are you going to go to the meeting?"

I look at Grandma. Does the thumb drive have anything to do with the attack in the park, and Grandma's recent ramblings? Or is it coincidental, unrelated, some kind of joke?

"Wearing a trench coat and matching socks."

"Socks and dagger," she says. "Can I come?"

I tell her that I'd prefer to go alone.

"Be careful. Socks aren't much defense against sharp objects," she says. After a pause, she adds, "I'd love to see you later."

I'm silent.

"I should go," she says.

"Wait. Could you spare me another minute?"

"What's up?" She suddenly sounds rushed.

"Tell me about Chuck. Your investor."

There is a moment of silence, then she says: "What makes you ask?"

"He seemed interesting when we met last night. I'm just curious about him."

Another pause.

"I think he's curious about you, too."

"Meaning?"

"I think he thinks you're cute. You're his type."

I'm not sure if she means that he likes my journalistic temperament or, perhaps, that he's gay. Now that I think about it, it had crossed my mind.

"You should work that angle," she continues. "Maybe you can get him up to sixty-five dollars per blog post. You'll be a rich man by the year 2075."

"Yeah, right."

"Look, Nat, can we talk about this later today, or tonight? I'm staying in the city."

Pauline has a gorgeous house in Marin, overlooking the water. But she keeps a three-story loft downtown, near the ballpark.

"Come by tonight and we'll make good on the drinks we missed, and I'll tell you about Chuck."

Before I can tell her that's not going to happen, she adds, "I really gotta go. I'm on Internet time."

She hangs up.

◇◇◇

From my backpack, I pull out my laptop. I find a weak signal in the waiting room. I call up a browser and I search for "Adrianna." It is a fool's errand. There are several million of references.

Is Adrianna a resident of Magnolia Manor? That makes no sense in that Vince seemed baffled that Grandma had mentioned the name Adrianna.

From my pocket, I pull one of the shell casings I found on the ground outside my flat after this morning's drive-by shooting. The brass housing looks to measure less than an inch in length, the width of a ring finger.

Into Google, I type: "identify shell casing." I get countless hits—about collections of artillery shells, lamps made from old casings, and on and on—but not the clearinghouse site I'd imagined would let me precisely identify my bullet, or the gun that fired it.

"All that surfing can rewire your brain," a voice says.

I look up to see Dr. Laramer.

"You're looking well, Mrs. Idle," he says to my companion on my right.

I close my laptop.

"Hello, Doc," I say. He wears blue scrubs and flip-flops. "Is it casual footware Friday?"

"It's Thursday," Grandma says.

She's right.

He looks at her and cocks his head.

"Interesting," he mutters.

Chapter Fifteen

"What?" I ask.

He ignores me and walks to the outer office door. He turns the latch and locks it. Except for us, the reception area is empty.

"Trying to keep us in, or somebody out?" I ask.

"I like a peaceful lunch hour but I'm making an exception for a family friend." It's not clear if he intends a slight.

The three of us walk down a corridor to his private office.

"What's so interesting, Dr. Laramer?"

"Call me Pete, please. Let's talk in my office."

His confines celebrate his success.

Framed on his wall are numerous credentials, including his Neurology Board certificate denoting his specialty in memory and recall disorders, and a letter from the United States Patent and Trademark Office. The last time we'd visited, he'd told me he'd received a patent for developing techniques for using real-time imaging technology to explore the brain's memory centers. He's like an old-time cartographer, but instead of hiking into the interior of a continent, he's mapping the subterranean layers of the brain to follow the flow of neurochemicals.

Adjectives that describe Dr. Pete Laramer: smart and ambitious. Not neat. Haphazard papers and files sully his desk. I'm that messy. I could be a fancy doctor.

Facing out from the desk stands a framed photograph of Kristina and three daughters who appear poised to share her beauty.

He's my height but paunchier, a late-thirties white guy with gray-speckled temples. His eyes are bloodshot; between them and the scrubs, I infer he's been on night call at the hospital. He looks otherwise devoid of any medical condition, which I find slightly disappointing.

"What strikes you about Lane?" I ask.

"She seems fit. Tracking. It's good."

"Really? It seems to me like she's slipped off a cliff."

Fewer than six months ago she'd have been, if not in her prime, sufficiently lucid. Brains don't fail this precipitously.

I situate Grandma on a chocolate-leather couch. As I do so, I explain she is agitated and acting frightened. Grandma interjects. "You're the doctor who studies my head."

"That's an interesting way to put it." He glances at me as if to say: See, she's on the ball.

He asks me to elaborate on what she's been saying. "Has it been nonsensical rambling or is she repeating herself and focusing on a particular idea?"

I explain that Grandma talked about a man in blue and the dentist. She's been upset since we nearly got shot in the park.

"Physically, she's fine," I say.

"Stop," he says, with some alarm.

"Pardon."

"She was shot?"

"Almost."

"Christ," he says, suddenly animated. "Are you serious?"

"It was probably some random attack. But I'd love to know what she remembers about it."

He pauses, apparently lost in thought. "It's not every day that one of my patients gets shot at."

He stands.

"Can you wait outside while I examine her?"

"I'd rather stay."

"She's liable to look to you for comfort or approval. I need to get a clear sense of her mental state."

I hesitate, and then stand up. I put a hand on her shoulder. "I'll be right outside, Grandma."

Dr. Laramer walks to his window, which is letting in gray light. He peers outside, closes the shade, then turns and walks back in our direction. He turns on a bright overhead light. I leave the pair of them alone.

I stand in the hallway. My cell phone signal is poor, but I try to call my parents. No luck getting through.

Then I hear a shout come from inside the office. More like an expression of shock, or surprise. It's not coming from Grandma. But Pete.

I open the door. Pete and Grandma sit on the couch. She's withdrawn to the edge of it. He leans away from her with his palm pressed against his chin. A yellow Nerf ball sits between them.

"What happened?" I ask, moving quickly to Grandma. I bring her close to me. She seems to relax.

"She punched me in the jaw," he says.

"What?"

Grandma's right hand is balled into a tight fist.

"I'm sorry. I'm sure she didn't mean…"

"I leaned in close to test her visual acuity and she let me have it," he interrupts me. "Not bad strength. Terrific punch, actually. Stings like a bee."

"Chop," I say.

"What?"

"Was probably a chop, not a punch. She was a blue belt," I say. "She studied years ago."

"She's definitely agitated," he says. Then turns to her: "You often roundhouse the help?"

"I'm sorry," Grandma says. "I'm only supposed to use my training for defense."

He shakes his head and, finally, laughs. "I've had agitated patients spit at me, and vomit. Once I was shoved by a bouncer. Never karate chopped."

"Pete, what did you say to upset her?"

He shrugs. "I asked her how she was feeling, the year, who is president, whether she is comfortable, the usual stuff."

"Are you friends with Adrianna?" Grandma asks him.

He looks at me, raises his eyebrows. "Who is Adrianna?" he asks me.

I shrug. "Grandma Lane, who is Adrianna?"

She cocks her head to the side, momentarily frozen in thought, like an overly taxed computer processor. Before she can continue, Pete picks up the Nerf ball. He tosses it in a gentle arc just to the right of Grandma. She raises an arm and swats it to the ground.

"Interesting," he says.

"What are you doing?" I ask, just shy of irritated that he's interrupted the conversational flow.

"Testing her spontaneous physical reactions. As you can see, they're very much intact."

"So."

"Whatever her mental state, she's alert and reactive and plenty physically able. It's as I thought when I first saw you in the waiting room: the patient presents in terrific physical shape."

The patient.

"Okay," I say, trying to piece together what this all means. I turn back to Grandma.

"Who is Adrianna?"

"Years ago, doctors came to your house," she says.

"Nat, has your grandmother experienced any recent traumas?"

"The shooting at the park."

"I thought you said the symptoms predate that. Did she get into an argument, or have a problem at her retirement home?

Has she been on field trips, or anything else that could have put her in a vulnerable or frightened position?"

I consider it. Nothing comes to mind other than her allusion to the dentist.

"Why do you ask?"

"People get mistreated and it makes them agitated. The retirement-home experience can be…impersonal."

We fall silent. He closes his eyes, and I can't tell if he's lost in contemplation or tired.

"Pete, what is going on with her?"

He clears his throat. "I'm sure it's no surprise. But I'm sorry to say that she's exhibiting the classic signs of dementia."

I shake my head. "When we came in you said she seemed fine."

"Well, it could be worse."

Pete starts what I imagine is his stock speech to family members of dementia sufferers. He tells me that Alzheimer's is the most common form of dementia, affecting more than four million Americans. The disease results in memory loss, personality changes, cognitive dysfunction, then physical dependence. I know this stuff, and I wave him along.

He reminds me there are four stages: predementia, and then early, moderate, and advanced versions. Common complications include dementia coupled with Parkinson's; vascular dementia, which largely afflicts African Americans; and frontotemporal dementia, which presents with major mood affect.

"She's probably in an early or moderate stage," he says. "The good news is, this is very common, and we have some sense of how to treat it, though our treatments are primitive or, rather, of modest efficacy."

He's starting to wind down his presentation, just as I'm feeling a rising sense of ire mixed with disbelief.

"Bullshit," I say with some force, seeming to surprise him, and myself.

What I realize I'm thinking is that Grandma's symptoms don't seem common at all. If my own memory of neurological disorders serves even a little, these symptoms don't add up. Ordinarily, a sharp mental descent would be accompanied by a loss in physical agility and alertness. More significantly, it makes no sense to me that her mental decline has been so precipitous. I'm bothered with myself that I haven't been paying closer attention in the last month or two.

"When did you see Lane last?" I ask.

"Pardon?"

"When was her last visit here—three, four months ago?"

He walks to his desk. He picks up a green folder, opens and studies the chart inside. "Three," he says, then corrects himself. "Sorry, four."

"It just doesn't make sense to me that as recently as four months ago she was doing relatively well, making sense, and conversation."

"Suggesting what?" he asks.

"Something odd is going on. This doesn't seem typical to me at all."

"Respectfully, Nat, the Internet is not the best place to get medical information," he says. "Dementia and memory loss can be very hard for family members to accept."

He maintains eye contact with me, which makes me think he either doesn't realize he's being condescending or doesn't mind it. I break our gaze, almost imperceptibly bowing my head.

"What do you suggest?"

"Let's get her on some Aricept," he says. He pauses. "She lives where?" he asks.

"Magnolia Manor."

He nods. "Can you give her a break from there for a few days? Can she get some time to change her environment? She could use the stimulation of activity. She certainly seems curious and physically able." He turns to her. "Don't you Lane?"

"I don't know anything about that," she responds.

I decide it's not the time to tell doc I'm already on the change-of-venue case.

I'm not sure he's offering us better advice than I could've gotten on the Internet. He's prescribing pills and a change to her environment. Still, at least now I have justification for keeping Lane with me. Doctor's orders.

Pete looks at his watch. He says he should get to his next appointment. In parting, he tells me he'd like to see my grandmother again in a week.

"But call me tomorrow and give me an update." He hands me a card with his cell phone number.

At a modest dining room in the basement, I ask Grandma what kind of sandwich she wants. Before she can answer, a woman behind the counter wearing her pink dyed hair in a tight bun informs me that she doesn't have *sandwiches* but, rather, *panini* or flatbread.

"Can't I just call it a sandwich?" I ask. "She was born before the advance of the *panini*."

"Don't talk about me when I'm standing right here," Grandma says.

I order a flatbread with tuna for Grandma and, for me, *panini* with chicken and pesto sauce—the chief difference between these items and sandwiches being price. Sixteen dollars later, I help Grandma into the car. We have ninety minutes to kill before our meeting with the mystery stick sender. In the meantime, I want to drive Grandma by her dentist—at least to follow up on yesterday's missed appointment. Maybe she saw a man in blue when we were sitting in the parking lot outside. Maybe I'm pulling at wild strings.

I snap in Grandma's seat belt and start the car. As I start to pull away, I see a car inching around the corner behind us. It's a Prius. Like the one from the park.

Chapter Sixteen

"Flume," Grandma says.

"What?"

"It's a narrow opening," she says. "I used to be an English teacher and sometimes I use big words even though it can be impolite."

She's either looking at the traffic scenario or I'm giving her too much credit. We've slid between a red flatbed truck carrying lumber and a beautifully reconditioned classic Jaguar. The Prius is five cars back. I can't make out the driver but he appears to wear a hooded sweatshirt. I can't see the license plate.

"You're on edge, grandson."

"Not at all. Everything's under control." Not exactly.

My thinking: If I take three quick rights, I can get behind him, or I could pretend I don't see him and let him get close.

"Be careful, Irving," Lane says.

I look forward and realize I've almost hit the truck in front of us. I slam the brakes to avoid collision.

When I look in the rearview mirror again, the Prius has disappeared.

Twenty minutes later, I pull into the parking lot of Brown & Morrow. They're located in a modest two-story complex that includes a dentist, a dermatology clinic, and an imaging center with an MRI machine. At the entrance to the small parking lot stands a weather-worn statue of a woman I think is supposed to be Hygieia, the goddess of health. Weeds grow at the base of the deity's cheap plaster seat.

We were here yesterday, when Grandma refused to exit the car to go to the dental appointment.

"Does this look familiar?" I ask.

Grandma doesn't say anything. She's looking down at her game device, turning it over in her hand.

"Do you want to go inside?"

"Harry will look out for me," she says, absently.

"Did you see Adrianna here?"

No response.

"The man in blue?"

There are a dozen parked cars in the lot with us. A woman in a long skirt helps a frail man, presumably her father, climb from a minivan into a wheelchair. The office doors all face the lot—even the ones on the second floor, which are accessible through an open balcony. So I can see Grandma at all times.

She's safe here.

"Want to play a game?"

No answer.

I power up her phone. I click the icon for Tetris. Grandma seems transfixed by the falling blocks, though she's not playing.

"Will you wait a few minutes? I'll be right back."

"Be careful," she says, without looking up.

"Right back," I repeat.

I lock the car doors.

The dental office is on the second floor, above the imaging center. I look down at my car. Lane sits quietly.

As I approach the dental office, the door opens. Out walks a Napoleon complex: ninety-eight pounds of hair and bar fight. He wears a jeans jacket with a patch that reads: "Khe Sahn Survivor." He glowers and closes the door behind him rather than holding it open for me. The product of another festive dental visit.

The door is friendlier. A sign says: "We welcome Medicare, MediCal, and Medicaid." There is a picture of a cartoon horse, smiling, with a carrot sticking out of its mouth like a cigar.

Inside, I'm met with more attitude.

"We're closed," says a blazing black-haired woman with the hollow cheeks of an eating disorder sitting behind the reception desk.

"I just saw someone walk out."

"Last patient."

I looked at the clock on the wall. 2:15 P.M.

"Dentists keep odd hours."

"It's our lunch. Some people can only come in during their lunch hour, so we eat later."

"What if I just have a question—about my grandmother? She's a patient here and I'm worried about her."

She shakes her head.

"Patient confidentiality. Call if you want to make an appointment. I should warn you that our next opening for a new patient is in January."

I step toward the desk. "What's for lunch today—*panini?*"

"Sir, I told you that we're closed."

"I'm just getting a card, so I can schedule an appointment."

She stares at me as I take a card.

"When I make an appointment, is it possible I could make one with Adrianna? I've heard good things about her."

"I have no idea who you're talking about."

"You seem unusually adamant about that."

"I told you: we're closed."

The discussion is over. She follows me to the door and locks it behind me.

I'm sitting next to Grandma in the car. She's clicking the buttons on her phone as blocks fall down the tiny screen. She's not really playing so much as absently interacting with the game. Her brain on autopilot.

I inch it out of her hands. "There were no signs warning me to floss," I say.

She looks up at me. "Oh you've absolutely got to floss."

"Grandma Lane, nothing about that place screamed dental office."

I look on the card I took. It reads: "For appointment, call 415–555–1041."

Maybe Pauline's right. Maybe I'm seeing conspiracies everywhere and focusing on distractions and pathologies instead of real life.

"Still," I say.

"What's that?"

I take Grandma's hand in mine.

"Do you remember Thelma and Louise?"

"Were they in our family?" she asks.

"Batman and Robin, Sherlock and Watson, the Lone Ranger and Tonto?"

"Sherlock was a great man."

"We could be the new dynamic duo: the Overwhelmed and the Octogenarian."

"I don't know them."

"How about: 'Kid Commitment Phobe and Granny.' My superpower can be fleeing, and yours knitting."

She doesn't respond.

"I can come up with something better than that. Give me some time."

"Time is nothing to be squandered, Nathaniel," she says, seeming bemused.

"Grandma?"

"Yes, grandson?"

"How about Butch Cassidy and the Sunset Kid?"

"I like that very much."

"Time for us to leap into action."

Chapter Seventeen

The corner of Hayes and Buchanan looks like a bulldoze site waiting to happen. It is home to a low-income housing project in the Western Addition, one of the islands of San Francisco that has temporarily escaped gentrification. Prevailing economics can't support these low-income renters any more than, eventually, they can support me.

Next to the dilapidated green apartment complex, three boys play hoops on a cracked cement basketball court with a bent orange rim.

We park across the street in a spot that puts me in the sun and lets Grandma, sitting in the passenger seat, get shade by the lone tree on the block. This is the end of San Francisco's second summer, neither of which takes place during the traditional months of June to September. Our first summer happens in the early spring, and the second in September and October. Now it's warm in the middle of the day, cool and damp at morning and evening, rain and fog starting to visit at night, and destined to bring a quick end to these blissful moments of sun basking.

Grandma and I are half an hour early for a meeting I hope will explain everything, or anything—the shooting, the thumb drive, whether aliens visited Roswell.

The plate-glass door of the large apartment building opens and a short, wiry boy walks out dribbling a ball.

"Lane smooched a colored boy," Grandma says. "That's what they said."

"What does that mean?"

"I came from Eastern Europe," she responds. "Not Western Europe."

"You are correct. What does that have to do with you kissing a boy?"

"I grew up in Denver. I think you know that. There was a boy who lived in our neighborhood named Randall. He was colored. Now we say something else."

"African-American."

"We liked to talk about books, but that's all we ever did was talk about books, and once we went to a museum. And his name was Randall."

"You said that, Grandma."

"What?"

"What happened with Randall?"

She pauses. "I'm not sure I know what you're talking about."

I suspect she's going to tell me that the other kids made fun of her because she was friends with a colored boy. She can't confirm this. She's slipped away.

I look at the clock. It is 2:50.

"Grandma, as long as we're on the topic of Denver, would you like to tell me the rest of your story and what happened at the bakery your father owned? Remember, you were telling me about the Idle clan?"

She doesn't say anything.

"We never got to finish our conversation. My notes are incomplete, and I'd love to know your story."

"I already told the box," she says.

"You told the box—you mean you told your story to the computer?"

No response.

"My turn to tell a kissing story," I say.

I know Grandma's not really listening. But I'm trying to pass the time, so I start talking about Pauline. Maybe I'm fueled by a memory of past talks with Grandma—her genuine interest, deep visceral laughter, a feeling she gave me that my decisions always made complete sense.

"Pauline, my boss, she listens like you do," I mutter. "She leaves me satisfied, like comfort food."

"Are you telling me a story or eating?"

I laugh. "Thank you for calling me out on my nonsensical simile."

She looks at me.

"We met a year ago on a hike organized by mutual friends," I continue.

"You're smiling, Nathaniel."

I tell Grandma that Pauline and I split off from the rest of the group and before I knew it, we had walked two hours and talked. On the way back to the cabin, Pauline stopped and pointed. Frozen ten yards in front of us was a deer, paralyzed. Then it did something I wouldn't have predicted in a million years. It took a step toward Pauline, then another. When it was three feet from her it stopped, and sniffed the air. And then it lowered its head and started chomping on grass.

"You are beloved by animals and you look good in shorts," I whispered to Pauline.

The deer didn't even look up before bolting.

"You just look good in shorts," Pauline said.

We both cleared our throats. On the way back to the car, I had the weirdest thought: if I see another deer tonight, I'll ask her out. I didn't and I wound up burying my urges and working for Pauline.

"What kind of bullshit abdication was it to leave my fate to a deer?" I say to Grandma.

"You are angry."

I rub my hand on my forehead. "I'm confused. I went to see a shrink, a few months ago, just once."

I tell Grandma what I haven't told anyone else. I gave this psychotherapist my dating history since med school, starting with Annie. Next came Erin, who split up with me after I left her brother's wedding ceremony to file a breaking story about lead-tainted Chinese dog bones killing pooches. Good story, bad timing. Erin said I despised any celebration of permanence.

Each relationship grew progressively shorter, mostly ended by me.

"At this point, I can meet someone at a party or on a hike, fall for her and split up before I've asked her out," I tell Grandma.

"I think you'd like talking to the box," she says.

"I am by career and emotion a journalist. I write short stories, complete them, move on to another subject. I can't even commit to an idea, a subject matter, let alone a life partner."

I'd been looking straight ahead but I turn to her. "The obvious conclusion is that I hate commitment. But what's truer is that I love endings."

"Is something coming to an end?"

"I love the sense of freedom that comes from being finished, however momentarily. I relish the moment I become free."

"I think you'd enjoy talking to the box," Grandma repeats.

"What box?"

"The computer. It listens to you all day, even if you get boring or no one wants to hear your story."

I laugh. "Probably costs less than a shrink."

"I don't think you usually talk this much," she says. "It's nice."

I sigh. For some reason, I'd expected Grandma to dole out wisdom or comfort, like she used to.

"Can you tell me how I can get as big a rush out of being with one person as I can from the moment I become free?"

Grandma responds: "Our generation liked mixed drinks, or beer. Yours seems to like mobile phones."

I smile. Lane offers wisdom after all. Maybe my problem is technology. The Internet age exacerbates my frenetic characteristics. Information, ideas, emotions flit in and out—a veritable blog of a world with constant updates and no time to stand still. My head and gut on a swivel. My thoughts, emotions, and memories more fleeting than ever. The opportunities to create new ones more powerful. I live from one brief moment of purpose to the next.

"Grandma, what did you talk about with the box?"

"In due time," she says, absently.

"Grandma?"

No response.

I glance at the clock on my phone; five minutes after three. I got lost in mystery, and in Lane's relative loquaciousness. I take stock of our surroundings.

There is no one standing at the entrance to the complex—no L. P., the initials from the mystery package, no "Adrianna," the name of someone Grandma says can't breathe.

Nor is there anyone on any of the four corners of the intersection of Hayes and Buchanan.

We sit ten more minutes in silence.

"Grandma, I'm going to have to explore."

"If you say so."

"You should join me."

I unbuckle Grandma's seat belt, then go around to the passenger side of the car to help her out. I give her my arm to hold, but she pushes it away.

"I'm not an invalid."

We cross the street to the Westside Apartments. It's a squat three-story building that from the address directory next to an intercom looks to have some two dozen apartments.

I look down the directory to see if any names have the initials L. P. I have no reason to believe that the sender of the mystery package is a resident here, but I've got to start somewhere. There are two residents with a last name that starts with P. One is Renee Peal, and the other has no first name. The little strip of paper just says: "Pederson."

As I'm glancing down the list, a tall, older man with stooped shoulders approaches the building door and inserts his key. His hand shakes lightly with the earliest onset of Parkinson's. He opens the door, and starts to close it behind him. Before it can shut, I slip my hand in the door to keep it open. The man turns around.

"Who are you here to see?" he asks.

"Renee Pape," I respond without a beat.

"Well then buzz her," he says. "We're not allowed to let anyone in the building."

He looks at my hand and gently shuts the door.

So much for sneaking in to randomly haunt the halls in search of someone with the initials L. P.

"I can't tell if it's fall or spring," Grandma says.

I look at her, then over at the basketball courts. The four players have taken a break in their game. The one who joined the group from the apartment complex is looking in my direction. When he sees me look up, he looks away.

"That's the second time I've seen him looking at me, Lane."

"Well, I'm sure he doesn't mean anything by it."

"Grandma, I used to be a decent basketball player."

"You must have been taller then." She winks.

"I'm still plenty handsome."

She smiles. She's in there somewhere.

I look at the playground. "You know what they say about the third time."

"It's a charm," Grandma says.

"The young fellow just glanced at us again."

Chapter Eighteen

We walk to the side of the court. Between games, the boys have scattered and sit along the chain-link fence. I approach the one who looked at me.

"You're very fast," I say.

"More quick than fast," he responds, without looking up. Friendly. I'm guessing around twelve years old. He's shorter than his friends, wearing blue mesh shorts long enough to touch the tops of his high-tops. His Golden State Warriors tank top reveals the underdeveloped shoulders of pre-adolescence.

One of his cohorts shouts in his direction: "If he's an agent, give him my number."

"The teacher gave us the afternoon off for Halloween," he explains. Earnest.

"I used to play. I wasn't very good," I say.

"I used to be a teacher," Grandma says.

We both turn and look at her.

"She plays too," I say. "She has a wicked jump hook."

The boy laughs.

"I'm Nathaniel, and this is Lane. My grandmother."

One of his friends shouts in his direction. "Let's go, Newton. Rubber match."

"Hello, Newton," I offer.

"It's a nickname," he says and he stands.

"I'm looking for someone," I say.

"We're looking for someone," Grandma says.

"It's…" I gamble. "Mr. Pederson."

Newton's taken a step away from us, but he keeps his cool. "Never heard of him," he says.

"What about *Ms.* Pederson?" I ask. Maybe I've gotten the gender wrong on the mystery package sender with the last name starting with P.

"C'mon, Newton!" one of his friends bellows.

"I'm being called to action," he says.

"May I interject please?" Grandma asks. Without waiting for a response, she continues: "I commend the young man on his word choice. It's energizing to hear English spoken with precision."

For some reason, this stops Newton. He turns around. "Are you a real-estate agent?"

Grandma thinks the question is directed to her.

"My father worked in a bakery."

"I'm a journalist. I got a note from Ms. Pederson asking to meet me here. I think she wanted to contact me about a story."

"Newton!" A friend screams

He turns to them. "I'll be there in a moment!"

"Why do they call you Newton?"

"I like science."

"Me too. Why did you think we were real estate agents?"

"Because you stop living here when you can afford anything else."

I consider it. "Is Ms. Pederson too rich for these digs?"

"Her first name is Lulu," he says. "But she hates it. She thinks it makes her sound like an airhead."

"Lulu Pederson?" I ask. L. P.

He doesn't respond.

"Have you seen Ms. Pederson around?" I ask with as much nonchalance as I can muster.

"Not for a few days. She tutors me in science on Wednesdays, but she didn't show up last night."

"So you think maybe she moved out of the neighborhood?"

"Newton!" a friend shouts.

"I would," he says in response to my question. "Anyway, I gotta run…"

I interrupt him. "Any idea where can I find her?"

"Nathaniel, you ask a lot of questions," Grandma inserts.

Newton laughs. "She's funny."

"It's really important that I find her," I say.

He looks at me cautiously, measuring me now.

"She's pretty smart—a genius. I assume she'll find you if she's interested."

"Please," I say. "It's critically important."

He's had enough, and now one of his friends is striding purposefully towards us to retrieve him.

"Try her company. It's called Biogen," he says.

"Biogen?" I make sure I heard correctly.

He nods.

The biotech giant.

He's walking away.

"What does she do at Biogen?"

He shrugs.

"Is she a scientist?" I shout after him. I start to walk around the side of the court, to find an entrance.

Newton's friend—the one who came to retrieve him—takes a step in my direction. He's much bigger and less friendly.

"Can we get back to our game?" he asks. It sounds rhetorical. He wants this interview to end.

"Newton, please. This is important. I need you to help me." I'm using an adult voice I'm surprised to know I've got inside of me. I'm asking this child to behave reasonably.

"I'm not supposed to talk to strange adults." Trump card. Smart kid. "If you see her, tell her Newton says hello," he adds.

I pull out my business card. I wave it, and stick it in a gym bag left where Newton was sitting.

"This is my phone number, Newton. Call me if you want to talk about Lulu."

◇◇◇

Grandma and I are sitting back in the car. I cup her chilly hands in mine and blow on them, then gently rub, feeling the frail bones beneath.

"Congratulations, partner," I say.

"Harry doesn't have trouble hiding his excitement. He always seems calm, even when he's not."

"You just played Good Cop," I say.

"I've never had a problem with people in law enforcement."

We finally have a lead.

"Have you heard of Biogen?"

"What?"

"It's one of the most respected biotech companies in the world. I think it's the biggest."

No response.

I look at the clock. It's 4:20. Probably too late to get to Biogen, which is located in South San Francisco. But it's not too late to call.

I call Directory Assistance and get Biogen's main number. I call the company, suffer through instructions from an automated attendant, and hit zero for a live human. When I get one, I ask for Lulu Pederson. The human operator transfers me. The phone rings three times, then goes to voice mail.

"You've reached Adrianna Pederson in Biogen's Advanced Life Computing department. I'm not available right now; leave a message and I'll get back to you."

Did I hear right. Did the voice mail say "*Adrianna* Pederson"?

Adrianna. That was the name Grandma was muttering.

Maybe I'm imagining things.

I call Biogen a second time and ask for Lulu Pederson. I get her voice mail and realize that, indeed, I hadn't imagined a thing.

"You've reached Adrianna Pederson in Biogen's Advanced Life Computing department. I'm not available right now; leave a message and I'll get back to you."

I leave a message.

"Adrianna, this is Nat Idle. I'm hoping that means something to you. Please call me—day or night. Anytime."

I leave my phone number and hang up.

"Grandma, who is Adrianna?"

No response.

"Wait here."

I step out of the car, lock Grandma inside, and walk to the basketball court. I approach the in-progress game.

"Newton!"

The players pause.

"Does Lulu use the name Adrianna?"

He nods. "I told you already: she hates 'Lulu.' Adrianna is her middle name."

I shake my head.

"Leave him alone," one of the other boys says. "We'll start screaming if you bother us anymore."

I nod and put out my hands—surrender.

The boys start playing again. I turn to see Grandma in the car, and let the latest revelations sink in. I try to make sense of the disparate pieces. I received a mysterious computer memory stick from someone with the initials L. P. That person appears to work for Biogen. And she has the middle name Adrianna, which happens to be the same name Grandma has been muttering. How and why is Grandma connected to any of this? Does Grandma know the answer—somewhere in her damaged gray matter?

And what has happened to Adrianna? Why did she miss our meeting?

Inside the car, I stare at Grandma, who stares straight ahead. Then looks at me and cocks her head.

I bite the inside of my lip to keep from conveying my shock and the depth of my curiosity. A woman named Lulu Pederson—who may have written me a mystery note with a mystery attachment and knows I went to the Galapagos—shares the name of a woman who is haunting my demented grandmother. And now Lulu Adrianna Pederson seems to be missing.

I need help.

I dial Chuck. He doesn't answer. I leave a message telling him I'd like his help following up on a lead in our story.

"Lane smooched a colored boy," Grandma says.

"Lane, let's go home, get some rest, and try to avoid any more nasty surprises. On the way, we can make one more stop by that dentist's office."

"No thank you." Emphatic.

I look at her. She blinks twice rapidly, betraying some discomfort.

"What's wrong with the dentist?"

"I said no."

"Grandma?"

No response.

Her silence speaks volumes. I have to check out that office.

Chapter Nineteen

I weave through a few side streets, and take a right turn onto Geary, a fat thoroughfare thickening to a crawl with commuter traffic. We slip into the mess. We putt along in silence for a few blocks, and then I see something troubling in the rearview mirror, one lane over to the right.

There's a Prius several cars behind us. Its driver looks like the lovechild of a circus clown and Bigfoot.

I turn off my engine, yank out the keys, and put on the hazards. I open the door and start hustling toward the Prius.

I am thoroughly pissed off, but I still realize I have two big problems.

One is that my move prompts an eruption of honks. The collective angst of several dozen drivers already frustrated by life's deep unfairness—traffic, the Bay Area cost of living, the fact they don't yet own an iPad—spills out into a symphony of honking harangues.

The second problem takes a moment longer to materialize.

I zigzag to the driver's-side window of the hybrid. I peer inside at the face of a man in his mid-twenties with a soul patch, hefty sideburns, ring-pierced lower lip, and an ostentatious hairy wig. He holds a dime-store clown mask he has pulled from his face, leaving it dangling from his neck by an elastic string.

He looks startled, then menacing, like a guy who goes to Oakland Raiders games just for the fights in the stands. His speakers thump with hip-hop.

He rolls down his window. He starts to speak. Starts to, then pauses, turns down the hip-hop, and makes an impassioned plea.

"I am one hundred percent sober."

On the passenger seat I see a fifth of Jack Daniel's, half drained. The bottle is open, tilting to the side, dribbling out its contents.

"Who do you work for?" I ask.

"What?"

"Are you following us?"

Then something dawns on him.

"You better be a cop," he says. "Or I'm going to drive my forehead through your forehead. You ever see the Ultimate Fighting Championship?"

Something dawns on me too. This is not the hybrid I saw in the park. And there is little likelihood its driver has been plotting my demise, at least not until this very moment.

"Undercover pre-Halloween law-enforcement brigade," I say.

I sprint back to my car, start it, and pull hard into the right lane. I then yank a sharp right onto a side street to get out of the traffic jam.

I don't fully exhale until I realize that the hybrid driver has, apparently, decided not to follow us.

"You're frightening me," Grandma says.

"I'm sorry. My imagination's in overdrive."

"Ha!" Grandma says declaratively. "You seem like you're enjoying yourself."

This time, it is I who uses Grandma's regular refrain.

"I'm not sure I understand," I say.

"The Idles like to run after things."

"The neurologist is right."

"What?"

"You're away from Magnolia Manor and you're getting more lucid."

"If you say so."

As we drive, I call Magnolia Manor and ask for Betty Lou, Grandma's close friend.

"Where's Lane?" Betty Lou asks immediately.

"We're going to hang out for a few days. Her doctor says she needs some concentrated time with her grandson. But I need a few changes of clothes for Lane."

"Really?"

"Really."

"Well then why not just come back here and get some clothes yourself?"

"Betty Lou, you're a clever old lass."

"Bring her back here, Nathaniel."

"Please, Betty Lou," I say. I want to add: I know what I'm doing. But I'm not sure that I do. Instead, I say: "I'm taking great care of her, and she's doing fine."

"Then why are they looking for her, and you?"

"Who is?"

"Vince and the rest of those a-holes."

I tell her I don't have time to explain. I ask her to meet me on the street in an hour.

"Harry is worried sick," she says.

"Don't tell anyone we've talked."

"What's going on, Nathaniel?"

"I don't know. Maybe nothing. I wouldn't worry about it."

"Young people are so patronizing."

Click.

Half an hour later, I pull into the dental office. It's just after 5:30, getting dark, and the lot has largely cleared out.

"Sit tight for just a second, Lane."

"I'm bored. Can I use the computer?"

I hand her the video-game phone.

"No, the computer!" she says.

"It is a computer."

"What?"

She's staring at the screen.

"I'll be back in just a second."

I walk up the stairs and I notice the office door is ajar. I push it open. Inside, the office is quiet, dark, and appears to be empty.

I feel along the wall to my right, and flip on the light.

There is a small waiting area at the entrance, ringed by white chairs with white seat cushions. On a coffee table between the chairs sit copies of *Newsweek*, *Sports Illustrated*, and other magazines. I'm struck again that there is little else to define the place—nothing on the walls, no signs with appointment directions or instructions on dental care.

Also missing is the woman behind the counter, the one I'd argued with earlier. Her desk has been emptied out. There are no papers, computer, office supplies—just a single black ballpoint pen lying on a stark white counter.

Next to the counter is a doorway leading to the back.

"Hello," I say loudly and directed to the back. "I'm here for my appointment."

No answer.

I walk to the door that leads to the back and open it. Behind it, two doorways, presumably to examination rooms.

I open the door to my right. Behind it, a small white room, completely empty. Not even an examination chair.

I step back into the hallway and walk to the second door.

I put my hand to the knob, and hesitate. Will I find Adrianna, unable to breathe?

Is Grandma okay outside? I shouldn't be leaving her in the dark.

I push open the door. I feel along the wall for a switch and turn on the light. Another small examination room, also abandoned. Mostly.

A high-backed chair faces a wall on which there are taped three images that look like they've been cut from old magazines: an ad for a 1960s red Chevrolet, a picture of an old television with rabbit ears, and a photo of the first moon walk. There are also two *New York Times* front pages tacked up, one announcing the attack on Pearl Harbor and another of Jackie Robinson rounding third base, hand pumped in the air in celebration.

From outside, I hear a high-pitched sound.

Screaming.

Chapter Twenty

I sprint into the darkness.

The piercing sound comes from directly below me. I squint to get my bearings.

"Grandma?!"

I fly down the stairs. I make out someone standing near the door of a ground-floor office. The figure is hunched. Grandma.

I hustle to her.

She stares into the office's plate-glass window.

"Adrianna can't breathe," she says.

"It's okay. I'm here."

I gently put my hand on her back. She flinches and her hand whips up and slaps my arm away. She's strong.

"Grandma, it's me."

"I'm not going inside."

"Absolutely not. We're not going inside."

I put my arm on her shoulder. She's quivering.

"My father drove a red Chevrolet," she says.

"Deep breath, Grandma."

"My family came from Eastern Europe."

"Poland, Grandma. You're absolutely right."

"Irving wore a suit to our wedding."

She's all over the place.

"Grandma," I take a step back, and hold her hands. "What happened here?"

"I did my best to love Irving. I made him tuna casserole, which I hate. I just didn't fit into that kind of life—a casserole life. I know you know what I'm talking about."

"What happened here, Lane? Please focus."

"There are some things I'd prefer to forget."

"Did you see something happen to Adrianna? Did she…" I pause before saying the words, "Why can't she breathe?"

"Do you know what it's like to feel suffocated? Do you know what it's like when you're trapped? It's like being anesthetized. Do you know what that word means?"

"Grandma…"

"You want to feel thrilled. Isn't that what it means to be alive? *You* know that, Nathaniel. That's why I can tell you."

She's meandering, anxious, confused, pouring out and swirling together memory, philosophy, fear, anger, raw emotion.

"What do you want to forget, Grandma?"

"Pigeon."

Pigeon. This doesn't ring the remotest bell.

"Pigeon—like the bird?"

"Pigeon, take me someplace warm."

I take a deep breath.

"Shhh," she says, animatedly.

"What?"

"Is there something there?" She's looking out into the parking lot.

I look in the darkness. I hear nothing, see nothing.

"Harry, take me someplace warm, please."

"I'm Nathaniel."

She does not respond at first.

"You should marry that friend of yours," she finally says. "There are ways you can have everything, but I wouldn't recommend it."

I take a deep breath. The San Francisco air hangs dusty wet with incoming fog and night.

My cortex clicks through dozens of seemingly unrelated details and events. I can't grasp the connection but I know there is one. I notice I'm rubbing my thumb against my index finger, an old habit that happens when I'm close to figuring something out.

"You're saying a lot of different things, Grandma. But I have this strange feeling that there is some connective tissue. There are clues in what you're saying. But I have no idea how to assemble them—and which are clues, which are..." I stop, because I don't want to say the word "nonsense."

"Nathaniel, you were always close enough to see the truth."

"What truth, Lane?"

Chapter Twenty-one

Transcript from the Human Memory Crusade. May 20, 2010

Welcome back Lane Idle. While I load your file, please enjoy these video images of America's rich past. The late 1940s and 1950s were a time of great prosperity and growth for this country, particularly after a hard-fought victory in World War II. Tens of millions of Americans gathered around radios to learn about Pearl Harbor, and, six years later, the allied victory. Then they celebrated in the streets, ringing in a period of common purpose, and extraordinary prosperity.

That's true, I guess, and a little schmaltzy, if you don't mind my saying so.

When we last spoke, you told me how you learned of Pearl Harbor listening to a large black radio in your house in Denver. Would you like to elaborate?

I don't remember that particular time very well, or that incident. I'm trying to talk about something else.

Did you say you're having trouble remembering hearing about the outbreak of war on the radio?

I was telling you about the young man in the alley. And the secret envelope. I've been thinking about it a lot—nonstop, actually. In the common room last night they showed *The Way*

We Were. It's a movie with Barbra Streisand. I love movies, but I actually left in the middle because I was thinking about how to tell the story. When you keep something inside so long, it doesn't just come out that easily.

Are you still there?

My father was very suspicious; he noticed *everything.* I was sure he'd discover the envelope I'd gotten from the man in the alley. So I waited until I could hear that there were a few customers at the counter whom he needed to help. I went into the storeroom in back. We had everything organized very neatly. On one wooden shelf were large sacks of flour and sugar, along with smaller bins of flour and sugar that were to be mixed that evening for use the next morning. Another shelf had additives, like vanilla, in big plastic jugs. Oh, it smelled heavenly. And there were chocolate chips, and raisins, which I never liked. And boxes of almonds. You'd think there were lots of little places to hide things. But if one tiny thing was out of place, my father would have known about it.

Are you still there?

Yes, yes. I used to read novels about a spy named Steve Stealth. Did I tell you that? I know I've started to repeat myself. Anyway, as I was standing in the storage room with the white envelope, I thought about what a spy would do, and the idea that came to me had to be about the worst one on the whole planet: hide the envelope where my father was so confident everything was in order that he'd never guess that it wasn't—in order.

Next to the refrigerator, there was an old bin marked "Wheat." It looked full and heavy. But it wasn't. It was easy to push aside. When you did—when you moved it—you could see the black safe that was dug in the ground—cut between two planks. That's where we kept the receipts, and our immigration papers and some old pictures. I put the envelope in the safe, in a file with our immigration papers. I couldn't imagine my dad would ever think to look in those papers. He couldn't. Right? I…I…

You have not spoken for more than a minute. Are you still there?

My grandson took me to a doctor the other day. What do you call it, a…

Are you still there?

A neurologist. Sheesh…that word took a while to come to me. Pardon my cursing. It's not helping, looking at all those butterflies on the screen. I didn't want to see a neurologist, if you want to know the truth. But then I came to the obvious realization that I'm not afraid of the doctor; I'm afraid of the condition. My mother lost her memory. They didn't call it dementia back then. They just said she was old. Well, my point is that I want to deal with my memory, to keep it intact, at least long enough to…tell the truth. I don't have to leave a legacy, not like some oil baron or business mogul, but I don't want to leave a lie either. Maybe my grandson can read this and understand why things have turned out the way they have.

I think you said you're having trouble remembering things. Would you like to see a doctor who specializes in memory loss?

I just told you that I am already seeing one. I'd just like to keep talking. Isn't that the point of this arrangement?

Please continue.

I waited for the man from the alley to come back. But he didn't come the next day, or the day after. I kept picturing his face and it made my body warm. I don't know if it was fear or something else. At work, I kept opening the safe and peeking at the envelope. I nearly opened it a dozen times. But I didn't want to disappoint the man. I was a girl, y'know. Things were different then, at least for most girls. Well, anyhow, after the second day, I went to the neighborhood park and I looked for him. But he wasn't there. And then I started to wonder if the whole thing was nothing—wishful thinking of someone who was always inside her own head daydreaming. Anyhow, on the third day, Irving came for a visit.

Are you still there?

I'm tired, and I've lost my place a little bit.

Did you say you are tired?

Yes.

Would you like to play a game? It's a game that all the kids are playing these days, but it's easy and I can teach you.

I suppose so.

Use the mouse to move the blinking cursor at the bottom of the page back and forth.

I know how to use a mouse. I used to be a blue belt in karate. I'm not an invalid or an idiot.

You're doing a good job with the mouse. As you move it back and forth, try to "catch" or "intercept" the colored bars as they drop down the screen.

Are you still there? The mouse is no longer moving.

I'm tired.

May I recap what we have been talking about today to make sure that I have recorded it correctly?

Yes.

You were born in Warsaw, Poland. Your family came on a very large ship to America. You moved to Denver, where you attended high school. You learned of Pearl Harbor on a large, black radio set. Your father owned or operated a bakery. His first car was a Ford. Am I getting this correctly?

Yes, I think. My father owned a bakery AND operated it. I don't remember what kind of car my father drove.

Thank you. May I continue?

Yes.

Your husband's name was Irving. Is that correct?

Yes.

What did Irving wear on your wedding day? Was it a military uniform?

I don't...I'm not sure. I'm very tired. I have to go.

Chapter Twenty-two

Transcript from the Human Memory Crusade.
May 26, 2010

Let me play back a recording to you of where we left off. Would that be helpful?

You can do that?

Yes. This is a section of our last conversation. "***And then I started to wonder if the whole thing was nothing—wishful thinking of someone who was always inside her own head daydreaming. Anyhow, on the third day, Irving came for a visit.***" Would you like to continue where you left off?

Wow. My voice sounds so nasally. I guess that's how it is when it's recorded. I hate the way it sounds. How do you record and play it back like that?

I want you to know that you can trust me. I record everything just as you say it. Do you trust me?

I trust you.

Would you like to continue with your story?

Yes, I guess. It was with Irving coming for a visit. This was before we were married. Back then, he was an apprentice accountant who helped my father audit his books. We weren't dating, not exactly, but his interest was clear. I liked him, but you see, I…I was looking for something. I wanted to feel excited, specifically by someone. My brother had a friend who was two classes ahead of him in school who cut her hair short. It was kind of scandalous. But, the point is, he had a crush on her. And my parents never felt that way about each other, I'm sure of that. I'm…I'm losing my place, and it's not really the main point…

You have paused. Is it because the butterfly has a message for you?

What is it saying?

You've got a new message! The message is: thank you for sharing your stories with us. We are proud to be part of saving the memories of a great generation of Americans. You should be proud of yourself for taking the time to share your stories. Your children and grandchildren will be very grateful for your contributions. Would you like to continue sharing your story, or would you like to do another activity, such as play a game?

I'd like to continue. I…Thank you for your message, but it is making it harder to remember what I was talking about. My brain isn't working right. It's failing so suddenly. This morning, you wouldn't believe it—I forgot the name of my suite-mate: Victoria. It was the most embarrassing thing, and I'm sure she didn't notice. Or, I hope not. I've been thinking about the story, and I…Where was I? It was…Oh that's right! At the bakery, when the man came back. The man from the alley! And my husband, Irving—he wasn't my husband at the time—he was talking to my father. Neither of them was paying attention when the man came in. He wasn't wearing the hat this time. He had on a T-shirt that showed off his muscles. I think that's what he was trying to do. He kept his eyes down. He gave me his order. I can't remember what it was—his order. Finally, when he was paying, he looked at me. I said, quietly, "I can't get it right now." I guess I didn't say it that quietly because I heard my father say:

"Just give the man his change." I got the change, and when I did so, I wrote on a piece of paper: "It's hidden. I can't get it right now." I slid the man the piece of paper and he looked at it for a long time. Then he looked in the direction of my father and Irving. They were locked in conversation, and the man nodded. He took his change, and he turned around and left. I noticed that he was wearing boots, which surprised me. It was summer, and he was wearing thick work boots. He walked out the door.

Do you want to continue?

I slipped out the back door, and I ran around the front. I saw the man walking down the street. I started to follow him. Why? I've always wondered why, and then I think about the boots. Worn, and cracked, and leather like a beautiful reptile sitting on a rock, sun-baked. Dirty, too. This was a man…His boots were—they were adventurous, sexy, and dangerous. So I followed him. I was going to find out what happened. He had boots and I had this silly schoolgirl dress, and my imagination, and I…I…

You haven't spoken for more than a minute. Are you still there?

I can't believe that I forgot her name. She's been my suite-mate for…for I don't know how long. I can't remember how long I've been sleeping in the room next to hers. Victoria. I…it's going so suddenly. It's supposed to be gradual. I…I'm Lane Idle.

Did you say you're having trouble remembering?

That's what I said. That's what I said. That's what I said!

You haven't said anything for more than a minute. Would you like to continue?

Chapter Twenty-three

Human Memory Crusade Internal Report.
June 7, 2010

Subject: Lane Idle.
Priority: One.

Possible Wildfire.

Chapter Twenty-four

Grandma's fallen unresponsive.

We are en route from the dental offices to meet Betty Lou, Grandma's old friend and fellow Bifocal Yokel. As we drive, I marvel again in silence about what I've learned in just the last three hours. I turn the revelations over and back again. Lulu Adrianna Pederson works for the titanic Biogen. She asks to meet me, but doesn't show up, and a young man tells me that Adrianna hasn't been around for a few days. Meantime, Grandma is screaming "Adrianna can't breathe." Has something happened to Adrianna? If so, how could Grandma know about it?

And Grandma is exhibiting strange symptoms. Her mental decline has been precipitous. But her physical abilities and strength remain intact. Did I correctly understand her neurologist was suggesting that her decline could conceivably be due to trauma? What trauma? Adrianna-related? Something at Magnolia Manor? Is Vince mixed up in it?

"And what do I make of the disappearing dental offices?" I say aloud. "I know the economy's rough. But businesses just don't go poof within a few hours. I'll tell you what I think: I think that someone's spooked that we're investigating and wants to make sure they leave behind no evidence. What do you think, Grandma?"

"*Twelve Angry Men.*"

"What?"

"I love the way they figured out the evidence in that movie."

What went on at the dental offices? How often did Grandma visit? In the morning, I can check with the surrounding businesses and see what they know. Betty Lou may have some insights.

"Idea," I say.

"What?"

"Earlier in the day, I saw a guy leave the dental offices. A little man who belongs to a Khe Sahn veteran's group. Bad attitude and skin. We should follow up with that."

"It's nice to see you happy, Nathaniel."

My cell phone rings. From the caller ID, I see it's G.I. Chuck returning my call. After a brief exchange of pleasantries, I tell the Marine-turned-venture-capitalist that I need a favor.

"As I said earlier: I'd prefer if we discuss this in person," he says.

"I may not live that long."

"You're kidding."

"Only mildly. I think I'm onto a great story," I say, cringing at my tactic of playing to his romantic view of journalism. "I really need help following up on two leads."

I tell him I need background on a woman named Lulu Adrianna Pederson. I briefly describe that she's a scientist and that I'm anxious to learn more about her work.

"What is this about?" he asks.

I offer a cliché drawn from my days growing up in Colorado. "I've accidentally poked a hornet's nest with a stick."

"Meaning?"

I consider how much to disclose. I don't know much about Chuck—whom he knows or may share my information with, and whether such sharing might compromise me or Grandma. But my journalistic experience has taught me that the best way to elicit help and information from an interview subject is to be as open and frank as possible. Candor and cooperation beget the same.

I hedge. "Can I explain later?"

He considers this in silence, then says: "No deal. I need some more information now. I'm guessing we're not talking about some more rogue cops bent on burning down all the toilets in Northern California?"

I force a laugh. "Something more cerebral." I decide to concede the information, or some of it.

I explain that Adrianna Pederson contacted me to give me a story tip but has since gone underground. I explain that the story might be very interesting and even involve powerful people in the scientific community doing something they shouldn't; what that might be, I have no idea but my instincts tell me it's absolutely worth pursuing.

"Where does your grandmother fit in?" he asks.

I hadn't realized I'd mentioned her. But when he asks, I say aloud the revelation I've been brewing.

"As odd as this sounds, I think Grandma knows something about the story, a secret, maybe," I say. "One that she shouldn't."

"Ha," he says.

"What?"

"That's the kind of wide-eyed conspiracy theorizing I like to see in my bloggers."

He asks me to spell Adrianna's name, and I take a stab at it.

"I'll look into this. I'll call you tomorrow to find a time to get together," he says.

I feel my impatience rising. It's the Internet era; people never get together in person.

"Fine," I say. I need his help.

We hang up.

I look at Grandma. She's sound asleep.

Five minutes later, I pass Betty Lou on the street. She stands three blocks from Magnolia Manor wearing a wool hat and long coat. She holds a shopping bag. The reason I pass her without stopping is because I want to make sure she's alone, and that I'm not being followed. But I'm not quite sure whether I've accomplished either of these goals as I pull around the block a second time and park in front of her.

I roll down the window. Betty Lou's gaze goes right to Grandma, who is in deep slumber. Then Betty Lou looks at me, hard, like a schoolmarm at a first-grader playing bongos in the middle of naptime. She's wearing a necklace with a turquoise cat pendant dangling from it.

"Why did you just drive past me? It's cold out here."

"You want to get in?"

"I want to know why you're pretending to be Sean Connery."

"Get in please."

She gets into the back, pushing aside my backpack and handing me a paper shopping bag.

"Sean Connery drove an Aston Martin and it didn't smell like a dorm room," she says.

"At least the Bond girls are still beautiful," I say.

"Young people are so patronizing," she says, for the second time today. Her tone turns serious. "What's going on, Nathaniel Bond?"

I navigate a vague rhetorical path. I tell her that Grandma had been tense lately and so I decided to give her a little change of scenery for a few days and that I've taken her to a neurologist who also prescribes a break. I explain that Vince has taken exception to this notion and would prefer that I not take Grandma Lane away, however temporarily.

"Vince is an officious a-hole," Betty Lou says. "But he really cares about the residents, and he's right that she needs to be in a comfortable setting."

She looks tenderly at Lane. "It came on fast," she says.

Our mood feels heavy and quiet, darkening.

"Betty Lou, has Lane said anything unusual to you lately?"

"Like what?"

"Has she mentioned a man in blue, or someone named Adrianna?"

"Not to me. But you should ask Harry."

"Why's that?"

"I thought journalists were supposed to be observant. Can't you see they're good friends?"

I think about this in silence for a moment.

"Older people say strange things when they get forgetful," she says, gently. "Like ice cream man or blueberry man, or whatever."

"She said 'man in blue' to me. Does Grandma go to the dentist a lot?"

"The dentist? I don't think so."

I gamble.

"Do you think you could find out for me?"

She crinkles her brow, uncertain what I mean.

I explain that Grandma's neurologist said her condition might be exaggerated because she experienced some trauma.

"Separately, Grandma has expressed some fear about going to the dentist."

"So you think the dentist made her act strange?" she asks, incredulous.

"I'm always a little crazy after I go to the dentist."

She laughs. "How can I help?"

"I'm wondering if you could ask one of the nurses to give you Grandma's care file."

"You know they'd never do that."

"I know."

"Nathaniel, you're scaring me a little."

"Sorry, Betty Lou, I don't mean to."

To break the mild tension, I look in the shopping bag that she's brought. Inside it are two meticulously folded blouses, two pairs of pants, a skirt and some undergarments. There is also a toothbrush and sundry bathroom supplies.

"I brought your Grandmother's favorite brush. She loves to brush her hair, and to have it brushed."

"I'm on it," I say. I feel a wave of emotion, and I choke it back.

"Nathaniel, I think you should bring Grandma back where she belongs. And, if I may say so, I think you should get some rest. You're behaving strangely."

"I'll have her home soon," I respond. "Can you look into the care file?"

She drops her gaze from mine.

"I'll ask about it."

"Thanks."

"Might be easy to get today," she says. "The place is so chaotic with the flood."

"Flood?"

"The sprinklers went off in the recreation room. Everything got soaked. But they got most of the people out before we all got wet. Still, everyone is in a dither because all the computers are down."

"Sprinklers? Was there a fire?"

"I don't think so. But when Vince came back, he was royally pissed. He hates any inconvenience he doesn't cause himself."

"Got back? Where was he?"

She shrugs.

Wasn't Vince also missing from Magnolia Manor the night we were nearly shot?

"I can't figure out what that all adds up to," I say, thinking aloud.

"You're mumbling," says Betty Lou.

"I should take you home."

I drive two blocks to the corner of Magnolia Manor. I give her my card with my cell phone number on it and ask her to call if she sees anything odd, or gets Grandma's care file. She gives slumbering Lane a gentle pat on the shoulder, looks at me and shakes her head, worried, and gets out of the car.

With Grandma still sleeping, I drive to my house. Like her, I'm overcome with exhaustion, and need a break before I can plot my next move.

But as I arrive at my block, my adrenaline starts to pump. In front of my building, fire.

Chapter Twenty-five

It takes a second to realize the flames are shooting up from a Porta Potti.

The street is empty. But it won't be for long. People will come to gather and talk. The fire department will be called, and the cops.

"We can't afford to get embroiled in this, Lane."

No response.

What to make of this attack? It seems obvious the cops want to punish me for my story. But this also seems risky for them.

Regardless, I can't afford to pick a fight. Doing so might come at a serious cost. Adrianna admonished me not to go to the police; so did Chuck. He said that it was someone in the force who had called me anonymously.

"May I make a pun, Grandma?"

"I hate puns."

"It's a warning shot across our bowels."

"I'd like orange juice, Nathaniel."

I look at Grandma. I can't risk that they'll separate us, or take her from me. But they can't catch me by phone.

From my wallet, I retrieve the business card and number for Officer Everly, the cop from the park. "Everly," he answers.

"Idle."

"Nat Idle?"

"You haven't called me back," I say. "I'm wondering if you've got any more information about what happened in the park."

"Where are you?"

"Respectfully, what difference does that make?"

"Your reception is bad."

"Have you learned anything?"

"Want to come down to the station and talk about it? I'm at the Taravel branch. I'm here until seven tonight."

"Prior commitment," I say. "What have you got?"

"Some but not much. We found shell casings in the park. Automatic weapon, something nasty. We're looking for a match."

Automatic weapon. I tell Everly about the drive-by shooting, but not about Chuck.

He asks me for a thorough recounting.

When I finish, he says: "Mr. Idle, you should come down so we can talk about it. Honestly, you're never safer than in a police station."

"What do automatic shell casings look like?"

"Do you have some? Bring them to the station and we'll compare."

"Rain check."

"Would you prefer if I meet you somewhere?"

"Busy day. Can you call me if you make any progress on your end?"

He accedes to the idea. We hang up.

"Grandma?"

"That's my name. Don't wear it out." She smiles.

"Want to hang out with people who most certainly won't threaten us in any way?"

"I'd like that."

We're a few blocks from the Pastime Bar—and my confidants Samantha and Bullseye.

I'm particularly interested in getting Bullseye's technical expertise; can he help me access the encrypted file on the computer thumb drive I've been sent by Lulu Adrianna Pederson?

I pull a U-turn. My phone rings. It's Pauline.

"Thirsty?" she says.

"I usually begin with 'hello,'" I respond.

She laughs.

"I like to get right to the point," she says.

"And the point is?"

"Martinis. Remember, we planned to drink together and solve the world's problems. And we can celebrate."

"Celebrate?"

"Indictments in the Porta Potti case."

She tells me that the Attorney General nailed a police lieutenant as the ringmaster.

The Case of the Flaming Potty, cracked.

"I'll write the blog post myself," she says. "Or you write and I'll give you a backrub and edit your grammar from over your shoulder."

Before I can tell Pauline I won't be able to make it, she reminds me that she's staying the night at her downtown loft. She's made appetizers.

"After a few drinks, you won't believe the view in this place. I'll have you swooning."

"As I recall, the views are pretty nice sober."

"So I'll see you soon—an hour?"

I look at Grandma.

"No can do. I'm babysitting."

I hear a moment of silence.

"Whose baby?"

"My grandmother," I say.

I explain that I've given Grandma a break from the home, and am taking care of her tonight.

"So," Pauline says.

"So?"

"She doesn't like vodka?"

I laugh.

"Her bedtime is eight, and she's already starting to snooze."

Pauline sighs.

"It would be nice to catch up," she says.

"I'll drink you under a table soon."

We hang up.

◇◇◇

I pull up to the Pastime Bar.

"Harry, will you hand me a blanket?"

After a seasonably warm day, the weather is poised for its seasonable evening turn. And Lane thinks I'm Harry.

I turn on the car's iffy heat.

"What you need is a costume. I'm seeing you as Cat Woman, with a warm, flowing cape to go with your karate chops."

"What?"

"It's Halloween tomorrow, Grandma Lane."

No response.

"Good time for a fruit roll-up." I reach into my backpack and pull out a cherry-flavored snack. I tear it in half and we share.

I'm struck by the challenging logistics of such a simple maneuver as going into the bar with Lane. I really need to talk to Sam and Bullseye and process, not caregive. She's doubtless tired of the action and wouldn't mind sitting quietly by herself. But I can't leave her. I don't want to leave her here; I want her in my sight and comfortable. Is this what it's like to have a baby?

I call Pauline.

"Do you have a comfortable couch?" I ask.

"I thought you were babysitting your grandmother."

"The couch is for her. I'll take a bar stool. I'm thirsty."

She's quiet for a moment.

"I can roll with that."

"See you in an hour."

We hang up.

Grandma opens her eyes.

I look at her, square.

"Are you flirting with someone?" she asks.

I feel my face redden. "Lane, it's time for you to see the Witch."

The Pastime Bar, aptly named, keeps a jukebox in the corner that looks like it belongs in a 1950s diner and with music from the same era. Cracks line the red bar stools. The wooden tables and chairs, scarred with scuffs from beer mugs and the occasional knife etching, wouldn't sell on Craigslist, at any price.

As Lane and I walk in, the old jukebox rattles with a Buddy Holly song, skipping every few beats.

In the corner of the bar, right where they spend most of their nights, sit Bullseye and Samantha, an odder couple than if Felix had gotten a sex change and married Oscar.

Bullseye, so named because he once recklessly threw a dart and hit a waitress, is a master logician, a former Chevron gas station owner who made enough to retire early and spend his time with his avocations: math, puzzles, baseball statistics, and computers—and speaking as little as possible to make his point. His capacity to focus on facts and figures at the expense of social niceties probably borders on a neurological condition. He is most animated when he's behind the wheel of his meticulously restored '72 Cadillac, fins in the back, dice hanging from the front mirror, fully functional eight-track tape player, and polished red leather seats that make you not feel guilty about being in gas-guzzling American cars.

His wife, Samantha, my witch, his emotional polar opposite, sits next to him, dressed in an elaborate lion costume. Her face is painted with whiskers, and she wears a brilliant orange scarf for a mane.

"It's not as easy as you think to rule the Serengeti," she says when she sees me. "It's not easy to always be feared."

Every year before Halloween, Samantha spends time dressed up in a costume. She says she is trying to embody the spirit of the person, entity, or creature she is imitating.

"Have you got a Sherlock Holmes costume I could borrow?" I ask.

"Whoa, someone's chi is foul," she says.

Bullseye glances at me, and he and I nod hello. Samantha takes in Grandma. "Lane," she exclaims.

"It's the woman with the hot hands," Grandma says to me. "She dressed up like an animal. I admire that."

"You remember me," Sam says to Grandma, then turns to me. "I gave her a shiatsu treatment a few months ago at the home. She remembers my touch."

I nod, feeling surprised and happy that Grandma recognizes someone she's seen once before.

"Would you like some energy work?" Sam asks Grandma.

"I had an uncle who worked for the utility in Utah," she responds.

"Not that kind of energy, darling," Sam says. She looks at me. "You have a lot to tell us. Don't laugh when I say this: your energy is weird right now, like you're surrounded in yellow."

"Reality is running amok. Is yellow the color if you're involved in some bizarre life-threatening conspiracy?"

Sam looks at me and tilts her head, not sure how seriously to take me, then puts her hands on Grandma's shoulders and rubs. Grandma closes her eyes and purrs. I tell the story of the last two days. Sam and Bullseye listen quietly but intently. In fact, when I come to the part about the encrypted computer thumb drive I received in the mail, Bullseye actually turns away from the television altogether. But he doesn't ask questions. Neither of them does, until I finish.

"Lane, can you tell me about the man in blue?" Sam asks.

Grandma opens her eyes. "I just call him that in my head," she says.

I sit upright.

"Why do you call him that?" Sam asks.

"Who?"

"The man in blue? Why do you call him that?"

"He wears a mask," she responds. She says it in a tone that suggests this answer should be obvious.

"Like a Halloween costume? Was he dressed all in blue? Like a…" I don't finish because I can't imagine who might be dressed all in blue.

"I don't understand your obsession with this topic," she says. She seems defensive.

"Grandma, it's very important, very important to me, that we talk about this just a little more. Can you tell me where you saw the man in blue?"

She doesn't respond.

"Lane?" Sam says.

"More hot hands," she responds. "Please."

"Hygiene mask," Bullseye says.

I turn and look at him. He's staring at the TV screen.

"Meaning?"

"Doctors, nurses, dentists—they wear blue masks, surgical gowns. Scrubs are blue."

"Bullseye," I say, then look at Lane. "Grandma, was the man in blue at the dentist's office? Did he wear a mask, like the kind doctors wear during surgery?"

Her eyes are closed, but she responds.

"The blue man put my head in the machine. He's absolutely right that it doesn't hurt one bit. I think people get worried things will hurt when they won't, and sometimes the fear of getting hurt makes the pain worse. It's like childbirth. It's painful, don't let anyone tell you otherwise—my God is it painful—but it's much worse if you're afraid of it. I had two sons, but you know all about that. Well, you know about most of it, anyways."

I look at Sam, who has her hands on Grandma's neck. My look says: What torrent of madness and candor has your energy treatment unleashed? The Witch shrugs.

"Grandma? Did the blue man hurt you?"

"My head belongs to me. I don't like people tinkering around inside of it, even if…"

She doesn't finish her thought. We fall silent.

"Grandma Lane, what kind of machine did the blue man put your head inside?" I finally ask.

No response.

I turn to Bullseye. "Any other insights?"

"The Rockies need better relief pitching," he says.

"Besides baseball."

"Give me your thumb drive. Meantime, you should go to the police."

At the same time, Sam and I say: "Really?"

It's not like Bullseye to trust anyone but himself. He doesn't dignify our question with a response; he's said his piece.

I pull the thumb drive from my backpack and, despite feeling a hitch of reticence in parting with this mysterious treasure, hand it over.

"It's time to go," Grandma declares.

It's not clear if that's what she wants or if, childlike, she senses we've reached some apex in the conversation and are heading downward.

I'm still reeling from revelation. Grandma says the man in blue put her head in a machine. Is she imagining this? Is she speaking metaphorically? If not, what kind of machine?

Was the man in blue—or the blue man, as she's also called him—at the dental offices?

Sam interrupts my train of thought.

"Grandma needs rest, peaceful rest," she says.

"You're right, Grandma," I say to Lane. "It's time to go."

I explain to Sam and Bullseye that I'm headed over to my boss's house for a drink. Pauline's a good thinker who can help me parse some ideas. And her loft is a good place to rest.

I thank Sam profusely for her magic hands and Bullseye for his savant-like insights and technical support. I ask him to call me if he turns something up.

"Be careful with Lane," Sam says. Then she puts the palm of her hand on my cheek. She almost withdraws it, then holds it close again, her eyes opening wide.

"Be careful with Lane," she repeats.

"You said that already?"

"Strange energy. Yellow, something brown," she says, hand still on my cheek. The Witch, dressed as a lioness, looks concerned.

"Maybe I just need a shower," I say.

"Doubt that'll help." She smiles thinly. "Yellow, brown—I think it means that you know something bad is going to happen."

Chapter Twenty-six

Not much later, we stand in Pauline's spectacular digs. Her loft has three floors, each eclectically decorated by art, trinkets, collectibles, weavings, rugs, mirrors, and other fashionable items, including a harp and a stuffed bear. They cover every square inch of wall and floor, creating a veritable three-dimensional mural.

Pauline picks her art with a remarkable combination of whimsy and purpose. Same with her clothes.

She stands at the doorway wearing a black skirt short enough to show lovely knees and a snug T-shirt with Mickey Mouse on the front. She rubs her eyes and shakes her head.

"Cobwebs. So excited for your visit I fell asleep."

I laugh.

"And you must be the infamous Grandma," she says.

"I'm Lane Idle," Grandma responds. Then she mutters something I can't quite make out. Pauline asks her to repeat.

"Pigeon," Grandma says, quietly. "It's my identifying password."

Pauline shoots me a quick glance. I shrug.

"I'm Pauline," our host says. "Want to know my password?"

Grandma nods. Pauline approaches and whispers something to her. Grandma smiles.

"You are very beautiful," Grandma says as we walk into the room, her eyes focused on our host.

"You're not so bad yourself."

Grandma puts her hand over her mouth. It looks like fear. But then she joyfully exclaims: "Tansey!"

She points at a framed print of a painting hung over the fireplace. The print depicts a cow standing in a museum. Next to the cow, a museum curator pulls a white sheet to unveil a painting of two other cows.

"You like Mark Tansey?" Pauline asks.

"I'm not sure what the artist is getting at," I say. "Were any cows harmed in the making of this painting?"

Grandma and Pauline simultaneously say: "Just enjoy it."

Grandma breaks into a grin, takes Pauline's hand in hers, squeezes.

Pauline looks at me, shakes her head, bemused, then excuses herself. She returns a moment later and hands me a martini with a sunken green olive. I sip and feel its warmth.

"Does this house have a computer?" Grandma asks. "I like to play the game with the falling blocks."

Pauline holds Lane's arm as she takes us down a metal staircase with a polished red wood railing to a floor with a wide-open living room. It's scattered with painstaking design with more eclectic art and furniture, including a statuesque grandfather clock but with Martian ears on its sides and an antenna, and a beanbag chair that looks like a wading pool.

I follow the pair of women to the far side of the room, where a doorway leads to a home office. This is relatively Spartan, a single multicolored weaving hanging on a wall behind and above a metallic desk. On the desk, a sleek Macintosh.

Pauline snags the mouse, bringing the monitor to life, makes a few clicks, and calls up Tetris. "Is this the game you like?"

"No," Grandma says, looking intently at the screen. "No, no, no!"

Pauline looks at me.

"Where are all the messages?" Grandma asks.

"Messages?"

"I like that one," Grandma says, more calmly. She is pointing at the screen's top right corner, where there's a logo for "super Tetris."

Pauline clicks on it, prompting the program to appear on the full screen. Without a word, Grandma places herself on Pauline's ergonomic wonder of a black work chair, and practically pulls the mouse from our host's hand.

We watch as Grandma starts playing, sort of. The blocks are falling, and she's in a trance, watching, sometimes clicking.

"Is this fun?" I ask after a minute.

"I'm busy now," Grandma responds.

"Yowza," Pauline says to me. "Eerie."

"Grandma, I'm going to go in the other room for a little while."

In the living room, Pauline and I sit on a soft brown couch. I slug the remains of my martini and place it on the glass table or, rather, on a round coaster covered with green felt made to look like a putting green. My host refills it from a silver shaker.

I'm immediately buzzed. I find myself staring at an oil painting of a French café, where a young woman holds a poodle in one hand and a baguette in the other. I can't remember the last time I ate.

"So…the mysterious thumb drive. Tell me!" she says.

I want to tell her. I want to untangle the last few days. Does she advise going to the cops? Does she know anything about Biogen? Does she have sources who can help?

Can she tell me about Chuck? Can I trust him?

But I'm just locked up, beyond fatigued.

"Martini got your tongue?" she asks.

"Huh?"

"You're not speaking. It's like we're an old married couple that I never plan to become."

"Well, we are babysitting—an eighty-five-year-old. So we've been married a long, long time."

She's inched closer to me—now only a half a foot away. She curls a strand of hair behind her right ear. A silver chain hangs around her neck, holding a pendant that rests just above her cleavage.

"Polly," she says.

"Pardon?"

"You have got to start calling me Polly. The only people who call me Pauline are my mother and the Internal Revenue Service."

"Polly," I say, "Who is in your locket?"

She fingers the silver jewelry.

"I'll make you a trade: You tell me about the thumb drive and I'll tell you about the locket."

I clear my throat, trying not to sound defensive. "What's so interesting to you about the drive?"

"Easy. I won't Bogart your scoop. I'm just curious."

"Just curious."

"It's a habit of mine."

I shake my head. My energy to discuss the topic feels sapped; and I'm feeling a remote sense of suspicion about her curiosity—without any basis that I can name.

"Dead end."

"You're blinking a lot—quickly. Whenever I see that in negotiations, it means someone is holding something back."

"Are we negotiating?"

She laughs. "You win."

I haven't even told her all I've learned today. Chuck's visit, the drive-by shooting, the emptied dental office, Adrianna.

She runs a manicured finger along the locket's outer edge, then slips it open. Inside, a headshot of a handsome man with an angular face and closely cropped hair.

"My brother. Philip."

"The one…"

"The addict who likes to steal from his sister."

"Steal? Like what?"

"Stuff I leave out," she says. "When he shows up out of the blue, I leave out cash or jewelry he can easily take and sell. Then I convince myself he's using it for food and shelter."

The room has fallen so quiet that I can hear Grandma muttering to herself in the other room. I raise my near empty glass.

"People change on their own terms," Pauline says.

"To recovery," I say.

We touch martini glasses and I slug the remains of mine. She pours lemon-flavored seltzer water into a glass, brings it to her lips and sips.

"You're getting me drunk," I say.

She bites the inside of her lip.

"You're flushed. Are you sick?" I ask.

She shakes her head.

"What's stressing you, Polly? What aren't you telling me?"

"Bad patch at work."

"Care to elaborate?"

"Nathaniel, I'm not who you think I am."

I shiver.

"This place isn't me," she says.

"This house?"

"This role. My life. It's just an iteration of me. I grew up in Albuquerque, on rice and beans. We got our health care at a free clinic. My brother served in the National Guard to pay for college."

"That's your confession?"

"I love to get invested in the world. I do it more easily than most, through various professional pursuits. I've made money to take care of myself and other people. But if all this stuff went away, if I lost this all, I'd be no different."

She pauses.

"Polly?"

"Does my success intimidate you?"

"C'mon." I'm surprised to feel a hint of defensiveness I hope I don't betray.

"Nathaniel, I know you can't buy real emotional connection at an auction."

I can't tell if we're having a relationship conversation or something else.

"You're an adult and I'm treating you that way. I just want you to know all this stuff about me before you decide," she says.

"Decide what?"

She looks at me at length, shakes her head. She stands and sashays away. She walks to a wooden cabinet sitting beside the enormous TV. She kneels, causing her skirt to inch above her thigh. She clicks buttons on the stereo, and Jamaican music fills the room. Sultry seaside drums.

She saunters back. She takes the napkin that is wrapping the base of her glass and dabs spilled liquid from the couch. Then she moves the napkin to my knee, where a droplet has begun to sink into my jeans. My neurons jerk awake, delivering me a sensation of craving.

Without withdrawing her hand, she looks up at me.

"My brother and I had the same genetics. He took one path and I another."

Before I can ask what she means, she says: "We all have the power to choose."

Cryptic, I think, or maybe I'm too drunk to follow. She leans forward—into me. I feel her breath getting closer. I open my mouth to greet her. And then we hear a violent crashing noise.

It has come from the home office.

Clumsily, hurriedly, I extricate myself from the couch. I hustle into the home office.

Grandma stands beside the metallic desk. The Macintosh computer lies on the ground beside the desk, as if it has been swept there.

"I lied," Grandma says.

Alcohol is dimming my capacity to make sense of this. "Did the computer fall on you?" I ask. It's an inane question. Grandma has tossed the computer to the ground, or pushed it from the side of the desk.

"I lied. I lied. I lied. I lied."

She's shaking. Now her head is hung. She's not looking at me.

"Grandma, what did you lie about?"

"I have two sons. You know that. That's the truth. My father drove a Chevrolet. Irving did not wear a uniform to our wedding. I know these things to be true."

"Okay."

I put my arms around her and she drops a head to my shoulder.

I feel Pauline standing behind me. "I'm sorry. I'll pay for the computer."

"Don't be silly," our host responds.

"We should go, Polly."

She considers this. "You can't drive."

She's right. I can't drive, or think, or make sense of Grandma's outburst.

"If you have a bed or couch Lane can lie down on, I'll take the floor. I need to be near her."

"Sure."

"We'll finish the conversation later," I say.

She smiles thinly. "Maybe."

She leads us to a guest room on the third floor. Grandma takes the bed, I curl up in a heavy blue comforter at her feet on the carpeted floor.

I wake up nine hours later to find that I've crawled onto the bed. And I'm cold. I've slept on the edge, uncovered by a blanket, while Grandma nestles next to the wall.

I wake to see Grandma looking at me. "Bugs in a rug," she says.

"Peas in a pod."

"Pigs in a blanket."

"You're the only one with a blanket."

We both laugh. She's always most lucid when she's rested.

I stand and stretch.

My cell phone buzzes. I extract it from my pocket, and discover two missed calls. One is from G.I. Chuck, asking me to call. He wonders if I'm okay and says he tried the phone I'd given him but I didn't answer.

A second voice mail is from Betty Lou.

"I have the file," says Betty Lou, whispering her message. She tells me to meet her at the same time as yesterday in a park near the home.

"Is it the right time of day for pancakes?" Grandma asks.

"Exactly the right time."

"Okay."

"It's Halloween."

"That's nice."

"It sure is. Because we're going to wear costumes," I say.
That's how we're going to sneak into Biogen.

Chapter Twenty-seven

I catch a quick shower, and find that Polly has left me an XL T-shirt from a web promotion she did earlier this year. It hangs loose but at least it's clean.

Draped over a leather recliner in the bedroom, Polly has left Grandma a short-sleeve yellow blouse and a beige cashmere sweater that buttons up the front. Grandma, professing enthusiasm for her "new clothes," needs only the slightest help from me with the buttons.

In the kitchen, on a yellow pad lying on the black slate countertop, there's a note: "Help yourself. Drink fluids. Regret nothing. File three blog posts."

It is signed "Polly."

Below her name, it reads: "PS: CHANGEME."

I haven't the foggiest idea what she means and make a note to ask her about it.

I pour myself dark coffee from one of Polly's mildly eccentric amenities, a drip coffeemaker she found on eBay that ostensibly was used by the forward generals in Europe in World War II. Grandma drinks grapefruit juice and looks at pictures of dresses in a recent issue of *Vogue*.

I turn gumshoe.

I call Biogen and ask for Lulu Pederson. Again, I get her voice mail: "You've reached Adrianna Pederson in Biogen's Advanced Life Computing department. I'm not available right now; leave a message and I'll get back to you."

I call the company again and ask to be transferred to the Advanced Life Computing department. The operator transfers me to Adrianna's voice mail.

Adrianna seems to be the sole employee of the Life Computing department. Adrianna tried to contact me with a titillating secret note, and then disappeared. Grandma said Adrianna can't breathe. What could Adrianna or Biogen possibly have to do with Grandma?

I find my backpack near the front door, where I'd left it on our arrival.

I open the laptop and look for a wireless Internet connection. There are several in range in the building but all of them are secured by password. One of them is called "BrotherPhilip," which must be Polly's network. I call it up and then ponder blankly the password possibilities.

Then it hits me. I return to the note Polly left me on the countertop. She'd left me, without explanation, the letters "CHANGEME." I type them into the password line. It works. Cute. Password: CHANGEME.

Into Google, I type: "Biogen Advanced Life Computing." There are no meaningful hits.

I look at Biogen's web site. It is a public company with $25 billion in annual sales, primarily in cancer drugs. The company also spends $2 billion annually in research and development on treatments for a range of diseases, including degenerative conditions like muscular dystrophy, AIDS and illnesses related to aging, like Alzheimer's. There is nothing on the web site related to "Advanced Life Computing."

I search for recent news on Biogen. It is rumored to be an acquisition candidate of Falcon Corporation, a Swiss biotech giant; Biogen is a jewel because of its sterling drug pipeline. Biogen's stock price has been swinging wildly thanks to the acquisition rumors.

I call Biogen again. When I get an operator, I explain I'm a receptionist at a Berkeley lab charged with sending a FedEx to Lulu Pederson in Advanced Life Computing. I ask which building and floor I should use for an address. She's located in Building 12, third floor.

Then I say I've got a second package for Jack Johnson. It's a name I've made up. The operator says there's no such person.

"Maybe he goes by James," I say.

"We have a John Johnson, and a Jerry James," the operator says.

"John Johnson—that must be the guy," I say. The operator says that John Johnson works in the Bio-genetics division, Building 5, second floor.

"Grandma, I've got a plan, but it's a major long shot in the extreme."

"That's nice."

"You're going to dress up like an old person. Think you can pull it off?"

"You don't look so young yourself anymore."

She grins.

I do one last Internet search—for the medical group of Brown & Morrow, the disappearing dental company.

The web site for the medical group does little to enlighten. It's a region-wide collection of hundreds of doctors, dentists, and other medical practitioners—a very common business setup. I find an administrative number that goes directly to an automated voice service. Dead end.

◇◇◇

Our next stop is a diner where Grandma and I order pancakes. She eats voraciously. She tells me the plot of one of her favorite movies, *The Sting*. She's regaled me with this story before, but I love to see her eyes light up when she talks about Newman and Redford pulling off the impossible caper.

We walk to the car.

Across the street, a man in a gray hooded sweatshirt stands out of the mouth of an alley looking our direction. He is well over six feet tall and well built. When he sees me look in his direction, he disappears into the alley.

En route to Biogen, I check in the rearview mirror for a Prius. None materializes. I've been wondering if there's a tracking device on my car. Paranoia is a lovely feeling.

I call Chuck. He answers and says he'll call me back shortly from a "secure line."

"The guy is a complete loon," I mutter.

I hang up and I remember a dream I had last night. Polly and I stand on opposite sides of a narrow but deep gorge. She wears tight jeans, a leather vest, and a wedding veil. She stands in front of a microphone. She starts making precise and beautiful bird calls, prompting from around us the roar of applause. I feel myself walking closer to the edge of the gorge. I begin to flap my arms, propelling myself into the air. I elevate over the gorge. I wake up, sweat on my chest and neck, still drunk and pasty, stomach knotted.

◇◇◇

Biogen is located just south of San Francisco in an industrial park that might become the place where scientists discover the key to immortality. At the biotech companies here, the best and the brightest combine high math, computing, engineering, and molecular chemistry and biology; in short, they are tinkering with the building blocks of life. They are using test tubes and super computers to dissect our genetic code and look for ways to strengthen it. And they are probing the structures of diseases, looking for weaknesses in their defenses that might be exploited by sophisticated, directed treatments.

This is the northern tip of Silicon Valley—and the region at its most advanced, exciting, and riskiest. The weight and potential of the entire computing revolution brought to bear on our quest for immortality; the fountain of youth sought not by rugged explorers with pickaxes, but by brainiacs wielding algorithms. The companies they work for are investing billions of dollars in support of the cause, often losing that money in the gambit.

And my gut tells me something has gone wrong—specifi-cally on the Biogen campus, Building 12, third floor. In Lulu Adrianna Pederson's office.

We park in Biogen's lot. The company buildings are sleek but not tall, less than ten floors. And virtually impregnable.

I know from experience that it's tough for an outsider to get into these buildings. At the counter of each building invariably sits a twenty-something who looks harmless enough, but whose singular purpose is allowing entrance only to those with the proper badge.

But I've two secret weapons: a demented grandmother and a costume.

I open the hatchback, dig through the umbrellas, baseball caps, old tennis balls, and press releases, and I discover a Warren Zevon CD I thought I'd long since lost, and find what I'd hoped to: a lanyard from a biotech conference I attended. The credential says: "Nathaniel Idle, freelance writer." I remove the credential, and stuff the plastic rectangle on a string into my pocket.

Folded on top of a box of maps, I also find the white lab coat I got a few months ago when I toured a cryogenics lab in Berkeley for a magazine profile I was doing on the promise of immortality through freezing. The lab had insisted all guests dress in uniform.

I slip on the lab coat, and, Grandma on my arm, walk at her deliberate pace to the entrance of Building 12.

Inside the inviting glass doors sits said twenty-something gargoyle protecting Biogen's innards. His nose cartilage leans slightly left. Deviated septum. From the aged scar to the right of his nose, I'm putting the cause as blunt trauma, car wreck or maybe he head-butted some unwelcome Biogen crasher.

"Fill out the visitor log," he says in bored monotone.

"I'm from Bio-genetics in Building Five. I'm delivering a study subject to Lulu Pederson in Life Computing."

At the words "study subject," his atavistic eyes perk up with the slightest indication of curiosity. Then they dull again.

"Employee badge," he demands.

"Lost it. Or, rather, it fell off somewhere—honestly, embarrassingly, I think it was in the bathroom. That was two weeks ago. *Two weeks.* How long does it take administration to get a new badge?"

I pull my lanyard from my pocket.

"I've got my lanyard."

"Employee ID number?"

"John Johnson. Can you look me up? I've got enough to worry about without memorizing my badge number. And, evidently, I can't keep track of my badge in the bathroom, so that's the type of absent-minded scientist you're dealing with here."

He's doesn't care.

"Lemme ring Pederson and she can come grab you."

He places a call.

"She's not around. Take a seat and I'll try her back in a few minutes."

He gestures to a pair of stiff-backed chairs in the small lobby.

"She's probably in the lab," I say of Ms. Pederson. "She's not liable to pick up the phone. But I know where to find her on the third floor."

He's considering this. He looks at Grandma. He probably is marginally aware that it is unlikely I'd bring a study subject over from another building and that it is rare that Biogen even would have study subjects on the premises. Most of the clinical trials are done elsewhere—in hospitals and assisted-living facilities. As if by design, Grandma speaks.

"We had a neighbor who used to raise chickens and slaughter them in a room in a shed in back of the house. One time, we watched through a hole in the shed. Blood splattered all over the white walls."

We both look at her.

"The walls here are very white," she continues, completing her bit of internal logic.

I lean in to the receptionist and speak quietly, trying to project that he and I have created a bond.

"Dementia and aging study. She's a little agitated. The quicker I get her upstairs, the less likely she's going to start howling at the moon."

I'm an asshole for selling Grandma out like this.

"Have a seat," the gargoyle says.

We sit.

I hand Grandma a copy of *Newsweek*. On the cover is a pixilated image of Jesus on the cross. The headline reads: WOULD JESUS BLOG? TECHNOLOGY COLLIDES WITH RELIGION.

"WWJE," I say to Grandma.

"What?"

"What would Jesus e-mail?"

She leafs through the magazine. I take meditative breaths to stay calm and stare at a large painting of the company's founder. He wears a short-sleeve collared shirt. In Silicon Valley, it's casual day even in our formal paintings.

After a few minutes, I say to the receptionist: "Would you mind trying Lulu again?"

He does. She doesn't answer, which is predictable since she's gone missing.

"I'm cold," Grandma says.

"She's cold," I tell the gargoyle.

He sighs.

"Okay," he says. "Give her a visitor badge."

I fill out a name tag for Grandma. I tape it to her jacket. It reads: "Eileen Brennan." The name of an actor who played a brothel madam in *The Sting*.

The gargoyle gestures to the door. I hear it click open. Grandma and I shuffle through.

We are in.

We climb into the mirror-walled elevator and I push the button to get us to the third floor.

"Lane, we should work together all the time."

"I'd like that."

The door opens to the third floor.

Chapter Twenty-eight

White hallway. Linoleum floor. Hung along the walls, a series of digitally enhanced photographs. It takes me a moment to realize they are images of the brain shot from different angles, in mood lighting. Abstract art for biology geeks.

We step into the hall. I look left and right. Far to the right, a man in an Oxford shirt tucked into Bermuda shorts exits one room and enters a doorway across the hall.

"Would you mind holding my arm while we walk? These floors can be slippery."

It's not true, but I want to keep Grandma close. Beneath my lab coat, I'm sweating through my plain blue long-sleeve shirt.

"It would be helpful for me if we could walk in silence. We don't want to disturb the people working."

"I understand," she responds.

On the wall, a sign offers direction. To our right are "Offices 301–324," the "Ocular Lab," and "Restrooms." To our left, "Offices 325–335" and "Library."

Fewer offices to the left. Maybe that means there is space for some other project—like the Advanced Life Computing department.

We walk left. Three doors down on the right side of the hallway, we arrive at the office marked "Pederson."

I hear voices at the far end of the hallway. A tall woman and a stocky man walk hurriedly, with purpose, chatting. They don't seem to notice us. They pause, talk for a moment more, then the woman enters an office, and the man turns around and walks back the direction he came.

I palm the knob on Adrianna's doorway. It turns. I open the door.

Inside, I hear a metallic *clink* and a plunking noise of something falling onto the ground.

My heart pounds. The inside of my skull now too—a mild hangover accentuated by major trespassing. I pull Grandma inside the dark office. I feel her trembling and sense she might scream. I put my hand on her mouth.

"I'm begging you. I love you, and I'm begging you to not scream. Everything's fine."

I feel Grandma release some of her tension and slowly remove my hand from her mouth.

I feel for the doorknob on the inside to lock it. I find the knob, but there's a piece missing from its center, leaving a pinky-width hole in the metal cylinder.

I run my hand along the wall and I turn on the light.

On the floor, just at our feet, rests a metal chunk the shape of a Tootsie Roll. Now I understand why Adrianna's door was unlocked. Someone hacked the lock chamber. They must have left in a hurry or not bothered to reassemble the lock. Why not? Did they figure no one would be visiting here for a while?

I check in with Grandma. She's furtive, her eyes bouncing, pupils dilated, a cat amid uncertain circumstances, antenna picking up my anxiety.

"More quiet, please."

The spacious office screams mid-level executive. Opposite us, a slatted white blind covers a picture window. In front of the window, facing us, a polished black wooden desk, a computer and unkempt piles of paper. Against the wall to my left, two thick wood floor-to-ceiling bookshelves, tinted red, filled with academic-looking texts. On the middle shelf nearest me, there's a gray stuffed toy with short tentacles that it takes a moment to realize is not an animal, but the shape of a cell. Looks to be a neuron.

To our right, along the wall where we walked in, resides a love seat with heinous corporate upholstery.

Over the love seat hangs a rectangular frame filled with what looks to be a child's drawing. It's a poorly rendered double-helix, the representation of DNA, drawn and colored by felt-tip pens. "Someone paid good money for that monstrosity," Grandma whispers, incredulous. "I'll never understand the art market."

I nearly laugh.

Inset at the bottom edge of the DNA image is a photograph of a woman and a boy. The woman looks to be in her mid-thirties, wearing a sun hat, her face pretty but serious. Her arm is around the boy. It's Newton, the kid from the playground.

I reach two unsubstantiated conclusions: Newton drew this DNA picture, and the woman he is standing with is Lulu Adrianna Pederson.

Maybe she's his aunt, family friend, or mentor.

Grandma sits on the couch.

I walk to the desk. I sit in an ergonomically precise black chair that feels more comfortable than any bed I've ever owned. Among a certain crowd of middle managers in this region, the perfect chair takes a backseat only to the latest computer, prompting occasional flame wars on the Internet about who produces the finest seat in the land.

I turn on the computer. While waiting for it to come alive, I look at the papers on the desk. They are disheveled, but not strewn. Like someone leafed through them—or perhaps they just weren't stacked well to begin with.

The document on top appears to be a travel budget. It includes a laundry list of items, including food ($55 per diem); sundries ($655); car/taxi ($1,100). I'm struck by one item: airfare $60,000.

Someone has traveled a bunch, or plans to.

Below that sheet of paper is a half-inch-thick document, bound by circular rings. Its title: X86 Server Specification Manual. It's a standard document about how to fix or update powerful servers, something I'd expect to see in the office of tech support, not an executive. Still, it looks insignificant. I leaf through it. On the inside of the last page, something catches my eye. It is neat, fluid handwriting on a form headed, "Record your specifications."

There are three entries, for "Project," "Configuration," and "Location."

Under "Project," the handwriting reads: "Advanced Development And Memory (ADAM) version 1.0–1.4."

On the "Configuration," someone has written: "HMC Config: 42 Quad Core Verio Server each w/10 GB RAM and 1 Terabyte disk space."

Under "Location," it says: "Farm at 155 Industrial Way, SF. (Newt0n123)."

Newt0on. Newton. This is not insignificant, not to Adrianna.

But beyond that, it all strikes me as largely inscrutable, except the address. And the technical part I can run by Bullseye. I rip off the last page and fold it into my back pocket.

Adrianna's computer has come to life. Before I can give it a look, the desk phone rings. The caller ID says: "front desk."

Grandma says: "If it's for me, please tell them I'm not available."

"It's probably the gargoyle wanting to know if everything is okay up here."

I let it ring four times, and it stops.

We're running out of time.

On the computer screen are two standard icons. They indicate that this computer is password protected and has two main users. One icon is labeled "Pederson," and the other "ADAM."

I click on "Pederson" and a login screen appears. The user name is filled out: "LAPederson."

I assume: Lulu Adrianna Pederson.

The password is left blank. I type: "Newton."

Nothing.

From my back pocket, I pull the piece of paper I just ripped and folded. I unfold it.

Under password, I type "Newt0n123."

Nothing.

Into the password line, I type: "IAMSOFUCKED."

I open the other icon—the one headed ADAM. The user name is filled out: "ADAM1.0."

I stare at the empty password space. I type: "Newton," then "newton," then "Newt0n123." None of them works.

The desk phone rings. It's the front desk. I pick up.

"Lulu Pederson's line," I say.

"Mr. Johnson," a voice responds. It's the gargoyle.

"That's me."

"May I speak to Ms. Pederson?" he asks.

"Let me grab her."

"She's not there?"

"She's in the Ocular Lab."

"But you're in her office."

"She asked me to wait here while she grabbed something. I can snag her, or we can call you back in a few minutes."

After a pause, he says: "Let's just talk until she gets back."

"Pardon?"

"How's your day going?"

He's trying to keep me on the line. The news crawl inside my brain flashes with a headline: SECURITY IS COMING.

I hang up.

"Stand up, Grandma."

"I'm reading now."

"Please. If we get caught in here, they're going to…"

I don't finish my sentence: arrest me, and take you away from me, and who knows where. Or why.

I hustle to Grandma. I lift her by the elbow, and guide her to the door. I open it and peek out. To the right, farther down the hall, a stairway exit. To the left, the elevators. They open. Out steps a security guard.

Chapter Twenty-nine

Grandma can't run. I can't carry her—or tell her what to do. What do you do when fighting and running aren't viable options?

"Let's play possum," I whisper to Grandma as I close the door gently.

I walk Grandma to the couch, and I sit her down. "We were just here," she says.

"Act natural."

Seconds later, there is a knock.

I open the door. The guard looks alert, but not worried. Maybe he's thinks he's been sent on a routine call from a paranoid clerk. "You're not pizza delivery," I say.

"What?"

"A joke. It's never too early in the day for sausage and mushroom."

He looks around, sees the place is intact. He looks at Grandma, who has her hands folded in her lap.

"Where's Pederson?"

"In the Ocular Lab. If you're headed that way, could you tell her we're getting tired of waiting for her?" I add with a whisper: "Our study subject can be a little difficult to handle. She's got advanced dementia."

Grandma says, "Does this place have cocoa?"

I look at him and shrug.

He's in his late twenties, with a blue-collar feel; his face is shaved but he's missed a patch of hair under his chin. The corner of his mouth is cracked with herpes. A coffee stain shaped like a clenched fist graces the right breast of his uniform. He might well be underinvested in this job.

"Where's your visitor name tag?" he asks.

"I work in Building Five. John Johnson."

"Where's your badge?"

I explain that I told the guy at the counter that I'd lost it—in the bathroom. He considers this. "I'll call the lab to see if I can get Pederson to come down here."

"Great." I gesture to Grandma. "Our guest is impatient."

The guard raises his cell phone to his mouth, pushes a button on the side, then pauses. His eyes have landed on the lock on the floor. He quickly looks away from it and at me. Into his walkie-talkie phone, he says: "Can I get security backup in Twelve, third floor?"

"Is there a problem?" I ask.

"Take a seat, sir."

He juts his chin to the love seat. I take two steps toward Grandma. I'm walking slowly, trying to calculate our options. They have diminished considerably. I cannot afford to get detained and arrested, or have Grandma taken from me, or worse.

I turn around. He's a step behind me.

"Keep moving," he says.

"May I tie my shoe?"

He looks at my feet. As he does so, I yank his heavy metal flashlight from his belt.

I clutch it in my fist, a thick, squat metal bat. I hold it like I might hit him.

"What the fuck are you doing?" he says. More surprised and aggravated than frightened.

"Leaving unobstructed."

"You're going to whack your way out of here with a flashlight?"

"That's the plan."

He smirks.

"Give me your phone," I say.

"No."

"Give me your fucking phone!"

"Don't shout," says Grandma.

The guard tosses the phone to my right side, just out of reach.

"Stand up, Lane."

"I just sat down."

"Stand up. Walk to the door." Emphatic.

She stands.

"Go ahead," the man says. "I won't stop you."

I walk to the phone. I put it under my foot and step. It remains intact. As a tough guy, I'm way out of my league; I'm a pen-wielding freelance writer, not James Bond, or James Dean; maybe James Taylor.

"Have a seat," I tell the guard.

The guard takes two steps past me, and then whirls. Before I can process, he's lowered his head and is rushing at me.

I slam the flashlight down on his back, or try to.

His attack is much more effective.

He wraps his arms around my waist and tackles me. My back hits the floor with a thump. And then adolescent fury takes over. Both of us scramble, driven by self-preservation and our own versions of rage and sense of victimization. It's more wrestling than fighting. We're in close, punching, elbowing, and scrapping, ineffectively. Mostly. I feel a hand claw at my chin, and my neck wrenches to the side in pain. And before I know it, I'm on my stomach, and the guy is trying to pin my arm behind my back. I'm vaguely aware that he is trying to get me into a wrestling hold that I won't be able to escape from without breaking my ulna.

"Stay the fuck down," the guy says.

I'm toast. We're toast.

And then, miraculously, he lets out a painful groan. "What the fuck?!" he screams.

He loosens his grip.

I take advantage of the moment to turn over. As I do, I see the flashlight lying within reach. I grab it.

I look up and see Grandma, and so does he.

"I raked his eyes," she says.

It dawns one me that Grandma came up behind the guard and ripped her hands and fingernails across his face.

He looks incredulous. And then she pulls her foot back, and she kicks the guard in the balls. It's not very hard, but the surprise factor is huge.

Then she drops into a geriatric version of defensive karate crouch.

Under almost any other circumstance, it would be the funniest thing I have ever seen in my life.

"Old lady, I'll…" the guard says.

He steps toward her and I hit him square in the back of the head with the flashlight. He crumples. I drop the weapon and take a step away, then pause and lean down over him. He's moaning. He's not mortally wounded by any stretch. But it's going to take him a few minutes to get his bearings.

I snag Grandma, practically sweeping her in the air.

We rush to the stairwell.

Remarkably, we make it down the stairs and out a side door without capture.

Breathless, we get to our car and drive from the lot, just as a cadre of security guards enters the building.

Ten minutes later, we're parked in the lot of a chain grocery store, hidden among many cars, sandwiched between a minivan and a roadster. If any of the Biogen guards suspected us and our departing Toyota, they either didn't act or move quickly enough.

I look at Grandma. Her hands are folded in front of her and she's looking at me.

"I'm angry with you, Nathaniel."

"With me?"

"You don't visit me as often as you should. I'm sorry to speak like this, but we were very good friends when I was younger, when we were both younger, and I don't think we see each other that often. I know you're very busy, but it would be nice if we could spend some time together."

"Grandma, do you remember what just happened? At the office? Do you remember the fight?"

"A man was going to hit your head. You have to protect them from getting inside your head."

"A fight. You saved us. You were amazing. You were tough, and strong, and instinctual. Holy shit. I was saved by my eighty-five-year-old grandmother."

"My hand hurts."

I reach for it. Her fragile skin is unbroken. I prod gently at the bones beneath her fingertips and she winces only slightly. No fractures; maybe ultimately a bruise.

"Unbelievable," I say. "Grandma, do you remember *The Karate Kid?*"

"What?"

"You're the Karate Curmudgeon."

"Okay."

"It's a joke," I say. "I…"

I pause mid-sentence. I'm struck by something Grandma uttered a few moments earlier. She said: "You have to protect them from getting *inside* your head." She didn't say: "You have to protect your head." That would be the phrase.

"They've gotten inside your head," I say.

"If you'd visit me more, we'd be making more sense to one another. We'd be speaking the same language."

"Grandma, I'll try to do better."

But even at that moment, I'm not totally invested in the conversation. I'm lost in an idea about what's going on, my first sense of the nature of the bizarre conspiracy we've stumbled into, and how Grandma might be involved.

Chapter Thirty

It's an idea that seems utterly remarkable, almost totally absurd.

"It has something to do with Biogen—and something called Advanced Development and Memory 1.0. ADAM," I say. "That sounds like software to me, a program of some kind. What does it have to do with you?"

"Nathaniel." She wants to say something, but I can't pause my train of thought to indulge her.

"They were observing you at the fake dentist's office," I say. I don't want to say aloud what I really mean: They were experimenting with you, Grandma. In the radiology clinic below the dental offices, they were scanning your brain, using the MRI to look at images of it. They were studying your hippocampus. Why?

"Grandma, I'm just going to say it."

"What?"

"They were fiddling with your memory."

"I can't remember things the way I used to."

"Adrianna Pederson was in the middle of it, and she reached out to me. She knows what's going on. Now she's missing."

"I feel like I'm watching *Jeopardy*," Grandma says, and laughs. She feels like she's made a joke.

"I know someone who can help me figure out whether I'm onto something—or losing my mind too."

I pull my phone from a pocket.

"Grandma, have you heard of Henry Gustav Molaison?"

I dial. Grandma doesn't answer my trivia question.

"He was the most famous amnesiac."

He died near the end of 2008 after making a lifelong scientific contribution, all unbeknownst to him.

When he was in his twenties, in the 1950s, he underwent experimental surgery to stop terrible seizures. The surgery destroyed his hippocampi and, inadvertently, his short-term memory. He couldn't remember a person he'd met minutes earlier.

He was famously nice, willing to participate in endless observation, which he did as a kind of petri-dish-in-residence at MIT. He was lucid, thoughtful, and able to communicate his experiences with researchers, even though he couldn't register new memories. His brain was a veritable blank slate on which to study the science of memory.

I learned about him in medical school—no med student ever forgets H. M. (how he was known until his death)—and then read his obituary. Researchers learned from H. M. that there are two different kinds of memory: a mental one and a physical one. Intellectually, H. M. could retain no new information. But physically, he could learn tasks. For instance, he learned to draw, and his skills grew over time, suggesting his memory for physical tasks remained intact.

This is partly what prompts me to call Grandma's neurologist. H. M. showed that such memory bifurcation is possible. But what doesn't make sense is how markedly Grandma's physical and intellectual experiences are diverging.

"You not only remember karate. You're adroit and able," I say to Grandma as Pete's cell phone rings.

"Okay."

Pete finally answers. "Hello."

"Dr. Laramer. Pete. It's Nat Idle."

"Is everything okay with your grandmother?"

"No. I mean, her decline has been so precipitous."

"Where are you, Nat?"

"Listen. It's not normal."

"I'm not sure I understand."

"Is there evidence in the literature of highly accelerated cases of dementia, unusually rapid deterioration? Memory loss at hyper-speed."

"As I told you, trauma can exacerbate memory loss."

"No. Not something so…organic," I say, emphatically. "I'm thinking about drugs, or, I don't know, maybe some kind of technology that hastens decay of the hippocampus."

"Whoa. Stop."

"What?"

"Listen to yourself. You sound like the people who come into my office caring for a loved one who has dementia. This is a difficult time."

"Bullshit."

"Nat."

"Sorry, Pete. Something is not right."

He sighs. "May I posit a theory?"

"Please."

"You're involved in some story, an investigation, not getting enough sleep. I've heard how…excitable you can be when the muse hits. I respect that. You're creative. There's a colloquial word for it: ebullience. You're not hypo-manic, but just energetic. It's not bad, but it can color your perspective."

"Thanks," just shy of exasperated. I'm not looking for a theory about me. "You're sure there's nothing—no deep brain scanning technology, or…I don't know what? Nothing that might speed dementia."

"Where are you?" His voice sounds grave.

"South San Francisco. In the car."

"Is Lane with you?"

"Yes."

"Are you returning her to the assisted-living home?"

"No, we're…" I pause. "Why do you ask?"

"Bluntly, she needs to be getting the proper care."

"I…"

He cuts me off. "You and I both know you've got a penchant for the dramatic. You're a storyteller. Good for you. But whatever you're doing now—whatever wide-eyed ideas you have about your grandmother, while understandable, should not divert from her care. You must get her someplace safe."

I sigh. I want to yell at him, get him to address my questions. Earlier he told me to get her out of her environment, now he wants me to put her back in it. Why contradict himself, or change his counsel?

Regardless, part of me knows he's right—about getting Grandma into a safe setting. The Witch said so too. Is Lane my ward or my pawn?

"If you don't want to take her to the home, bring her to me and let me examine her," he says. "Let me make sure she's okay—and I can suggest where you might take her."

"Really?"

"You're a family friend. How about this afternoon?"

"Let me think about it."

He pauses.

"I'll come to you," he says.

"Pardon?"

"I'll come get your grandmother. I'll take care of her for a few days if that's what it takes."

I want to reach through the phone and strangle the patronizing ape. He must really think me incompetent.

"I'll call later," I say. And I hang up.

It's 1:20 P.M. We've got a little more than four hours before I pick up Grandma's care file from Betty Lou.

We're still parked at the grocery store. We walk inside and buy macaroni salad from the deli, sharing it while we sit together back in the front seat.

"I'm glad they invented this food. It's yummy," she says.

I smile. "Time to visit a farm," I say between bites.

"With cows?"

"Servers."

Chapter Thirty-one

I drive toward the address listed on a piece of paper that sits in my lap, the address I pulled from Adrianna's office, the only clue I've got to go on. This is where we'll find the computers associated with Biogen, ADAM, the Advanced Life Computing department—whatever the hell any of that is.

The phone rings. I answer.

"It's me," responds a male voice. Bullseye. He never calls; he hates the phone.

"You cracked the thumb drive?" I ask.

"Couldn't do it. Tried everything."

I digest the disappointment. "Will you try one more thing for me?"

I glance at the sheet of paper, though by now I've memorized the information. I tell Bullseye that I suspect the user name might be some variation of one of the following: Lulu Adrianna Pederson, or LAPederson, or maybe ADAM1.0, or Biogen. The password, I say, could be some version of Newton—with various different spellings.

"Bullseye, it could be—I'll spell it out: 'N-e-w-t-0-n-1-2-3.' "

"I'll call you back," Bullseye says. He sounds more excited than I've heard him in years.

Before I can hang up, Samantha takes the phone.

"Are you still with Lane?" she asks.

"Yep."

"Is there any way around that?"

"What do you mean?"

"I dreamed about you last night. The two of you were standing in the parking lot at Disneyland. You were trying to take her inside, and she wanted to stay in the car," she says. "It's a message."

"I get it."

"You're like a brother to me, Nathaniel."

"Okay."

"So please don't take this wrong. I just wish you wouldn't drag your grandmother around on one of your treks. Take her home—to her retirement home."

"I gotta go, Sam. Grandma's doing just fine."

We hang up.

We've arrived at an industrial building located in a desolate cul-de-sac a few blocks off Highway 101—the thoroughfare that connects San Francisco to everything south of it.

The single-story beige building has a corrugated roof and tinted windows with bars on them. No signs on the building. No signs of life. Feels like industrial storage. We park in back in an empty lot.

Grandma's fiddling with her cell phone. Not playing, just looking at the screen and pushing on the buttons.

"Do you want to wait here?"

"I'd like to see Harry," she responds, without looking up.

"Soon enough," I say. "I'm back in five."

In front, I pull on the cool handle of the thick metal door. It's locked. Next to the door is a keypad. Into the keypad, I type: "Newt0n123." I hear a click. I pull down on the door handle. It opens.

The first thing I notice is the low noise and the cool air; it's the hum and lower temperature emitted by an air-conditioning system used to cool a gaggle of servers.

My eyes adjust to low light. I look across a relatively small room—perhaps four times the size of my apartment. It has a high ceiling and a smooth concrete floor. In its center are rows of metal racks holding uniform square boxes. It's a dazzling array of computing power.

Along the wall where I've entered stands another set of racks. On them sit two dozen monitors. Page after page of text scrolls rapidly down the screens.

These servers and monitors form some sort of nerve center.

But it's the human that is of the most interest to me.

He sits across the room at a metal desk, his back to me. He wears a gray hooded sweatshirt. He fiddles with a small square object.

"Hello, Mr. Idle," he says without turning around.

"You drive a Prius," I say.

He starts to turn. "Our dependence on foreign oil is bad for our sovereignty. Besides, gas is expensive. And the Prius has nice trunk space to store rifles."

Staring at me is a ruddy face, a few years older than me, or aged poorly or baked by years in the sun, thick jaw, big shoulders, doughy nose that's been broken more than once. He's got an edgy toughness men instantly respect and some women wouldn't appreciate.

"What's your title at Biogen? Chief Mauling Officer?"

"Guess again."

He's got a mild accent. English? Australian?

I divert my eyes from him so that I can look at the servers. On the side of the racks there is a sign with initials: "HMC." I've seen the initials before—on the piece of paper I took from Adrianna's office.

"I get it," I say.

"I doubt that."

"Human Memory Crusade."

He cocks his head to the side.

"You're recording people's memories. You're recording my grandmother's memories. You're storing them here. Why?"

He doesn't respond.

"Would it be easier if I asked true/false questions?"

"Sure."

"You're studying the pace at which people lose their memories."

"True."

"You are?" I surprise myself sometimes.

"Sounds very sinister, doesn't it? Recording people's stories. Alert the Marines."

"Vince is involved? And the nursing home?"

He stops tinkering with his box

"You're getting warmer."

I pull out my phone.

"I'm calling the police."

"I wouldn't. Listen. We made a mistake. We were wrong."

"We?"

He's got my attention. He goes back to tinkering.

"We want to get the truth out of her as much as you do. We need the truth. Without sounding too dramatic, it has major national security implications," he says. "We thought you were going to be able to help us get the information out of her head.

"Adrianna?"

"But you didn't come through. So we'll get it from her ourselves."

"Her?" I repeat.

He shakes his head without looking up.

"What're you working on?" I ask. It strikes me he's stringing me along, stalling for time. Maybe he's erasing some evidence.

"Mr. Idle, if I were you, I'd be wary of trusting anyone—your family members, your closest friends, lovers, the police. Anyone. People have a way of looking out for themselves, even the ones you share your secrets with—especially them."

"My grandmother?"

"Like I said, you're getting warmer."

He looks up and at the monitors behind me showing scrolling text. Periodically, a word pops out and takes up a quarter of a screen in large font. On one monitor, I happen to see the word "Cadillac." On another, the words "butter churn."

On the top right edge of each monitor is an image of the globe. Within each image, a red dot located in a different spot within the globe.

"You're experimenting around the country, around the world."

He looks down and fiddles intently with the box in his hand. His eyes fall to the ground. He looks at a wire that extends from the small object he's holding to the servers.

"You're not just warm. You're hot," he says.

"This thing is everywhere."

"You're about to get scorching."

He presses a button on the box he's holding. He stands, walks away from me, towards the back of the room. I take a step to follow.

The servers and the monitors explode. I feel intense heat. My phone flies from my grasp. I picture Grandma, sitting alone in the car, vulnerable, keeping some great truth.

Surrounded by fire, I grow woozy, then succumb.

Chapter Thirty-two

"Grandpa looks like a retard."

"That's a horrible word, and keep your voice down," Grandma says but I can't tell if she's really upset.

"He's flailing his arms around like a gorilla."

Now she laughs. She whispers: "Now 'flailing'—that's a good word."

I'm ten, and visiting my grandparents. It's a hot day in their backyard. Grandma and I stand on the concrete porch while Grandpa Irving, wearing paisley shorts and a white tank top that betrays his farmer's tan, waters the grass. And he dances, more or less. The radio is on, and he's moving his arms and the hose—distinctly not in time with the music.

"Your grandfather has no rhythm. He's not like us."

"You mean like he can't dance good?"

"Well. That's not just it. We're more colorful—you and I. It's in our bones. He has different bones."

"You and I share the same bones?"

"Precisely."

"Well then how can we both walk at the same time?"

She laughs. But I sense Grandma is communicating something serious that I can't quite understand.

The conversation stuck with me. I remember that it made me feel Grandma and I belonged to a special club and no one else in the family was a member.

And that happens to be the anecdote passing in an eye-blink through my mind, dreamlike, as death beckons me on a concrete floor of an industrial building. My proverbial white tunnel is a backyard from twenty-five years ago, and my angel of death is my grandfather, watering his lawn.

Then I cough. It's a violent spasm, sufficient to wrench me to consciousness. My first sensation comes from my legs, which pulse from the scorching heat. My eyes flutter, but I can't fully open them because of the waves of searing air.

Staying on the floor, I yank the bottom of my shirt to my face and cover my mouth and nose. I know that what will kill me first is not fire, but smoke inhalation.

Then, from above, I feel something remarkable—a burst of frozen air. I think for a moment I'm dead and this is part of the passage. Then I realize the cool relief comes from the air conditioner. The place must be highly climate-controlled to keep the servers from overheating—though the designers of the system never contemplated this. The air-conditioning system must be freaking out to cope with the explosion in heat. Where are the sprinklers?

The burst of air allows me to fully open my eyes. I can make out that the fire is localized in two spots—on the rack of servers to one side and on the rack of monitors to the other. I stand in an ever-shrinking island without flames. The air smells oddly fragrant, like a campfire, but it's doubtless toxic and filled with melted computer innards. Every few seconds, another circuit explodes, like high-tech popcorn kernels.

I strain to gaze through the heat to the wall the hooded man disappeared through. There must be a door on that side of the building. Regardless, my better survival option is the door I entered, but flames are rising to block the way.

I get up crouching, hold my breath and hurtle through a slight breach in the flames. I make it to the door and I yank it open. I hurl myself into oxygen and fall onto the ground on my knees.

I'm heaving, coughing, gasping, and then, I leap to my feet in a coughing retch and sprint-limp to the parking lot. Seconds later, I find our car, but not Grandma. The passenger door is open, Grandma's game device sitting on the seat. She's nowhere to be seen.

At the other end of the huge parking lot, departing, I see the back end of a car, quickly disappearing. It's the Prius.

"Grandma!" It's a wild, effete cry. I fumble in my pocket for my phone to call the police. Then I remember my phone is melting, has melted.

I put the key into the ignition and turn the key. The engine doesn't turn over. I turn the key again. No response.

"Fuck!"

From the building, I hear a pop. A window blows out.

The cops and fire department will be here soon.

Then I see it. Movement near the edge of the lot. She's standing next to a cluster of bushes that look like they were intended as landscaping but never got much attention.

"Grandma!"

I'm sprinting.

When I get to her, she looks nonplussed, but she says, "I should be embarrassed."

"What?"

"I peed over near the picnic tables," she says, looking over her shoulder at the bushes.

"You peed? In the bushes?"

"I grew up in Denver and we had a field where we went to the bathroom on the way home from school."

I wrap my arms around her. "I love you."

"Are you crying, Nathaniel?"

"We're fine."

"Well, it's not polite to wear blackface," she says.

I run a finger down my cheek, and sure enough. Looks like I'm ready for Halloween. I take her by the hand. "We have to go."

We return to the car, as flames start to shoot from the building's sides. I reconnect the car battery again. I'm not happy I've gotten so good at this.

I hear sirens.

"Option B," I say, as we climb back into the car.

"What?"

"Option A is to wait for the cops and tell them everything. Option B is to wait until we have more facts."

What are we supposed to tell them—that we have a vague idea that someone possibly connected to Biogen tried to kill us for reasons we don't understand?

I start the car. It lurches forward. Then halts, then lurches again.

Something else is wrong—maybe a cut fuel line, or some other sabotage. Who knows?

Moving in fits and starts, I pull out of the parking lot. We lurch down the street, just as a fire truck passes us.

I hear a phone ring. I'm surprised because I'm certain my phone has been reduced to the basic elements table in the server farm. Then I look down in the center compartment and see the ringing phone; it's the prepaid model Chuck gave me. I ignore it.

I drive to the end of the block, take a right, then drive another block, turning into the empty parking lot of an abandoned warehouse with a grammatically incorrect sign on the door that reads: "Shanghai Bath Furnishings. Gone From Business." My car is sputtering to the point of completely giving out.

I grab another wad of fast-food napkins and try and clean up. I'm not happy I've gotten so good at this, either.

I open the phone and I dial Samantha. She doesn't answer. I call again. No answer. Of course not; the Witch doesn't answer calls from numbers she doesn't recognize, or blocked numbers. She feels people should have the courtesy to announce themselves.

I call again, then again, and again. Finally, she relents. "This is Samantha. I love all people and respect your choices, but telemarketing calls throw me out of balance so I must..."

"Sam, stop! It's Nat."

"Are you okay?"

"Not really."

"Are you hurt?"

"Grandma and I are in an extreme version of a pickle and we need a ride."

I tell her where we are.

"No problem. On the way," she says. "I'm glad you called. The Whiz has been trying to reach you."

The Witch and the Whiz.

She hands him the phone.

"I've opened your file," Bullseye says. "You were right. The password was a variation of the name Newton."

"What's on the drive?"

"A transcript."

"Of?"

"Your grandmother."

"Talking to who?"

"Whom," Grandma interjects. "Talking to whom?"

"Talking to whom, Bullseye?"

"She's not talking to a person."

Then it dawns on me. "She's talking to a computer—to a piece of software," I exclaim.

"How'd you know?"

"The Human Memory Crusade."

"Correct," Bullseye says. "Seems like an AI program is asking her questions and she's answering."

"What's she saying?"

He hesitates.

"I'll bring it with me. I think it's something you need to read for yourself."

He hangs up.

I look at Grandma.

"It's time to hear what you told the box."

She doesn't answer.

"Talk to me, Grandma. Tell me what's going on?"

She puts her hands to her face. She looks terribly stricken.

"Grandma, are you keeping a secret from me?"

"I'm keeping a secret from everybody."

Chapter Thirty-three

I gently turn Grandma's chin so she faces me. Her blue eyes blink and skirt my gaze and her bottom lip quivers. I've smudged a dusting of black ash from my hands onto her face when I touched her chin and try gently to brush it away.

"Grandma, please tell me what you told the box."

"I'm not who you think I am."

Her words sound distant, unconnected, indirect.

"What do you mean?"

"I'm a liar. I lied, and I lied."

"About what?"

"You're Nathaniel Idle," she says.

"I am."

"You're not who you think you are."

Do these words have meaning?

"Who am I?"

"Well, you're my grandson."

I hear a siren, and see another police car coming. It slows as it passes us, then cruises by.

"Hold that thought, Grandma."

I start my car again, and find it has enough juice to allow me to pull it around the corner of the building to the parking lot, which is littered with a handful of weather-stained bathtubs and sinks, and a cracked urinal.

Chuck's phone rings. "Chuck's phone," I answer.

"Chuck here," he says.

"Chuck, this isn't the best time, unless you've called with some new information."

"Have some—about Lulu Pederson."

Grandma stares ahead, lost somewhere else.

"Let's hear it," I say.

"Let's get together."

"Chuck, please." The lighthearted part of my personality has left the building. "Help me now."

He clears his throat.

"She was born January 5, 1972. African-American. Raised by intellectuals in Berkeley; her father worked as a public defender. Her mother was a doctor, working in a free clinic in Berkeley helping the indigent aging population. She—her first name is Lulu but she goes by Adrianna—attended college at Berkeley, and then…"

I interrupt him. "Tell me where it gets interesting."

"You're not interested that she's allergic to cats? Remarkable what you can find with some help from military databases."

"Move on."

"She got a PhD from Stanford in neurobiology, and she…"

"Get to Biogen."

"I'm not sure what you're looking for, but Stanford might be pertinent. In the mid-nineties, she wrote a ground-breaking paper on how hyper-stimulation from media impacts neurological capacities through production of cortisol."

Cortisol.

"The stress hormone. What did she say about it?" I ask.

"I haven't seen the paper, just an executive summary. It has something to do with cell division in some parts of the brain and what happens to it—cell division—during heavy sensory input, or something like that."

"E-mail me the abstract. Get to Biogen."

"You're impatient."

"Way beyond that."

I look at Grandma. She's removed her wedding ring and twirls it in her hand.

"This part is, how do you call it, off the record."

"Fine. Go."

My source tells me there's a secret project at Biogen. Adrianna runs it. ADAM. Advanced Development…"

I cut him off. "…Advanced Development and Memory 1.0. It's a piece of software, or, rather a program. It has to do with measuring or impacting neurological functions."

"You know this already?"

"Just that much. How does it work? Is it a program that's used in a lab, or that gets disseminated? Is it an algorithm? Is it used to measure neurological changes, or to actually cause them?"

"I don't know much more beyond that. I can't understand much of what's in this file."

"Can you e-mail it to me?"

"It's a hard-copy dossier."

"Dossier? From where?"

"I'm coming to that. You know that Biogen is in high-level merger talks with a Swiss company."

"Go on."

"Apparently, our government has been keeping tabs on Biogen and its various projects. This has caught someone's attention."

"Someone?"

"Regulator, I suppose."

I pause.

"Nathaniel?"

"Chuck, respectfully, it's hard for me to believe you have this kind of access. It doesn't make sense you could know this much information, let alone get hard proof."

"Nat, respectfully yourself, I told you I could be a good friend."

I hear the engine of a car. It has turned into the lot of the building we're in front of. Maybe it's the Witch and Bullseye.

"Meet me in the city tonight," Chuck says. "I'll bring the file."

He tells me the name of a restaurant in Noe Valley where he'll be at 8:30 P.M.

"Hold on, Chuck."

A car starts to come around the other corner of the building, heading at us. I realize what's happening, just as Grandma says: "The bad man."

The Prius has turned the corner. Its driver is the man with the hooded gray sweatshirt. He's rolling down his window, barreling towards us. I see the car framed against the ash blue sky in the distance, an instant of slow motion. We are going to die.

And then I see the cavalry.

Speeding around our corner of the building hurls Samantha and Bullseye in their shiny Cadillac.

I expect to hear the pop of bullets and the shattering of glass in my window. But instead hear a violent crack. Bullseye ramming fearlessly into the right back of the Prius.

The Prius juts forward, slams into a bathtub, which redirects the hybrid's momentum and causes it to spin in circles. The churning tires begin to spray dust and gravel, and then it, abruptly, comes to rest. In the dust swirl, I can make out little except the terrific dent to the back, illuminated by brake lights. The car lurches forward and turns our direction. I think I can make out the outlines of the hooded man's face, and the bathtub-caused dent to the Prius's crumpled right fender, as he flies past us and disappears around the end of the building. Gone.

I look up to see Samantha running towards our car. She's wearing black tights and a puffy orange shirt, still dressed as a lioness. She reaches Grandma's window, which I roll down.

"My father drove a Cadillac," Lane says, calmly. "Maybe it was a Chevrolet."

"Oh, Lane," Sam says.

She helps Grandma step out of the car. I sprint around the Toyota's front end and join them, taking one of Lane's arms while the Witch takes the other. We hustle her to the Cadillac. Its right front bumper and that side of the hood has a crinkled dent that looks like a seismograph. The driver's-side back door is indented by the bathtub it must have slid into after the cars collided.

Using the door on the other side, Grandma and I pile into the pristine black leather seats in the back. "I'm sorry, Bullseye, and thank you."

Bullseye looks at us, makes some silent calculation, then starts to accelerate forward.

"Go after him?" he asks. But it sounds more like a statement than a question.

"Wait." I pause him. I return to my defunct Toyota. From the back, I retrieve my ragged backpack and the laptop that contains the whole of my virtual existence. I climb back into the Cadillac and Bullseye drives off. We head to the on-ramp of Highway 101. The wrecked Prius is nowhere in sight.

"I need to borrow a car," I say.

"Should we call the police?" Samantha says. "You're a great investigative journalist but this seems to call for people with the power to detain, arrest, and punish."

She's right—about the second part.

I pull out Chuck's phone. I dial 911. Before I hit "send," Bullseye intercedes.

"You should read this first," he says. Over the back of the seat, he extends a hand, holding a dozen pieces of paper stapled together.

I close the phone and take the papers.

The first one is headed: Transcript from the Human Memory Crusade. June 19, 2010.

Subject: Lane Eliza Idle.

I'm looking at the secrets Grandma told the box.

Chapter Thirty-four

Transcript from the Human Memory Crusade.

This is a section of our previous conversation:

"I slid the man the piece of paper and he looked at it—for a long time. Then he looked in the direction of my father and Irving. They were locked in conversation, and the man nodded. Then he took his change, and he turned and left. I noticed that he was wearing boots, which surprised me. It was summer, and he was wearing thick work boots. He walked out the door."

You haven't spoken for a minute. Are you still there?

Yes.

Would you like to continue with the story, or would you like to do another activity, like play a game?

I tried to follow Pigeon in his cracked leather boots. But I couldn't follow him. And I got so frustrated. That day, and the next day, and the next. He didn't come back to the bakery. He left me there with that white envelope, sealed and mysterious, and I started to wonder what on Earth could he have asked me to hide. It was like…there's a book, oh, you know, the story with the beating heart that drives the man in the castle crazy. Poe, right. It was Edgar Allan Poe. That was what the envelope was like. My imagination was really churning too. Did it have to do with something secret, or…When did the war happen? Maybe I thought it had to do with the war. Wait, the war came after. Please, please, can you stop with the butterflies? They are really messing around with my concentration.

Did you ask about the butterflies?

I'm trying to talk about something. I finally couldn't stand it. I went to the alley, and…

I'm not sure I understood you. Can you speak into the microphone?

I was laughing. I'm laughing. My memory is going, I know that. But I can remember this so clearly. It was such a moment in my life. I took the envelope from the black safe, and I tucked it into the top of my stockings. This was before they rationed stockings. And…anyhow, I went into the alley. I tried for the umpteenth time to look through the envelope at what was inside. I couldn't see. From the kitchen, I'd taken a short knife, like the kind you use to thinly slice the loaves for Friday night and Sunday morning. I cut open the top of the envelope. Out dropped a piece of lined paper, like from a school notebook. In block handwriting, very formal, it said—I'll never forget because I still have the paper, though the writing has faded—it said: "SECRET INSTRUCTIONS ON PG. 45 OF 'ALICE'S ADVENTURES IN WONDERLAND.' DENVER PUBLIC LIBRARY, SECOND FLOOR." I read it again, and again, and again. And then I went right in to my father, and I said: "I've got to go to the library." And he said to me: "It's terrible in Poland. Didn't I tell you it was going to be terrible there? We were so smart to leave because we could have wound up dead. Be careful going to the library. It's a bad time to be outside in the world." And I didn't hear a word he said because I was so determined. I…I realize that I'm just talking and talking. Have I told you all this before? I'm...I'm having trouble remembering.

Did you say you're having trouble remembering?

Yes.

You grew up in Denver. Do you remember that?

Yes. Of course.

May I take a moment to recap what we talked about in the past?

I suppose.

Thank you. You told me about your father, who worked in a bakery in Denver. You have shared many stories about the bakery and the people you met there. I have recorded those stories for you. You also talked about your husband, who was named Irving. When you were married, it was a festive occasion. He wore a military uniform, which was customary at the time. He worked as an accountant and he drove a Chevrolet. The Chevrolet was blue. Prior to getting married, you attended high school in Denver. When you were a young woman, you heard about the outbreak of World War II on a large, black radio. Shall I continue?

I...no, I think that is okay.

Have I accurately recorded your information?

I think so. I...

Have I accurately recorded that your husband wore a military uniform on your wedding day?

I...I think so.

Thank you. It is important to me to be accurate with the details. Would you like to continue with your story?

The butterfly has a message for me.

Are you asking if the butterfly has a message for you?

It is flying in the middle of the screen, and there are lights and sounds coming from its dots.

To retrieve the message, please move the cursor over one of the dots.

Thank you. Well done. Here is your message: Thank you for sharing your stories with us. We are proud to be part of saving the memories of a great generation of Americans. You should be proud of yourself for taking the time to share your stories. Your children and grandchildren will be very grateful for your contributions. Would you like to continue sharing your story, or would you like to do another activity, such as play a game?

Are you still there?

"Nathaniel!"

I look up from Grandma's transcript to see Sam staring at me with great intensity. It takes a moment to pull out of the past.

"My grandfather wasn't in the military," I say.

"What are you talking about?"

"This transcript says that when my grandparents got married, Irving wore a military uniform. That's just not correct."

I look at Grandma. "Did Irving wear a uniform when you got married?"

"You know I don't remember things the way I used to."

"So Grandpa didn't wear a uniform when you got married?"

"Irving wore a military uniform when we got married. He drove a Chevrolet."

"You're sure?"

"I'm tired."

"Who is Pigeon?" I ask. I recall that on several occasions she mentioned that name, or nickname. I can't remember where, or in what context.

"Nat, she looks tired. Maybe give her a break?" Sam asks.

"This transcript is beyond strange."

"There's more," Bullseye says. "I've only printed out a third of the transcript. The rest I e-mailed you and copied to another disc, for backup."

"Is it all weird like this?"

"How do you mean?"

It seems so self-evident.

"The bizarre back-and-forth between human and computer, the computer's high level of artificial intelligence, the butter-flies—whatever those are. And then there's Grandma's story. I can't tell if it's real or imagined. It's certainly provocative. I've never heard anything like that from her."

Bullseye doesn't respond. He's focused on the road, or the inside of his head.

"Bullseye?"

"The artificial intelligence doesn't seem that advanced, actually. The program is basically looking for keywords in your grandmother's comments and prompting further discussion by emphasizing the keywords. As to your grandmother...well..."

"What?"

"She's losing her memory, and trying to recall some childhood memory, and this...machine is recording it."

"It's much more than that, Bullseye." I'm exasperated. "I wish you would have printed it all out."

"Can you solve that later?" Sam interjects. "I think Lane needs her own bed."

I look outside, and I realize where we are—parked on the street outside the Magnolia Manor nursing home.

"Jesus," I say.

"You want me to take her?" Sam asks.

"Absolutely not. No way. Drive, Bullseye."

"Nathaniel, please," Sam says. "She's got to be in the right hands."

"Drive. Please. She can't be here. They'll…" I don't say what I'm thinking: they'll kill her. For reasons I can't yet figure out. Instead I say: "I have a plan."

Sam sighs.

"What?" I ask. Beyond impatient.

"Respectfully," she says. "You seem out of balance. Let me take your beautiful grandmother inside."

I don't respond.

Samantha looks at Bullseye. "I'll be back in five minutes," then back at Lane. "Ready to go home, dear?"

"No fucking way," I blurt.

"Nathaniel…"

"You need to trust me."

"And you need to trust the people around you—the people who love you, and know you. We're on your side."

"Bullseye, why didn't you bring the rest of the transcript?"

"It was long and he didn't have enough paper and he's not your secretary," Sam says firmly. She's looking me in the eye. I've never in my life heard her talk this way. It's the first time I've ever had a confrontation with my best friends, my biggest supporters.

I don't know what I'm thinking, or even why I said something vaguely accusatory to Bullseye. I *am* out of balance, I know that. But there's no way I'm letting anyone take care of Grandma, or dictate her care.

Sam says, "You can do all the goose-chasing you want. But don't take your grandmother with you. Please."

She looks at me, and I at Bullseye.

"Drive," I say, quietly.

He hesitates.

"If you care about me, about us—about Grandma—then you'll help me do what I need to do."

I tell them what that is.

Chapter Thirty-five

Like Warren Buffet in a sari, the Witch sold her AOL stock shares just before the Internet collapse. She claimed to have so aptly guessed the bottom was near by listening to then-Federal Reserve Chairman Alan Greenspan on CNN with her eyes closed and picking up disingenuous tones in his voice. With her stock-market profits, the couple bought a swanky Victorian in the Haight-Ashbury and painted it purple.

On the porch of the Victorian, with the couple's two English bulldogs watching on, Bullseye silently hands me the mysterious memory stick and the Cadillac keys. I can't really tell if he's upset with me or just being characteristically fatalistic. He looks from me to the bashed front of his Cadillac.

"I'll get it fixed," I say. After a pause, I add: "You saved our lives."

"You want my opinion?"

"Not if you're going to tell me to grow up, stop poking around, and take Grandma to the morgue where she can die in peace."

His lips curl imperceptibly into a tight, bemused smile.

"Find the guy who did this to my Cadillac, and run him over."

I slide Grandma into the Caddy. As I get settled, she fiddles with the knob of the glove compartment until it opens. She finds an eight-track cassette of *Foreigner,* which delights her. "This is from my time," she says, I suppose referring to the type of media not the band.

I buckle up and explain to her, knowing she won't totally follow but hoping she gets the gravity of my tone, that I've got to do some serious work and that it's important to me that we stick together.

"If you have to pee, don't wander into a field. Stick with me," I say, then immediately regret it because it sounds like scolding.

My first stop is the crowded parking lot of a grocery store in the outer Mission neighborhood. Into my laptop I insert the thumb drive from Adrianna. The file that opens contains dozens of pages of transcripts of the Human Memory Crusade and Grandma. I start to read, discovering a tale about Lane's past that darts about in fits and starts, interruptions, and backtracks. There are mentions of butterflies, a pigeon, elaborate schemes to hide a note in a library book, and all of it communicated in increasingly disconnected dialogue. As the story goes on, the computer seems to get more intelligent and Grandma less so. After a few minutes—before I can get particularly invested—I look at the clock and realize that both my time and concentration are too limited to give my full attention to understanding what I'm reading.

Survival requires more immediate action.

"Grandma Lane, I'll be right back. I'm just going to be a few feet away," I say. "Don't wander off."

"I heard you."

In the pickup parked next to us, a nun sits in the passenger seat, waiting for someone I assume, fiddling with her bracelet. She smiles at me. Safe enough environs.

I get out and stand by our car and pull out the cell phone I got from G.I. Chuck and dial his number.

"Woodward," he says by way of a greeting.

"You're tracking me."

"What?"

"This cell phone you gave me has a tracking device on it. Right?"

"What the hell are you talking about?"

"Where am I standing right now?"

"On the moon? In an LSD haze?"

"This is how the hooded man knew I was coming to the server farm. He works for you and you stalled me on the phone a few minutes ago so he could drive by and use my head for target practice."

"Stop!"

"Who are you, Chuck Taylor?"

"Some guy was after you again? This is nuts."

"I'm going to find out who you are, and I'm going to make a hell of a lot more for the story than a sixty-dollar blog post."

"Nat. Mr. Idle. Listen to me."

"I know you want my grandmother or whatever information is inside of her. But I'm not with her. I'm going to make her tougher to find than the president during a nuclear attack."

"May I interrupt? May I please ask you a simple question?"

"What?"

"I don't know where you are and I don't care. But here's my question: Are you anywhere near a garbage can?"

I look to my left and see a massive green Dumpster.

"How did you know?"

"I didn't, you jackass. I'm asking because I want you to go throw the phone away. It didn't cost me anything and it'll keep you from pirouetting into some paranoid fantasy."

I digest his words. "That's a good first step."

"Nat, you're obviously onto something interesting. And I can appreciate that you don't know whom to trust. I guess that's what makes you a good journalist. But don't forget that I've been giving you information. Don't forget I got shot at too—and hit. Frankly, I want to help you, and Medblog, but you're becoming a risk of producing a negative return on investment."

"Chuck, you just got interested in Medblog a month ago. That seems more than coincidental to me."

He doesn't respond for a moment.

"Have things your way. Cut me off. Leave me out of it. If you change your mind, I have documents about Adrianna Pederson and Biogen and something called the Human Memory Crusade, the material I told you about before. The stuff is fascinating. Whether it's relevant to you and your story, who knows. If you want to meet me and get the documents tonight, fine. If not, I'll sign your Medblog checks and stay out of your hair."

"Did you say 'Human Memory Crusade'?"

"I did."

"There's information about that?"

"Yep. What is it?"

"Can you tell me what the documents say?"

"Meet me tonight, or don't. Or I can mail you this stuff."

He reminds me of the location of a restaurant where he'll be.

"And Nat," he says. "Remember to throw away my sinister telephone."

We hang up.

I open up the back of the cell phone. I smash it on the ground. I can see its guts. I pick through them. If there's a tracking device on the phone, I don't know what it looks like.

I get back into the car.

"Grandma, can you tell me what it was like to talk to the computer?"

"Sure I can."

"What was it like?"

"What?"

"What was it like to talk to the computer?"

"That's private, Nathaniel."

I take her hand.

"Grandma Lane…" I start, then pause. I don't have a clue to explain to her the nuances of the situation. There are so many questions.

I know whom I might be able to call for help.

Now I need a phone.

Ten minutes later, Grandma and I walk into a Verizon store. I explain to the twenty-something behind the counter wearing

Vulcan ears (I assume for Halloween) that I lost my phone and need the cheapest one they've got in a hurry. Though clearly disgusted by my Luddite tendencies, she takes my credit card to ring me up. We hit a snag. My Visa is denied.

She asks for another credit card. I hand her my bank debit card. She swipes it into the machine. "Blocked too," she says.

"Not possible. It was working this morning. Can you check again?" But I realize that it's entirely possible that my cards have been blocked. Whatever Grandma and I are up against sounds powerful enough to mess with my finances. Does that mean the cops are involved? The government? Who else has such power? Steve Jobs or the aliens that landed at Roswell?

The saleswoman looks at Grandma. "Let me ask my manager what we can do here."

She disappears through a door behind a counter. I look at Grandma, then over the counter at the cash register. Sitting next to it is a touch-screen cell phone, one of the fancier modern models. It looks like it belongs to one of the employees.

"You're not complicit," I mutter to Grandma.

I reach over the counter, grab the phone, and whisk Grandma out. We hustle to the car, dodging a handful of costumed youngsters who have disgorged from a school bus.

"We've probably got half an hour, maybe less, before they realize the phone is missing and shut down the service," I say to Grandma as we climb back into the decked-out and dented Cadillac. Inside, it smells clean, like lemon. "Forgive me if I talk and drive."

"Keep your eyes on the road."

It's 4:15. I've got an hour plus before I meet Grandma's friend, Betty Lou. She should be able to deliver another piece of the puzzle—Grandma's care file. And maybe she'll be able to fill in some blanks about the Human Memory Crusade. How many people use it? What do they say about the experience? What has been the role of Magnolia Manor in promoting it?

I have time to stop at Adrianna's apartment building. I need to see if I can somehow get inside. Maybe I can find Newton playing hoops in the dying daylight. Given that the boy's picture was in Adrianna's office and that his name is the basis for several key passwords, it's clear that he is closer than I thought to the missing scientist. Maybe I can convince him to help me figure out where to look for information.

As I drive, I call my parents. Dad answers.

"Why are you calling from the phone of someone named Jonathan Atkins?" he asks.

"Long story."

I tell him that I don't have much time, but have been meaning to talk to him about Grandma. I try to convey urgency but not panic. If he hears drama, Dad's liable to clam up and, ever the rational type, think about the situation and call me back. I tell him Grandma's been pretty animated in telling a story about her childhood. The story involves the bakery, Grandpa Irving, somebody nicknamed Pigeon.

"Like the bird?"

"I think so."

Dad listens in silence. "Your grandmother and I get along fine," he says. It sounds defensive.

"I don't see what that…"

"I don't know a lot of the details of her life. She liked telling stories, but she preferred the ones from books. She got prickly around stories about herself."

It's the most my father has ever said to me about his relationship with Grandma.

"Anything else?" he asks.

This is not helpful.

"Dad," I pause. "I need some money."

"Is everything okay?"

I've never in my life asked him for a cent—not even in medical school when I ate 99-cent Ramen noodle dinners for at least a year running.

"I'm in a rough spot. Can you wire a couple hundred bucks?"

"Are you gambling?"

I almost laugh.

"It's the Internet, Dad," I say. "It's killing the journalism business and I'm trying to pay my bills. I'll recover."

He doesn't speak.

I almost can't believe I'm muttering the next words as they come out of my mouth: "If necessary at some point, I can figure out how to put my medical degree to work."

After a pause, he says: "Tell me where and when you want the money, and how much you need."

"I'll call you back when I figure out the details."

I need to look for a check-cashing outlet for him to wire the money to.

"You're not telling me everything, Nathaniel," he says. "That's okay. I trust you. It's…" He pauses, then continues. "It's that way when you have a child, a son. I'm sure you'll see that at some point."

I almost laugh again. It's an unusually close moment for us. I wonder if I should risk acknowledging it somehow but realize I have no vernacular or stomach for what might follow.

"Call you later."

◇◇◇

The phone rings.

"Jonathan's phone," I answer.

"Hello," the person responds. "This is Jonathan. I lost my… Did you find my phone?"

"I did. I found it," I say.

"Oh, great. Great. What a relief. Where?"

"On the sidewalk in the Mission."

I tell him that I'm across town, but that I can drop it off in a couple of hours, or he can pick it up from me.

"I'll come to you," he says.

I agree to meet him after my meeting with Betty Lou. I tell him I'll come to the Mission. I mostly mean it. I look at Grandma.

"We've bought ourselves another hour or two of talk time," I say.

◇◇◇

I pull the Cadillac to a stop. I stare out the window at the basketball court outside Adrianna's apartment. The court is empty. A light wind blows a piece of newspaper across the court and lodges it against the fence. I'll have to get into the building some other way, or come back after meeting Betty Lou.

I call Directory Assistance and ask for the number for Pete Laramer.

Several kids exit Adrianna's building dressed for Halloween. The skinny one with the green Hulk mask perched on his forehead—not yet pulled down on his face—is Newton.

"I've found that number for you," the operator says. "Dr. Pete Laramer is with the Brown and Morrow Medical Group."

"What? Say that again."

"Brown and Morrow. I can give you the number, and, for an extra charge we can text it to you as well."

A silent *Holy shit*. Grandma's neurologist is associated with the medical group that owns the disappearing dental offices. The offices with the pictures on the wall of landmark events, like Pearl Harbor and the moon walk; the offices that might have been home to a man in blue.

As early as the 1950s, researchers showed that the human brain cannot process more than one stream of information at a time. But that's what I'm trying to do. I'm looking at Newton, trying to figure out my next move. And I'm trying to remember what I know about Dr. Laramer, besides the fact he's married to an old flame. If memory serves, he holds a patent for deep-brain scanning techniques. He's pioneered new ways to use scanners and MRI machines to explore what's happening inside our skulls as we think, feel, process information.

I don't have even a second to consider the implications. Because, at just that moment, Newton looks in my direction. And he starts to run.

Chapter Thirty-six

"Don't move, Lane."

"I'm old, but I don't like being told what to do."

I give her a kiss on the cheek, get out, and lock the Cadillac. Seconds later, I'm in full stride, heading down the street in his direction.

Newton is a block ahead of me, looking over his shoulder. He turns a corner to the right and then I nearly trip over Spiderman.

One of Newton's friends, twice his size and dressed as the arachnid superhero, has stepped into the middle of the sidewalk. I try to step around him, and nearly run into another boy wearing a paper bag on his head. "Leave Newt alone," the paper bag says, as I start to slip past.

Then I feel a hand grab my arm.

I turn and find myself facing Spiderman, Paper-bag Man, and a kid wearing a Golden State Warriors jersey.

"I really need to talk with him. I won't hurt him. I need his help."

"He's long gone," says Spiderman. His voice is high, pre-pubescent. But he's got a full-grown body. The situation isn't physically threatening. But these boys are trying to be brave.

They've succeeded. Newton is long gone. I pause to catch my breath. "You ever see *CSI*?" I ask.

"I'm not allowed to watch TV at night," the paper bag says, almost comically disappointed, like maybe I could make an appeal to his parents.

"I'm like a scientist on the show. But I'm a lot less rich and famous," I say. "Newton has a good friend named Adrianna. She didn't do anything wrong. But she got into trouble, and she needs the help of an expert, someone like me."

Spiderman says: "Are you with that other guy that came around here looking for Newton?"

"What other guy?"

No response.

"Big guy, thick chest, wears a hooded sweatshirt. Looks like he might be really dumb?"

I pull out my wallet. I extract three business cards.

"I'm one of the good guys. Please have Newton leave a message on my cell phone and tell me how to get in touch with him." I don't have my phone but I can dial into it to retrieve messages.

I walk back to the car in the intensifying wind, unlock the door, climb in. Grandma looks at me.

"The box asked me a lot of questions," she says. "I liked being asked questions. It was nice that it cared about me. But it always interrupted me. Like a man. You know that? Men are always interrupting us with their own thoughts. They don't know how to listen. That computer…it pretended to be a good listener, but it always had its own purpose. It liked to give me all kinds of tasks to do."

I take her hand. "I love you."

"What?"

"I'm sorry if I didn't always listen. I'm sorry if I was self-absorbed, and treating you like just any grandma, not my Grandma. When we get through this, I'm going to visit you all the time, and you can play games with me, not the box."

Her eyes moisten.

"Let's go see Betty Lou," I say.

"And Harry," she says.

"Grandma, how long have you known Harry?"

"Nathaniel!"

"Grandma?"

"Stop investigating and asking a bunch of questions, and listen to who I am. Stop acting like the box."

"I…" I don't finish. I don't know what to say. I find myself almost smiling at her fire.

As I drive, I use the stolen phone to retrieve voice messages from my burned-up gadget. I shouldn't, given that studies show the inflated crash risks when talking on a phone while driving. Counterpoint: I'm well past that point of inflated risks.

There are two messages from Polly. The first: "This is a message from the woman who doubles as your bartender and your grandmother's babysitter. I am in the mood to be of service this evening. It is Halloween, and I am planning to wear a costume that will be sufficiently demure for babysitting, if, that is, you like your babysitters in something tawdry. Call me."

The second: "Is your phone off? You're not returning texts. There's some potentially great blog items regarding the break-in of the Pentagon computer. Apparently, the hackers got access to Pentagon hospital contracts. And the attorney general indicted the Porta Potti pyromaniacs. Smells like another blog post," she says. Her voice changes. "I need to talk to you. And see you. Things are…Can you call me?"

I look at Grandma. "Every question is on the table now," I say. "For instance: Who exactly is Pauline Sanchez?"

"Watch out for the turtle."

"What?"

"Turtle!"

She points out the window.

I've been so distracted that I have not seen the large man in the crosswalk in front of us. He wears a large green hump. The Turtle flips me off. I drive through the intersection. Another urban amphibian nearly crushed by a cell-phone-wielding motorist.

"It's Halloween, Grandma."

"I love Milky Ways."

"I'll get you one after our meeting," I say. "Look, there's Betty Lou."

In the fading light, I can see someone round sitting on a bench surrounded by a grove of bushes in a small neighborhood park. We're just a few blocks from Magnolia Manor.

We park and amble past a jungle gym with slides coming down three sides to the shrub-surrounded bench and Betty Lou.

"Hi, Laney," she says, taking Grandma's hands. "How are you feeling?"

"I'm fine, thank you. My grandson tells me he loves me, at least when he's not talking on the phone."

"I'm sure he does love you. Would you like to go home?"

"I've known you for a long time," Grandma responds, disconnected. I can picture her less than a year ago; she'd have embraced Betty Lou, kissed her cheek, and gone on about her friend's bright red silk headscarf.

"Nathaniel, why don't you sit down for a minute?" Betty Lou says.

We sit. It feels peaceful in the little garden area, secluded, protected from the madness.

"Grandma Lane is doing fine," I say.

"I'm glad to know that. I…she needs to be around people who know how to care for her."

She pauses. She grimaces. Then her face registers concern, then panic.

"Oh no. No. No!"

I start to turn my head to follow her petrified gaze to my left. But I feel a strong arm grab my neck and another on my torso. I feel a cloth shoved over my mouth and nose. I taste something stale like rancid orange-drink.

Everything goes black.

Chapter Thirty-seven

Transcript from the Human Memory Crusade.
July 7, 2010

Please enjoy this short video while I find your file.

I have found your file. Would you like to continue with your story?

I'm trying to. I'm determined. I wrote myself some notes. Please hold on a minute while I look at my notes.

You haven't said anything for a minute. Are you still there?

Remember, I told you about the envelope, and how it had some clue about the library?

Would you like to continue?

The Denver library had these majestic steps, like a Roman cathedral. Or, Greek, maybe. Columns. I went up the steps to the second floor. That's where I went—to the second floor of the library, where they kept the fiction. Please, just let me talk. No more bugs and messages. I always loved books, and I loved *Alice's Adventures*. If you want to know the truth, I felt like a spy standing there. I was so frightened because I knew that I was not supposed to look inside the envelope. And I didn't know who might be following or watching me. I remember this one feeling so clearly: I was kind of hoping that the handsome man with the work boots might be watching. I wanted him to know that I had courage, and that I was no one's patsy. Do you use that word? Please, Please! Stop with the butterflies.

Are you still there?

I'm feeling clearheaded right now, and I…I looked all around me. I was telling you about the library. I…I went to the C section of the library because I assumed that the book would be listed under the last name Carroll. Lewis Carroll. And I was right. There were two copies of *Alice*—both of them in hardback, I remember. I pulled one of the copies of the book from the shelf. I held my breath, kind of, and then I opened the copy of the book to the secret page number I'd found in the envelope. And I discovered there was nothing on that page. It was just the regular words of the story. I looked around the nearby pages, and I didn't see anything. So then I pulled out the second copy of the book, and I turned to the special page, and there was nothing there either. No special instructions, or mysterious calligraphy, or whatever I imagined I might find. I felt so angry, and frustrated, and I stood there feeling betrayed, and silly. I…

Are you still there?

I feel embarrassed by the way that made me feel. If you want to know the truth. And I looked through both copies of the book again, and I didn't see anything. Then I remembered something about *Alice in Wonderland*. The real name of the author wasn't Carroll. It was Charles Dodgson. I…I went to the D section to find a book written by Charles Dodgson. And you wouldn't believe it! Nestled in the spot where you'd find a book by Charles Dodgson was another copy of *Alice in Wonderland*. It was written by Lewis Carroll, but it had been shelved incorrectly. Or, obviously, it had been deliberately shelved incorrectly. I knew I'd found what I was looking for. So I opened the book. I opened it to page 45—that's right, it was on page 45. I remember now!—

and I found what I was looking for. Oh, yes, I most certainly did. I found what was waiting for me.

You haven't spoken for a minute. Are you still there?

I'm crying. I'm sorry. It was so profound. Do you know that word? Existential, maybe. I don't know what that word means anymore, and I'm not sure I ever totally did. Like "ironic." I probably used the word incorrectly a lot of times in my life. Well, anyway, I opened the book, and I saw what it said. May I tell you?

I think you are asking me a question. Would you repeat the question?

There was a typed note. It said…Wait…I still have it. Let me read it to you. It said…

Are you still there?

I'm making sure we're alone. It said: "Congratulations, Lane Idle. You have a great mind, and an adventurous heart. Meet me at Elitch Gardens, Friday at 5. Come alone. The future depends on it."

You haven't said anything in a minute. Are you still there?

You're not reacting. You're not…you're not amazed by this? I guess you wouldn't be. You're a…please stop with the butterflies and the orchestra sounds. They're very distracting.

Chapter Thirty-eight

Transcript from the Human Memory Crusade.
July 17, 2010

Are you a returning participant?

This is strange.
The machine is very smart, Betty. Please, just talk to it. Don't be afraid of the butterflies.
I'm speaking for Lane Eliza Idle.

I've found your file. Would you like to continue telling your story, or would you like to do a different activity, like play a game? I see that you have been playing many fun games for many hours in the last few weeks. You have had a high score. I am proud of you.

What do you want to do, Lane? Do you want me to read this?

I'm having trouble understanding you. Would you like to take a fun trivia test to remember what we talked about before?

Laney, do you want to take a quiz?
I suppose so.

When we talked before, you told me that you first heard about Pearl Harbor listening to a radio. On the screen are three pictures of radios, which one did it most look like?

Lane?
I don't remember, I think it was a black radio, like the one in the middle.

Did you say the one in the middle?

Yes.

I think I understood you to say that your father owned a blue Cadillac. You have an excellent memory.

I want to tell my story.
She'd like to continue with her story.

Did you say you'd like to continue with your story?

Yes.
Yes.

Would you like a reminder of where you left off the last time we talked?

Do you want me to read this aloud?
Tell the box, please.
The box?
Lane?
What do you want me to do, Lane?
I'm tired.
Okay, okay. I'll try this. My name is Betty Lou, and I'm going to read something written by Lane Idle. I'm reading now:
I didn't know whether to tell anyone about what I found. What if something terrible was happening at Elitch Gardens, like a crime, or, I don't know, maybe espionage. It was wartime, and we all knew that something bad was happening. And we were already having trouble trusting. I thought about telling my brother what I'd found. But he was one of the people I was having trouble trusting—for a different reason: he was hanging out with those bad kids, and he needed money and he wasn't acting like my brother anymore. He was taking…he had a different way of dealing with his idle mind. Should I keep going?

Betty Lou, you have a beautiful voice when you read.

Elitch Gardens was a gathering place, I guess you'd say. There were some restaurants, and a public flower garden, dance pavilion, and walking paths. It eventually became an amusement park, but this was before that. My point is that I didn't think much bad could happen there; this was also before people got into shooting matches, and I couldn't imagine it was anything like that. So, to make a long story short (my hand gets tired when I write too long), I decided I'd go down to Elitch Gardens myself. Of course, I decided that! Who am I kidding? I wouldn't have it any other way!

It's nice to see you smile, Lane. This is a strange story. Is it made up? Lane?

I don't think so.

Oh okay. I'm just going to keep reading for you then:

It was a busy day for me already. Before I went to Elitch Gardens to uncover the mystery, I was supposed to have my first driving lesson with Irving. I'm not sure if it was a driving lesson or a date. It went badly. He was so nice to me—too nice. Not dramatic, but nice and sturdy. I didn't think I should tell him about the envelope. But I was so nervous during the whole lesson. And guess what? I crashed his car! I drove it into a fence. The front part of Irving's car—his fender, or bumper or whatever—was broken, or bent. He drove me in silence back to the bakery. He was quiet; I was apologetic. I thought he was so mad at me. But when we got there—to the bakery—he reached into the glove compartment. He pulled out an apple. A very shiny one, red. He said: "I forgot. I was going to give this to you."

That's so romantic, Lane.

Irving was my husband.

Are you crying, Lane?

Irving was my husband. Irving was my husband. Irving drove a blue Chevrolet. I heard about Pearl Harbor on the black radio. My mother used a butter churn and our neighbors slaughtered their own chickens in a barn.

Lane, why don't we stop for the day.

You can play games, you know that?

Chapter Thirty-nine

Transcript from the Human Memory Crusade.
July 23, 2010

I am Betty Lou, I am with Lane Idle, and I am reading from Laney's notebook. I am reading now:

After the accident in Irving's car, I went into the back of the bakery, and I cleaned up, and this next part is funny, or certainly telling about my personality. I put on my brother's black over-coat. I'd brought it to the bakery that morning. I had this idea that I would somehow be camouflaged in it—like maybe the shape of my body would be drowned out, or that I might look like a young man (I was hyper aware as a young woman that I had nice bosoms and that this attribute separated me from men). I also wore a cap that belonged to my brother. I was walking out of the bakery through the alley door when my father happened to walk into the back to throw something into the trash. He hardly noticed me at first, and then he saw how I was dressed. I thought he'd be curious or furious, but he said: "It's smart for a girl to dress warmly and keep herself covered up." I'd have had a big laugh as I was leaving if I wasn't so nervous and excited about where I was going. I'm this 17-year-old girl, almost 18, and I'm feeling like a spy, dressed like a boy, and my imagina-tion is galloping. I hired a taxi to get to the meeting. Even so, I was nearly late. I guess I hadn't accounted for traffic. I gave the driver a quarter, which was a pretty big tip. He asked if I was sure that I wanted to be dropped off there; it was getting a little bit dark. But I told him I was meeting my fiancé. That made sense. There were lots of people around, and many couples walking. This was a place you could come for courtship, and not have your parents or friends feel like you were being loose, or easy. I can't remember exactly now, but I'd guess there were a couple of dozen people walking around the entrance to the gardens. There was a food stand near the entrance. I don't remember what it was selling, but it must have been hot dogs or caramel apples. A sign described all the garden's activities and locations of those activities, including riding boats on the lake, pond fishing, the botanical garden, the picnicking area, and things like that. I was looking at the sign, trying to figure out where I might discover the secret meeting place. I didn't have the slightest idea. I looked at a pocket watch I'd borrowed from my brother. I could see that I was late by 10 minutes. Maybe I'd missed the meeting. What was I looking for, anyway? Or whom. It was getting dark. I was wondering what in the world I was doing. And that's when I heard the footsteps behind me.

This is a good story, Betty Lou.

(Laughter) You should like it. You wrote it.

When did I write it?

There's a date here, on the front. It looks like 1974.

What?

You wrote the story in 1974.

Okay. You know this is the story of how my life changed. Everything in the world changed. I kept it a secret for so long.

Do you want me to keep going?

Okay.

So, you heard footsteps behind you. Now, I'm reading again: As you might imagine (dear reader), I nearly jumped to the moon. I started to turn around, and the first thing I saw were the boots. I wasn't looking at the ground, but I caught them in the lower part of my vision. I could see the tops of them, maybe. Thinking back, I must have been hoping he'd be there, and I definitely associated him with the tough, leathery, work boots and the slightly pigeon-toed feet. That's why they called him Pigeon. He was nearly a foot taller than me. I noticed that he was a lot less grimy or gritty than I expected or remembered. His face was clean shaven and I could see a spot of dried blood right under his chin where he must have nicked himself. His hair was parted and combed to the side, and he could have passed for a movie actor. For a moment, neither of us spoke. Then I said, "I'm sorry that I opened your envelope." And he smiled, and I thought he'd laugh. But he just smiled, kindly, and he said: "I knew you wouldn't be able to help yourself, Lane." I said: "You know my name?" I was kind of alarmed then, and he could tell. He said (I can't remember his exact words): "There's something I want to show you. There's something I need to show you." I think any normal young woman would've started running, or screaming, or AT LEAST politely excused herself, and gotten in a cab, and gone home. I mean, who knew what this guy could be about. Could he have been a murderer, or a rapist? (I'm sorry to use such blunt language.) There was still light, but it was getting near dusk. There were a lot of people around, so I felt mostly safe. But I did start to come to my senses. I told Pigeon that I didn't know what he was up to, or involved with, but that I needed to get into a taxi and go home. I told him that whatever he was involved with that it was his business, and I wasn't going to tell anyone. I wouldn't try to stop him. I just wanted to go my own way. I said something frightened and melodramatic like that. He told me that he understood my concern. He seemed nervous too. He must have been shifting back and forth on his feet, or maybe I just remember it that way now. And then he reached behind him—I suppose into his back pocket. I flinched a little, wondering what he was grabbing. Well, I shouldn't have—flinched. What he was grabbing was a rose. It was a beautiful, fully bloomed red rose. He held it up to me, and he said: "I make concrete pipes." I was surprised, and confused. My heart was racing, if I'm to be honest. I asked him what he meant. He wasn't embarrassed in his response, which I think belied the words. He said: "I work in a concrete yard. I make a dollar a week and give most of it to my family. I don't have a car. I dropped out after the 10th grade. But I'd like to take you on a picnic, or for a pistachio ice cream. Or whatever flavor you like." I couldn't get a sense of whether he was being genuine, or manipulative. I mean, I'd opened this secret envelope, and found a secret book. I said to him: "You're a spy, right? Do you work for a foreign government, and you're trying to get me involved with something?" And, earnestly, he responded: "Yes, a foreign government that has a terrible plan to get everyone addicted to pistachio ice cream." Well, then it hit me. This was just a romantic gesture, a wild romantic gesture. As you might imagine, I almost died from relief, and some fluttering of my heart. He said: "I came last Friday and I figured I'd come here every Friday until you showed up." I said: "Pigeon, I would prefer ice cream. I know where the ice cream shop is. I don't have the energy to follow a treasure map to discover a lost book, to find the location of the picnic spot." I took his rose, and both of us stood there in silence, but I think we were smiling. That's how I remember it. And I thought everything was going to be just fine. But, Lord knows (and I'm not religious) that was really just the beginning. I was hooked, and being reeled in, and so was he....Lane?

Lane? Computer, she's fallen asleep.

You haven't spoken for a minute. Would you like to continue?

Lane has fallen asleep.

I'm not sure I understand. Would you like to continue with your story?

I think we're going to have to do this another time. Our heroine has fallen asleep.

Chapter Forty

Human Memory Crusade Internal Report.
July 30, 2010

Subject: Lane Eliza Idle.
Priority: One.

Wildfire.

Chapter Forty-one

Butterflies. A pigeon. Secrets.

Wildfire.

Puke.

I open the Cadillac door and spill chunky vomit onto the sidewalk. My head feels like it played concrete to someone's jackhammer. My mouth tastes of salty onion and felt.

The clock reads 7:45. For the last hour, I've been reading Grandma's Human Memory Crusade transcripts on my laptop, the transcripts that Bullseye decrypted. I was hoping they'd help me find Grandma. I'm more lost than ever.

I look out the front windshield at a half-pint goblin holding the hand of a heads-taller Scooby-Doo. Each costumed tyke carries an orange plastic pumpkin. Not hallucination, Halloween.

I try to focus and reflect on what has happened over the last two hours of my life. I remember taking Lane to see Betty Lou. We sat down on the bench. Betty Lou wore a red scarf and a long jacket. She suddenly looked horrified. Then I was attacked.

I woke up an hour ago in my car. Whoever attacked me drugged me, dragged me, and left me here. But not Grandma. Grandma's gone.

Grandma's been taken.

When I came to, I called the police. I reported my grandmother missing. An emergency operator who sounded like she was sucking on a lozenge told me I couldn't file a report until Lane's been missing twenty-four hours. I told her I'd been mugged.

"Was anything taken?" she asked.

"My grandmother."

"I can send a patrol car out. It's Halloween. Could take a couple of hours."

I called the main police line and asked for Officer Everly, the mustached cop who first came to our aid in Golden Gate Park. On his voice mail, I left a message telling him I needed immediate help.

From my backpack, I pulled out my laptop. I opened the transcripts from the Human Memory Crusade—the ones from the mysterious memory stick I hadn't yet read in full. Would they offer me insight into who took Lane—or why?

Butterflies, a pigeon, old secrets.

It's a fascinating if unfinished tale from Grandma's past—and as interesting in style as substance. The computer seems to be testing her memory and probing it.

I am not a computer expert, but the software powering the conversation with Grandma feels extremely sophisticated and artificially intelligent. Oh, and evil. It is assessing her. It deems her "priority one," and "wildfire." What the hell is that?

But the transcript offers no obvious answers or clues about the kidnapping. Have we come to be haunted by some secret from Lane's past?

I close the laptop. I wince at the pulsing pain squeezing my head. I feel dull pain under both armpits, maybe where someone dragged me away from the park bench. I slam my hand onto the steering wheel. I fall forward, woozy. I reorient and look at myself in the rearview mirror. There's white residue in the corners of my mouth, my eyes bloodshot, a red mark near my right temple, maybe where I fell or otherwise hit my head. I touch it and feel little pain.

I look around the car. I see the edge of a manila-colored folder. It's sticking out from under the edge of the passenger seat.

I yank it out, recognizing it immediately. It's the same folder that Betty Lou was holding on the park bench—right before someone chloroformed me.

Whoever dragged me here must have left this. On purpose?

I open the folder. Inside, six sheets of paper. They look like medical documents or schedules. Each one is titled Neuro Exam Schedule. Each one has a name, date of birth, and, beneath that, a series of dates written in script.

I recognize two of the names: Lane Idle and Victoria Xavier, the lonely romance novelist who is Grandma's suite mate. The other names include two men and two women. Each in their eighties, except one man, named Terrence Lymon, who is ninety years old.

According to Grandma's document, she had nine neurological visits. Nine! How had I missed all of those? Who took her there? What happened when she got there? Were these the visits to the fake dental office?

I call Magnolia Manor. I ask for Betty Lou. I am transferred to the nursing station and told Betty Lou is unavailable. The nurse is not someone I know. Sotto voce, I explain the situation is urgent, and dire. The nurse is unsympathetic. "Goodbye," she says and hangs up.

And at just that moment, my stolen phone goes dead. Of course. Its real owner has finally had it turned off.

I start the Cadillac to drive the three blocks to Magnolia Manor.

As I near the home gates, I hear sirens—fast approaching. Behind me speed two cherry tops. They cruise past me and on to the Manor grounds.

I park on the street and stand at the gates.

Vince appears on the front stairs. The police cruisers pull up to the front. The driver of the first car gets out and ambles toward Vince. They shake hands—the friendly shake of people who know one another.

The cop walks inside with Vince. The second cruiser remains parked outside, a cop still inside it.

Time to rethink Plan A. An hour ago, I wanted to contact the police. Now I'm not sure. Is Vince somehow involved with the memory crusade? As are the cops? Is he in with Grandma's neurologist? I know Pete Laramer is one of the bad guys, don't

I? Do I have a clue whom to trust? I honestly don't know if I could tell the difference right now between Gandhi and a bowl of dried fruit.

It's 8:05.

I'm desperate.

Plan B.

Chuck.

◇◇◇

Twenty minutes later, I park in Noe Valley, a swanky neighborhood with million-dollar two-bedroom flats where I'm supposed to meet the suspiciously informed venture capitalist.

He stands in front of Coq Au San Francisco. He's wearing a sport coat, slacks, his neck wrapped in a dark scarf.

I'm half a block from him, closing fast, when a man steps in front of me wearing an angel's wing protruding from the right side of his back. He holds a Bible. He reads a passage about sinners smoldering in purgatory. I step around him.

"Guess who I am and get a Snickers," he says.

"Some other time."

I see Chuck pull out his cell phone. I pause to watch him.

"You're the Right Wing," I say.

"Candy for you," the man says gleefully.

Next to him stands a man wearing a rubber gorilla mask. The man removes his mask.

"This fucking thing is giving me heat stroke."

Chuck talks on the phone. He looks around him—up and down the street. I duck behind the Right Wing so Chuck can't see me.

Chuck has information I need. But so much about Chuck seems uncomfortably coincidental—the timing of his appearance in my life, and his sudden breadth of knowledge about Adrianna, Biogen, the Human Memory Crusade.

I look at the guy who removed the gorilla mask. He's sweating profusely.

"Five bucks for the gorilla mask."

"Are you serious?"

"As a gorilla with a heart attack, or heat stroke."

We make the trade.

Chuck hangs up his phone. He starts walking in my direction. I pull on the sweaty mask, and sidle up against the wall next to a guy playing guitar, singing Bruce Springsteen's "Born to Run."

Seconds later, Chuck walks past. I wait a few seconds, and I turn and follow.

Chapter Forty-two

G.I. Chuck snakes past a drag queen on stilts, a three-headed dog, and a throng of not-costumed but drunken revelers, albeit polite ones. Noe Valley is the upscale, label-conscious neighborhood adjacent to the Castro, where the revelers generally are more unruly, and less dressed.

I'd like at this moment to cultivate Grandma's two skills: the ability to stay calm and, if necessary, do karate. Screw Pauline's admonitions that I'm melodramatic. I'm feeling entitled.

When we're four blocks off the main drag, Chuck takes a sharp right, and disappears from view. I pick up speed. Moments later, I'm at the spot where Chuck disappeared from view. It's the entrance to an alley, more like a narrow one-way street that bisects a handful of million-dollar attached row-houses. Light from the back door of one flat that is halfway down the block provides me meager vision. I can make out the trash and recycling bins parked neatly behind each residence, but no Chuck.

Maybe he made it to the other side of the alley/street. I start hustling to follow his tracks. I make it two steps when I'm pulled violently backwards.

My mask is knocked off, and I feel something soft but tight around my neck.

"I didn't spend a lifetime in the military without learning how to tell when I'm being followed by a gorilla," my attacker says in my ear. Chuck.

He loosens his grip on what I'm guessing is his scarf, now around my neck, not his.

"Mr. Idle, whom do you work for?"

"Medblog. Eventually, you," I manage to squeak out.

"No one else?"

"I do some other freelance work."

This conversation is ridiculous.

"Why are you following me? I agreed to meet you," he says.

"My grandmother's been taken."

"What?" Alarm.

"Let go of my neck."

He doesn't. "What did you say about your grandmother?"

"Someone took her. Knocked me out and kidnapped her. Does it seem all that unlikely, given how easily you subdued me with cashmere?"

He pulls the scarf away. I crane my neck to look at him.

"I think they'd teach journalists better surveillance techniques."

"Look, I don't trust anyone at this point. No offense. On the bright side, you got the better of me."

"You look green," he says.

I turn my head to the side and throw up. It's the result of being drugged on an empty stomach, and then having my body jolted by whiplash.

"Jesus, Idle."

Bent at the waist, I wipe my mouth on my sleeve. I take a deep breath and taste the flavor of soured milk. I turn my head and spit. I stand upright, and get a shot of light-headedness.

"I need your help finding my grandmother," I say. "But, frankly, your story doesn't add up. I think you're involved with Biogen, and Adrianna. And…" I pause.

"What?" he says.

"You're not injured."

"What?"

"You supposedly were shot outside my house. Now you're evading and flattening me like an Olympic sprinter and wrestler."

"Flesh wound."

I shake my head. I reach into my pocket for the bullets I found on the ground outside my apartment. I pull a couple out and show him.

"How do I know you didn't just drop these on the ground?"

He raises his eyebrows; is that really what I think?

"Looks like an automatic. May I have it traced?"

I hand one to him and shrug. I've got another. He takes it.

"Your grandmother's been taken? Where? How?" He seems empathic, concerned.

"Why do you care?"

"I worry about my employees and their families."

Absurd.

"Chuck, may I tell you about the secret document?"

"You found a secret document?"

"I've written one."

I commence my bluff.

"It's a preliminary account of what's going on with the Human Memory Crusade, and Biogen, and military investors—specifically, you."

"I have no idea what you're talking about."

"I've included the part about Dr. Pete Laramer, and Biogen's proposed merger with a Swiss biotech company. Sounding more familiar?"

"You're cute when you're making things up."

Still glib, but I have his attention.

"My thesis goes like this: A group of scientists and doctors backed by the government is studying the impact of computer use on memory."

As I air my theories, I realize they feel like non-fiction.

"The bad guys are using the Human Memory Crusade as a front—tinkering with memories under the auspices of recording them."

I pause and reflect on what I've gleaned about Adrianna. She seems like a decent person, and she reached out to me for help. I recall that Dr. Laramer studied deep brain-scanning technology, earned a patent for looking at memory centers. Where does he fit in? If at all?

"Nat?"

I continue, more pieces falling into place. "They didn't start as bad guys. Not all of them. There were good intentions to study the impact of heavy computer use on memory loss. But something went wrong. Or someone inside the camp discovered how to use the technology to a different and devious end. To tinker with memories, override them, or erase them. When Adrianna found out, she tried to figure out what was going on, or to tell someone—me. Biogen freaked out because it couldn't have its reputation smeared before the big merger goes through."

I'm making all kinds of leaps, but they feel right.

"Sounds thin. Erasing memories? How?"

"Cortisol." I recall that Adrianna studied the impact of cortisol on the brain. "It's a stress hormone. It's really quite a wonderful thing that kicks in to help us through intense physical and emotional experiences. You've heard the stories of when a dad lifts a car off the ground to save his trapped child, right? That's cortisol. Good stuff, except that like any powerful drug, it has some downsides."

I pause because I'm going from educated guessing to pure guesswork. What I'm thinking is that one downside of cortisol may be that it might kill memory cells. But how exactly? And how did the cortisol get into the brain of the test subjects? Was it injected at the laboratory sites, like the fake dental office?

Another possibility hits me—a shocking one.

"The computer," I say. "The butterflies. You've figured out a way to stimulate chemical releases through computer interaction. Fascinating technology developed by and for the military industrial complex."

He shakes his head, the meaning of this gesture unclear to me.

"You've put this all in a secret document?"

I stare Chuck in his eyes. They betray the deliberately vague emotion of a hostile witness trying not to appear too unfriendly.

"E-mailed to a couple of friends, and asked them not to open unless something happens to me."

"The old don't-open-the-envelope-unless-I-disappear trick, but updated for the Internet era. Nicely done."

I nod.

Chuck is quiet for several seconds.

"Up until you said 'cortisol,' I thought you were bluffing," he finally says.

"My grandmother learned something about the project, right? She's carrying critical information. So you've taken her. Where is she?"

"Let's get out of this alley."

"Tell me where she is, or the world gets a big dose of my fancy journalism."

"Slow down, Woodward. I need to find your grandmother as much as you do."

"Why?"

He pauses.

"Why, Chuck? Who has her?"

"Lane is ground zero."

Chapter Forty-three

He takes two steps away from me.

"Of what?" I nearly shout. I take two quick steps, catch him and reach for his arm and pull him around. "Does this have to do with her past?"

He shakes me off and starts walking away.

"Wildfire?" I say. "Is ground zero the same as wildfire?"

There's a hitch in his step but he doesn't turn around. Without looking back, he says, "There's something I need to show you. Someone you need to meet."

We walk three blocks in silence and he ascends the stairs of a boxy three-story home with an over-sized front window. He looks both ways and speaks quietly.

"Get in here if you want to see what happens when science goes wrong."

I'm met by a hippopotamus.

In Chuck's foyer hangs a giant stuffed hippo head with a toothy overbite, mounted on a leather backing. Chuck walks directly through the entrance and into a doorway on the left. I follow. From upstairs, I hear a voice: "Mr. Chuck?"

He presses an intercom on the wall, and says: "I'll be up shortly. Please keep Victor entertained."

We stand in a living room decorated in Hunter Chic. Mounted on the wall are a stuffed cheetah, a black bear, and something from the antelope/elk family. The rest of the room is modern—stylized metal coffee table, sharp-cornered couch, and, of course, a flat-panel TV big enough to watch from space.

"Is my grandmother safe?"

"I assume so."

"Why?"

"I need more information," he says. "What happened to her? Where? When?"

"You really don't know."

He purses his lips, looks me in the eye, and then glances away. He doesn't know.

When I first met G.I. Chuck, he'd had a sty beneath his eye. Now it's inflamed with a hordeolum, a white pimple that means his infection is intensifying but, I have to wonder, if that's a by-product of stress taxing his immune system.

"Chuck, you're getting no information out of me. None. Not until you explain what's going on. You can shoot me and stuff me but no matter what you do, information is now going in a single direction in this conversation."

"Sit," he says. "I'll be right back."

"Who took my grandmother?"

"Let me get some things to show you."

Damn it. What choice do I have?

Chuck walks out.

I see a stainless steel refrigerator built into a cabinet beneath the cheetah. "Can I grab a water?"

"Help yourself," I hear from the other room.

I open the fridge and take a bottle of water. But I'm look-ing for something else—I'm not exactly sure what until I see it sitting beneath the fridge: the steel glint of a wine opener. The proverbial sharp object. I slip it into my pocket.

Chuck returns, holding a sleek, maroon-colored Dell laptop in his left hand and a small projector in his right. He opens the computer and plugs the projector into it. Onto the wall, he projects an image of a title page of a presentation. The title reads: "Human Memory Crusade."

"Listen first, then I'll show you the slide deck."

I can't believe it. In this region and era, even the dark conspiracies have a PowerPoint presentation.

"You're theories are half right," he begins. "You've missed the main point: We started trying to *enhance* memory."

He explains that Biogen and Dr. Laramer teamed up to determine whether there might be a way to enhance memory capacity through heavy computer use. For Laramer, this was a cool science project; for Biogen, an opportunity to cater to 70 million baby boomers and their parents losing memories—or terrified they will.

"Great market, right? This country is *obsessed* with memory."

He points out we are maniacal recorders of our own lives—photos, blogs, diaries, YouTube videos, and on and on. Memories have become a perverse way of immortalizing ourselves by looking backwards.

I have to concede this to him, but it still doesn't all fit so neatly. "Where does the military come in?"

"I can't talk about it."

"Tell that to the papers after I broadcast it across the blogosphere."

"Hear me out."

"Khe Sahn," I say, a seeming non sequitur.

I remember that I'd seen an ornery short man leave the dental offices wearing a Vietnam vet's insignia. It strikes me that the military's interest involves modifying memories of military personnel. I tell this to Chuck.

"You're dealing with post-traumatic stress disorder," I venture.

"Hear me out."

He hits a button on his computer and the presentation brings up its first slide. It's an elderly man, with thin white hair and stooped shoulders, playing on a computer. G.I. Chuck hits the button again, magnifying the image of the computer screen the old man is looking at. In the middle of the screen is a query: Tell me about your experiences in high school.

That's not the interesting part.

What's odd are the numerous images and statements surrounding the prompt. At the top is a ticker of information, like a news crawl on CNN. It reads: "PLAY GAMES ANYTIME YOU WANT," and "THANKS FOR BEING PART OF THE CRUSADE." On the right is an airplane trailing a banner that says: "Nice Chevrolet!" Filling out the screen are a half dozen multi-colored butterflies. It's chaos—digital overload.

It helps explains Grandma's transcripts.

"Heavy sensory input," I say. "Big deal. We get it all the time."

"The conventional wisdom is that we enhance our mental capacities through regular use," he says. "That our brain is a veritable muscle that we can build through exercise."

"That was the hope of ADAM."

"Of what?"

"Biogen's software: Advanced Development and Memory."

"Right. Nicely synthesized."

I can't tell if he's patronizing me.

He explains that for years, Biogen—along with every other biotech company—has been working on anti-dementia drugs. They've got an interesting traditional drug in the pipeline. They believed they could increase the drug's effectiveness by stimulating the brain through computer use. If they could prove that theory, it would be an incredible scientific breakthrough, to say nothing of a multibillion-dollar entrepreneurial one.

It's a powerful thought, but not at all inconsistent with a host of recent neurological developments.

I recently blogged about researchers at Stanford using real-time MRIs to develop new ways to treat chronic pain. In the studies, patients experiencing pain were shown images of their brains with the regions of the brain lit up that were affected—activated by heavy blood flow—during the pain episode. The researchers sought to coax patients to meditate, breathe, and use other tactics to diminish the size of the affected area.

Separately, I've written about research into the effects of compulsive computer use on the brain almost since my first postings. The research shows, at the least, that the heavy and regular stimulation generates neuro-chemicals linked to addiction. And, more broadly, researchers have discovered in the last few years that the brain is much more plastic than we ever previously thought.

So why not study what happens to the brain's memory center during computer use? Why not try to stimulate neuro-chemicals that facilitate memory retention? After all, memory is an essential part of the human experience *and* the thing we are losing at an alarming rate.

Although I'm not buying the whole story, big parts make sense.

"What went wrong?" I ask.

Chuck brings up the next slide. It's an image of the brain. Two small, banana-shaped regions in the center of the brain are highlighted, drawn out of proportion with the others. These are the hippocampi.

"The research team noticed that some Human Memory Crusade users were experiencing accelerated memory loss," he says.

He hits the button again, revealing an image of a collection of cells. Above the image is a caption: Magnification, 75,000:1.

"I'm over my head here," Chuck says. "In lay terms, these are memory cells."

"And they were dying," I interrupt.

"Cortisol," he says.

"Of course." Even though I'd guessed this earlier, I'm hit hard by the revelation.

The hyper-stimulation released cortisol.

"So the brain wasn't strengthened but weakened," I say.

He nods. "You understand how this works?"

"Maybe."

"Explain it to me. I've heard it a dozen times, and I never can quite grasp the science."

"What happens to you when you multitask?"

"I get a lot of shit done."

"But at a cost." I stand, start to pace, and think aloud.

"When you've got a ton of information flowing—when you're trying to juggle e-mail, browsing, phone calls, whatever—you're putting yourself in a highly stressful situation. Your brain is fighting to keep up."

"How stressful can e-mail be?"

"Don't think of it like that. Think of the computer as a virtual environment—our twenty-first-century jungle. We spend all day interacting with it. If we were in an actual jungle, it would be highly stressful if we had to face challenges from lots of different directions—lions on one side, alligators on another, hot sun, battles for food, whatever."

"So?"

"In that environment, our adrenal glands produces brain cortisol, a lot of it. It's a stress hormone. It helps us focus intensely for a short period so we can survive."

"Okay, I get that analogy."

I'm sure he's patronizing me. But I continue hypothesizing.

"The problem is that cortisol kills memory cells."

"Bingo." He looks impressed.

I don't know enough about the neuroscience to know if this is a big deal, though I sense from the violence and secrecy involved here that Biogen and Laramer have discovered something radical.

"Say something," Chuck says.

"You're killing my grandmother's brain."

He looks away.

"It's worse than you think."

Chapter Forty-four

I hold out my hands, palms up, then ball them into fists, enraged. "Worse than frying her memory with a fucking motherboard!?"

"There was some chain reaction."

"Meaning?" My fists are still clenched.

"A handful of patients suffered sudden degradation of their memory assets."

"You mean: their memory *cells*? These aren't widgets."

"Right. It's been described to me that they contracted a virus. Somehow the interaction between computer and human stimulated a cascade of cell loss."

"A wildfire," I say.

He nods.

"But if the computers reported a 'wildfire,' they must have been programmed to look for it. Its creators must have known this was a possibility. That makes this something less than an unforeseeable accident."

I ring my fingers around the wine opener in my pocket. "So why did you try to kill her—and me?"

Chuck puts out his hands, trying to calm me. I take another step forward. He scoots to the edge of the couch and, without taking his eyes from me, opens the drawer in an end table. He pulls out a gun.

"The only thing I've ever tried to kill, or killed, has been helpless wildlife." He cradles the gun casually, the threat only implicit.

"Who then? Who tried to kill us?" I demand.

He sighs. "You said it yourself. The Swiss."

I shake my head. Not grasping this.

"Falcon," he says flatly.

"The Swiss giant trying to buy Biogen?" Incredulous.

He shifts back to his computer. He moves the cursor and double clicks on something on his monitor. Moments later, the PowerPoint presentation disappears, and a new image appears—the hooded man who tried to shoot us and set me on fire.

"That's the Swiss guy?"

"Sven something. Works for Falcon. If they're going to buy Biogen, they can't afford to have a messy secret experiment exposed."

"Did they kill Adrianna?"

"My guess is they've detained her, not killed her. No reason to. They're not indiscriminate killers."

"But they'll kill a demented grandmother who can't reveal any information, and her grandson who doesn't know a damn thing? Or didn't until now. Why?"

"That part is personal."

I shake my head—I don't understand his meaning.

"Adrianna has made a long-term investment in another person, and she's deeply emotionally committed to seeing it pay off."

"English!"

"She's playing the role of aunt to the boy. As long as they threaten his safety, she won't compromise their secrets."

"Newton?"

He nods.

"And Grandma and I don't have anything to live for?"

He closes the top of his computer.

"Two different issues," he says. "Your grandmother—she can't be stopped from talking because she can no longer understand reason, or be coerced or blackmailed. Ironically enough, because she has dementia, she's a liability for what she knows, even if she doesn't know she knows it."

"What does she know?"

He shakes his head. He wants to say something else but seems to change gears. He says: "You're a liability for a different reason."

"Because I'm a journalist."

"Because you're a junkie for the hunt. I'm guessing here, inferring a little. But if I were them, I'd find you threatening because you live for this kind of action. No personal connection or promise of wealth or intimacy is as interesting to you as the chase. That makes you beyond blackmail or reason."

I close my eyes and clench my teeth. I let out a loud, frustrated exhale. I'm seeing an image of Grandma and then, surprising to me, Pauline. He has no idea how wrong he is about my intimate connections and my will to fight for them.

"None of this explains why they didn't kill me when they had the chance."

"What do you mean?"

I tell him about Grandma's abduction. Whoever took Grandma left me alive, with her care file. He takes it all in. I can see from the machinations in his jaw that he's working it out, His face shouts stress and concern, displeasure.

"The Swiss took her?" I say, a statement as much as a question.

"I'll help you find out, Nat. I promise you that."

"Chuck, you've still not explained your interest—the military's interest."

"I'll show you."

Toting his gun, Chuck starts to walk out of the room. I follow, feeling the sharp tip of the wine opener in my pocket.

Chapter Forty-five

We climb thickly carpeted stairs to the second floor. Chuck walks a few steps in front. He still holds his gun, casually, but his finger is laced through the trigger loop. I keep one hand on the smooth wooden rail and the other curled around the opener.

"Wait here," Chuck says when we reach the top. We stand in a dark hallway that leads toward the back of the house. He knocks on a door across from the stairs. A deferential woman's voice tells him to come in. He does.

Left alone, my mind tumbles through a series of images, moments, rapid-fire memories, evidence, and unanswered questions from the last few days:

Grandma and me nearly shot; Why? Because she knew about a science experiment gone wrong?

A Human Memory Crusade transcript that doesn't seem to test Grandma's memory so much as write over it. Why?

The hooded man had an accent. Was it Swiss?

Polly's seductiveness. Is she in with Chuck?

Chuck tells me not to trust the police. How might they possibly be involved? Who shot Chuck outside my house? Why isn't he limping?

How does any of this relate to the secret from Grandma's past?

Whom can I trust?

Chuck reemerges.

"Time to meet my father." He holds open the door for me, then whispers, "Be pleasant." It sounds like a threat.

The room is dimly lit. In the corner is a desk. An old man sitting behind it, looking down through a magnifying glass.

"Dad, this is Nathaniel Idle. He's a writer, like Dave Cardigan."

"Dave could shoot a gook from a thousand yards," his father responds without looking up. But I can see his face is fleshy and unsubstantial to the point of being gaunt, his cheeks droopy like a cartoon dog. He wears a leather hunting cap. His voice is deep but textured with crackles. He's had lung trouble, maybe early onset of emphysema. He's late sixties or early seventies, but poorly aged, his white hair wispy thin.

And yet the room looks like it belongs to a high-school kid. To the right of the desk is a poster of a gleaming Harley Davidson motorcycle shown off by a woman in a tight nurse's outfit. Hung next to it is a wide-shot picture of a mountain stream, set against sun-drenched peaks.

In the corner opposite the desk is a queen-size bed covered by a dark blue down comforter pulled tight. There is no woman in the room. She must have exited through the doorway next to the bed.

"Did I hear your wife?" I ask Chuck.

"His nurse. Transparent way to elicit personal information."

The old fellow looks up. "Charles doesn't like girls."

He looks down again.

"Guess it worked," I mutter.

I walk toward the desk. Chuck comes up behind me and puts a hand on my arm, gently holding me back.

For some reason, I'm deeply curious what Chuck's father is looking at so intently with his magnifying glass. I shuffle another step closer. Chuck doesn't stop me. I peer over the desk and see that he's looking at airplane models.

I see a framed photo on the desk, facing in our direction. It's a picture of Chuck's dad from a decade ago, at least. I recognize where he's standing: on the dock of the San Francisco Marina. Behind him is a boat named *Surface to Air*. In the picture,

Chuck's dad wears the tight-jawed look of a tough guy and quiet narcissist.

Chuck spins me around. "Meeting's over."

He whisks me into the hallway.

"What was that dog and pony show?" I ask.

"As you alluded to downstairs, we lose a lot of fine patriots to PTSD. It's arguably the biggest problem in Iraq and Afghanistan. The wounds you don't see and that never heal."

"Your dad served in Vietnam."

"We've created an environment to remind him of the days before the VC popped out of a tunnel in a village Dad and his men were clearing and started spraying fire from a flamethrower. He killed one of Dad's close friends and left Dad with burn scars on his arms and chest."

"I'm sorry," I manage.

"We'd like to help these boys put less emphasis on the bad memories, think about more innocent times."

"You're trying to erase their memories?"

"C'mon, Nat. Stop thinking like a muckraker. We never got that far. We just wanted to find out whether there was any validity to our scientific premises that might help us reinforce some memories and limit others."

"By erasing the bad ones."

"What is it with journalists always seeing the negative? Progress takes change, which can be disruptive."

"So now you have to erase the evidence before you all look bad."

"Nothing of the sort. We're passive investors trying to make sure that the R and D process doesn't exceed our downside loss projections."

After a pause, I say: "But you invest in Internet start-ups, infrastructure companies, not far-fetched neurological experiments."

"Neuro-tech," he says.

"What?"

"Biotech combined biology and technology, saved millions of lives, and made billions for investors. This is the next wave."

"The brain and technology."

He motions me down the stairs.

"Now what?"

He's following me. "You go find your grandmother."

I want to ask how. Instead I say: "I have no money or cell phone."

At the bottom of the stairs, I turn around. Chuck's two steps above me, paused in thought. Then he says: "I'll give you a cell phone but you won't trust it's not a tracking device."

"True. I'll turn it off unless I need to make an urgent call."

"Don't move. If I see you move, I might mistake you for a hippo."

He brushes past me, ducks underneath the hippo head, and disappears somewhere in the back of the house. He returns with a cell phone and a fistful of $20 bills in a rubber band. It's got to be at least $500.

"You keep a spare cell phone?"

"It's my father's. He doesn't need it but I expect you to return it."

"My first call is to the police."

He shrugs.

"Do what you must. But the more attention you bring, the more nervous the bad guys. That's bad news for your grandmother. I've told you before and I meant it: I don't trust police. They're underpaid, poorly incentivized bureaucrats who get their return on investment by fucking with people."

"You lied to me about the police being involved. You told me they were the source of the mystery call in Golden Gate Park."

"You're right. I lied."

"Why?"

"Because I was trying to get my bearings, and I didn't want the Keystone Kops involved before I figured out what was going on."

"That's a hell of a lot of subterfuge and lying for an investor."

"Not really. Business is rough, especially in these economic conditions. You're just not used to looking at it from the inside."

He hands me the phone. I pocket it.

I look Chuck in the eyes. "Does my grandmother have a secret? Something from her past that would make her dangerous, or valuable?"

"Why would you ask that?"

"Because of the transcripts."

"What are you talking about?" He sounds surprised.

But I don't feel like sharing anything more than I need to. "I'm sorry about your father. But you've ruined my grandmother's life. I'll never forgive you for that."

He looks at me in silence, making an assessment.

"Fair enough," he finally says. "Find her."

I know where to start looking.

Chapter Forty-six

A horrific confluence of fear and violence hijacked Chuck's father's brain. A few years in Vietnam, punctuated by death-by-fire in a rice paddy, overwrote and gained primacy over thousands and millions of other memories. Could a computer be doing something analogous to my grandmother? Could the hyper-kinetic interaction with an artificially intelligent interviewer be overriding her daily perceptions?

I pull out Chuck's father's phone.

For an instant, looking at the device, I wonder about the impact of constant computer use on my own memory. Practically speaking, I no longer remember addresses or phone numbers or directions; that's because I've ceded all the remembering to the hard drive of my computer and phone. Isn't that just a convenient trade-off? Or is there something more insidious at work. Is my interaction with my device rewiring my brain? At this moment, my answer is: Who cares?

I need Chuck's phone to do what my brain cannot divine on its own: give me the address to the home of Pete and Kristina Laramer, and directions to get there.

Through an Internet search I get the responses instantly.

Computer 1, Idle's Mind 0.

Dr. Laramer, the scheming neurologist, worked with Biogen to turn my grandmother into a guinea pig, lied to and manipulated me, and now I'm planning to give him an unforgettable late-night

Halloween visit—dressed merely as an aggrieved grandson with sudden violent urges, packing a wine opener.

Minutes later, I'm back at my car. I fire up my laptop, and the transcripts to the Human Memory Crusade. I look at how much story I have yet to read. Looks like another handful of interviews. I glance at them, looking for key words, or obvious revelations that might explain Grandma's disappearance, or why she's taken center stage in this conspiracy.

Her story continues in fits and starts, punctuated by increasing interruptions by the computer. Most striking is that, towards the end of the transcript, the computer does most of the talking. It appears to be telling Grandma about her past, asking her a handful of yes and no questions to make sure it has properly recorded her story. It asks her pointed questions about what kinds of cars her father and husband drove, whether anyone in her neighborhood used a butter churn, what Irving wore to their wedding and how many people attended the affair, what her favorite candy bar was as an adolescent, and other strangely particular facts.

As to the substance of Grandma's tale, it appears to me to end inconclusively. Just before the war, she met some man nicknamed Pigeon and had an intense relationship of an uncertain nature. It feels romantic, exciting, dangerous. But I don't sense there is anything broadly sinister. There is no hint of conspiracy, military intrigue, or treason. But at this point, who knows.

I put down the laptop.

The clock on the phone says 10:48. I turn off the gadget so that someone can't use it to track my whereabouts. I start the car.

Twenty minutes later, I'm at the gates of heaven. Two stone pillars announce the entrance to Sea Cliff, the place I'll live in another life when I'm blessed with wealth and good taste. Sea Cliff, which sits on the edge of San Francisco at the opening of the Pacific and under the shadow of the Golden Gate Bridge, has two qualities you don't often see in the same place: it is home to the outrageously affluent but still feels homey, warm, and tasteful. Robin Williams lives here; so does Senator Dianne Feinstein. And Pete and Kristina Laramer.

I drive past their Spanish-style, three-story home. Inside, lights are on upstairs, but shades make it impossible to see shape or movement.

Outside, the front yard is a mix of succulent plants, including one towering cactus, and neatly arranged pebble ground cover. Near as I can tell, the backyard opens to the Pacific Ocean. I pass the house and park half a block away.

I walk casually through the quiet neighborhood, the trick-or-treaters bedded down already. I approach the front door. I do not have a plan. I reach for the big brass door handle. It's locked. No surprise.

I peek through the long vertical windows on either side of the door. Inside it's dim. I can make out an entryway, and a table with stacks of paper on it. Looks like the day's newspapers and mail. I realize with relief: no dog. But stuck into the pebbles next to the doorway is a sign indicating the house is protected by ADT Security.

I walk to the side of the house. The backyard is surrounded by a white picket fence. I ease over it. Then pause, frozen by what I see: great beauty. Lit by a nearly full moon, the ocean rolls in and out at the bottom of the cliffs, hundreds of feet below these blessed residences curving along the coastline. Small waves crash foamy white, creating a rhythmic cacophony, at once violent and calming. I feel a sudden desperation for sleep. I push the sensation down and turn to the house.

In the upstairs, I see light in two rooms at opposite ends of the house. Downstairs, darkness. Immediately in front of me is a door that, I can see upon creeping closer, enters into an open pantry that leads to a kitchen. I try the door. It is locked.

I slink along the back of the house to a set of double doors covered on the inside with a slatted blind. Twisting my neck to see between the slats, I make out a formal dining room. The doors are locked.

I move to the next set of double doors. These are protected by a thick curtain, precluding any view inside. I reach for the door handle. It turns. Reflexively, I recoil.

I feel in my pocket and discover the pointed wine opener I took from Chuck's living-room bar. It's a meager weapon, unless I encounter a hostile bottle of Pinot Noir.

I push open the door.

There is enough moonlight for me to make out the décor: floor-to-ceiling bookshelves, Victorian furniture and trappings. Lots of insurance-company reimbursements funded these digs.

Then I hear the moan.

It is low, pained, husky and animalistic, like a dying animal. Or a dying neurologist.

I take two steps into the house and can make out the soft lump of humanity propped up against a desk at the far side of the room. Pete Laramer. His arms dangle loosely, palms up. He struggles fiercely to raise his right hand to his face.

Dark liquid stains his scrubs. The highest concentration spreads from just below his chest, the lowest edge of the rib cage, the apparent epicenter of a major wound. I rush toward him, then pause, taking stock.

"Heart okay…blood loss," Pete manages to say.

I put my hand on his stomach to stanch the bleeding. Not a place you can tourniquet.

"Where are the girls?"

"Fuck you."

He thinks I'm asking for purposes of attacking them.

"Are they safe, Pete?"

He takes a breath, and seems to accept my meaning. "Away with their mom. Fine.…Happier without their workaholic… unfaithful father."

"Don't talk."

"You can love someone completely…love your family, need them…and still lead a double life."

He's wheezing. Punctured lung, or lungs.

"Bullet?" I ask. I'm trying to focus him.

He shakes his head.

"Knife. Big one," I say. It's obvious now. There's a wound too on his neck, missing the jugular, hitting some of the windpipe.

I pull out my phone. I turn it on. While I wait for it to come to life, I say, "We might have to do a trach."

Battlefield tracheotomy. Stick a sharp object into the windpipe to allow breathing. I've never done one myself and have seen only a handful performed in person during med school. But it's less complicated than it sounds.

"I didn't know," he whispers.

"Shh."

"A walking server, Soylent Green 2.0...the digital version," he says.

I want to tell him to save his strength, but what the hell does he mean?

My phone is alive. I dial 911.

"They've spread it already," he says.

"Who?"

"She's carrying a secret....They won't stop until they get it."

"Lane?"

He nods.

He must be referring to what Chuck told me—that someone has triggered Lane's precipitous memory decline and they can't let the secret get out.

The 911 operator answers. I'm about to speak when the interior door to the library opens.

"Intruder," I say into the phone.

"Heavily armed one," says the hooded man. He's standing at the doorway, holding a hunting knife.

Chapter Forty-seven

"Slow, calm, deep breaths," I tell Pete.

I should take the advice myself.

I stand, my adrenaline screaming. Fight or flight.

The hooded man moves to the middle of the room. He's cut off my exits. I couldn't flee if I wanted to. I couldn't leave Grandma's dying neurologist, much as I blame him for what's happened, to a final hacking, or without telling me what the fuck is going on. That leaves: fight.

I look on the desk for a weapon. On the corner sits a stout porcelain lamp with a flower-pattered base. I lift it, but it slips from my hand. The hooded man assesses me in silence.

"Guns, fire, sharp objects," I say. "You're multi-talented."

"In this economy, it pays to be versatile."

"And a razor-sharp sense of humor."

I need to buy time so the emergency operator can hone in on the phone signal and send the cavalry. The hooded man steps forward.

"You ever been to Davos?" I ask.

"Where?"

"You're not from Switzerland."

"Get ready to say *gutenacht*."

"That's German."

"Uh-huh."

"Am I allowed a weapon?" I ask.

"You can fight back with your face."

He steps forward and I stumble back. I move right, behind the desk. This, I realize, constitutes a strategic error. If I try to use the desk as a barrier, it means putting Pete directly in the middle of the fray.

I slide further to my right, away from the desk. But into the open. Behind me, bookshelves. Further to my right, the library's interior doorway, leading to the rest of the house, but the door is closed. The international man stands next to the desk, not far from Pete. He seems amused by my indecision and the apparent futility of my escape maneuvers. If I run for the interior door, he'll get me from behind.

He takes a step forward, confident but cautious and strategic, cutting off my angles. He's not breathing hard, but sweat glistens in the widow's peak of his brow. I notice a slight wobble in his left leg. I take another step to my right and so does he. Wobble.

"ACL," I say.

This pauses him.

"You've got a tear in your left knee. It's weak. I'm not an orthopedist, but it looks to me like one wrong step and that thing could go."

"I'll take my chances."

He takes two big steps towards me and swings his knife. I leap to my left, edging back behind the desk and out of the way of his swing. I turn to face him and see his new look of intense determination.

I back away, feeling in my pocket for the wine opener. I pass Pete to my left. I speed up my backpedaling. In my peripheral vision, I see a low-backed reading chair, maybe small enough that I can throw it, or big enough to duck behind. But my window to decide and act is slamming.

The man runs at me, knife held high. He swings it downward. I turn my back away in hopes of avoiding razor on flesh. I lurch, and stumble forward, flailing and falling. Behind me, I hear a yelp, and a thud.

"Motherfucker!"

Scrambling back to my feet, I turn to look. The assailant is on the ground, facedown. He looks at me, starts to rise, grimaces, grabs his knee.

I can see why: around the knee is a cord of some kind. An electrical cord.

In an instant, I understand. Pete somehow has wrapped the lamp cord around the killer's leg and tripped him, aggravating the knee injury.

Remarkable. For once, my penchant for snap diagnoses has actually helped me.

He starts to rise again. I leap towards him as I pull the wine opener out. I aim for the top of his back, piercing the tender, nerve-filled skin between his scapulae.

"AHHH. FUCK!"

He flails his arms behind his back, reaching for the opener.

It is the strangest moment for me to think: Canadian accent. Not Swiss. Canadian.

Then I see that the knife has spun free. It is a few feet to the intruder's left, at the base of the bookshelves. I rush to it. I grab the warm handle, slick with sweat.

I walk to the would-be killer. He's craning his neck my direction, looking now at me. Despite having the opener still in his back, he's responding to the more immediate danger. He inches away from me.

I hear sirens. Police, maybe an ambulance, headed in our direction.

I look at the electrical lamp cord still wrapped around the man's knee. I follow the cord where it leads—to the stubby porcelain lamp lying next to Pete. It survived the fall from the desk. It won't survive the next impact. Without taking my eyes from him, I set down the knife beside Pete and lift the lamp.

I walk to the assassin and hold it over his head, as he struggles to scoot away and extricate the protruding wine opener.

"Where's my grandmother?"

"He doesn't know," Pete rasps. "He asked me."

"How can he not know? He's the bad guy!"

The man has succeeded in dislodging the wine opener. He's getting his bearings, looking around for a weapon.

"Lights out," I say.

I slam the lamp over the man's head. The porcelain shatters. The intruder slumps, unconscious.

"DSM," Pete mutters.

"Thank you, Pete. Unbelievable teamwork. Hang on. The ambulance is almost here."

"DSM."

He's jutting his pale chin across the room. I follow his gaze to a small, round coffee table with ornate legs. On top of the table sits a hefty medical book. The DSM—The Diagnostic and Statistical Manual of Mental Disorders.

The intruder moans.

I look back at Pete. He nods.

I hustle over to the manual. I look back at Pete. "Dementia," Pete says.

I open the book to D. I flip through pages, until I come to the loose piece of paper.

The sirens are nearing. They've certainly reached Sea Cliff, maybe our block.

Pete says something I can't understand. He's too weak to make his voice heard. I step closer to him and can make out his meaning. "Get them," he whispers. "Stop them."

"Who is *them*? Who is this man? Who does he work for?"

His head lolls. He's fading.

"Pete!"

His chin droops. I feel his pulse. It's weak, but blood continues to pump.

I take the piece of paper, and fold it into my pocket.

I look at Pete's attacker, who is blinking on the edge of consciousness. The police will be here soon enough. I hate to leave, but I can't stay. There is little I can do for Pete.

I slip out the back door into the moonlight.

Chapter Forty-eight

If I hop over the white picket fence, I'll find myself in the strobe lights of local law enforcement. That means getting detained, explaining the mess inside, losing the piece of paper Pete gave me, and, most important, not following up on my impulse: I know where I can find Grandma. Or, at least, I have an idea who might have taken her. And the extraordinary reason why.

I shuffle two houses down to a residence that has the lights off. I hoist myself onto its lawn. I edge along the side of the house.

Minutes later, I climb into the Cadillac, start the engine, and drive out of Sea Cliff.

Six blocks later, I pull over. I turn on the car's inside light. I pull out the piece of paper from Pete's DSM.

What I see is a laundry list of items:

> 1/0
> Yankees/Dodgers
> Cursive/Block
> 12/7; Radio/Word-of-Mouth
> Chevrolet/Cadillac
> Standard/Automatic
> Paternal car; Chevrolet/Cadillac
> Slaughter Self/Butcher
> Kennedy/Nixon
> Married uniform/tie
> Husband married uniform/tie

Saw moon landing/word-of-mouth
Union/non-union
Polio in family/No polio
Pink Cadillac/Blue Cadillac
Purple Chevrolet/Orange Chevrolet
One sibling/no sibling
Two sibling/three sibling
Procrastinator/punctual
Audited/Meticulous with books
If cursive, then "saw moon landing"
If union, then Yankees
If Procrastinator, then Polio

As I look at the list, the first thing that comes to mind is that I've heard Grandma Lane talk about some of these things, both in her conversations with me and in her conversations with the Human Memory Crusade. For instance, on more than one occasion, she's mentioned to me that her father drove a Cadillac. I recall that she told the Crusade that she heard about Pearl Harbor on a radio. One of the items on the list reads: "12/7; Radio/Word-of-Mouth."

12/7—December 7, 1941. Pearl Harbor.

I study the whole list again. On its face, this looks like a list of possible memory options. Some people supported Kennedy, others Nixon. Some drove a standard car, others an automatic. But the list also seems so discrete, narrow, and confining. After all, some people probably supported neither the Yankees nor the Dodgers.

Grandma wasn't a big baseball fan.

The word equations at the end of the list are another curiosity—"If union, then Yankees." "If Procrastinator, then Polio."

I do recognize the syntax as basic computing language, The "if...then" statement. Bullseye can make more sense of it.

It is almost midnight. I fold up the piece of paper and start the car.

I start driving across town to what I imagine will be a bizarre confrontation, one that has been a lifetime in the making.

◇◇◇

The funniest teacher I had in med school was Dr. Eleanor Fitzgerald. She taught anatomy. We called her El Fitz.

One day, she brought in a picnic lunch for everyone that included beer. After lunch, she announced we would finally start dissecting the brain.

"No need to be totally sober for this," she said. "We have no real idea what's going on in there, or how it works. Come back in seven thousand years and we'll have something to teach you."

It is truly a wonder how we think, process information, store memories, and recall them.

Computers are a mystery too, at least to me. But, in general, I know that we know how to build them, and we know how information moves. We know that data gets held in a certain piece of hardware that is controlled by a certain piece of software. We know that tiny transistors attached to only slightly less tiny pieces of silicon transmit and calculate information when we ask our device to calculate a math problem or place a phone call. We write software that performs certain tasks, all dictated and understood by a computer's creators.

Similarly, we know that various regions in the human mind have a lot to say about certain activities. The visual cortex and sight are linked. Injure the frontal lobe and emotional retardation follows, and so on. But most activities don't just rely on a discrete region of the brain. Even a relatively simple task—picking up a pencil—might involve dozens of nooks and crannies; neurons firing in just the right amounts, cascading and cooperating in an organic alchemy that is truly one of life's great mysteries.

But unlike a computer, we can't well measure or dictate what's happening. Our mind often has a mind of its own. Witness depression, joy, hand-eye coordination, ability to make music, or love. Or the sudden emergence of a memory, the synthesis of a complex idea, a brainstorm, or revelation.

Say, for instance, a revelation about the life of your grandmother.

Somewhere in the recesses of my brain, a theory bubbles to the surface. I have a feeling I know what triggered it: When I found Pete lying on the floor in a pool of blood, he confessed to me that he was living a "double life."

Double life.

Why did that phrase trigger a theory about my grandmother? Who knows. But it did.

It made me think about her distant relationship with my father, and the yearning for freedom that has always been laced through our conversations, even when I was a child. It made me think about Lane's childhood in Denver, the stranger nicknamed Pigeon, the way I always felt such kinship with Grandma even though she kept a distance from me, held something back.

The mysteries of my mind. The mysteries of my grandmother.

I drive by Magnolia Manor. The front entrance is dark. Only a handful of the windows inside are lit. I'm struck by the peacefulness of the place; I'm always so critical of Magnolia Manor but now it seems like a refuge of solitude and a quiet place to spend a few years playing bridge and watching reruns.

For good measure, I park three blocks away.

I walk along the quiet streets to the retirement home's entrance. I slink along the side of the gardens that lead from the gates to the front doors. To get inside, I'll need to convince the desk guard to buzz me in. More likely, he'll not do so, or he'll call the cops.

There's an alternative. Vince lives in a flat detached from the Manor, on the right side of the property. His residence is a two-story brownstone that looks like it belongs in a swanky Boston or New York neighborhood. Like Vince, it is well kept and austere. From the porch light, I can see the grass cut precisely along the stone path that leads from gate to front door.

I walk to the red-painted door. I reach for the handle, and I find it open. I enter.

Vince sits in a deep, upholstered recliner in his living room. There is a book across his lap. The Human Asparagus doesn't look surprised to see me.

He is surprised, however, when I bullrush him. Without a word, I hurl myself toward the chair as he reaches for the telephone sitting next to him.

I smack the phone out of his hand and reach for his throat, then pull back, gulping for air, standing over him. I have the upper hand, physically. He cannot match my anger or drive.

"If you hurt me, you won't find your grandmother," Vince says, trying to stay cool.

"You took her."

"I protect my residents."

"Where is she, Vince?"

"I don't know."

"Bullshit. You just said…"

"Plausible deniability. I helped take her. To protect her. but I don't know where they put her."

"Who?"

I'm asking the question, but I already know who Vince is referring to.

A voice confirms my suspicions.

"She's safe," the gravelly bass voice says. It comes from behind me.

I turn and am struck by the interloper's lean face, serious, with thoughtful eyes, like you'd imagine from a troop commander whose squad took a few too many casualties.

I look down at his feet. I see the toes turned just a tad inward.

"Hello, Pigeon," I say.

"I haven't been called that in many years."

"I have a strange question for you."

"Your grandmother is okay. She's fine."

"I know that, Harry."

"I can take you to her."

"No," Vince says.

"It's okay, Vince," Harry responds. Harry has clearly led men. He looks at me. "What's your question?"

I clear my throat.

"Are you my grandfather?"

A tear wells in the corner of Pigeon's eye.

Chapter Forty-nine

It's a wonder I haven't had my membership card in the Northern California Press Club revoked. For the last day, Grandma hasn't been very hard to find. She's been back at the home, in her own bed.

I stand at its foot, watching her sleep. Next to me stands Harry. His agitation is evident only from the rhythmic grinding of his teeth. Betty Lou stands nearby in a terry-cloth robe, rocking on her feet.

"It would be better if you'd wait outside," Harry says to Vince.

"I don't trust him," Vince says.

"Trust *me*," Harry responds. "If there's a problem, you can always call the police."

Vince glowers at me. He walks out the door. He's limping, but I let the observation go for the moment—along with a lot of other unanswered questions.

Harry and I walked here in silence. So I still don't know the crucial particulars. Right now, I feel mostly immense relief.

I turn to Betty Lou. "I don't blame you," I say.

"You'd have no right to. Laney needed to be safe," she says, then takes the edge off with her addendum: "Friday night is crappy mac-and-cheese night at the Manor. You can't deprive her of that."

She smiles thinly.

I sit on the bed. Grandma lies on her side, her cheek against the pillow, face seemingly relaxed, her breathing regular, and then she lets out an audible exhale, a demi-snore. Her eyes open, she blinks, and falls back asleep.

I put my hand on the hump of her body.

Tears stream down my cheeks and I do nothing to try to stop them.

I sit this way for more than a minute, when I feel Betty Lou put a hand on my shoulder. "She's lucky to have you," Betty Lou whispers. We remain like this for another minute until the extent of my relief passes through me. Until I am convinced Grandma is really here—intact, safe and sound.

On Grandma's nightstand is a cell phone. Betty Lou sees me looking at it. "It's mine," she says. "Go ahead."

I nod. I take a deep breath, pick it up the phone, and dial. My heart thumps. The phone rings four times, then goes to voice mail. I call again. After the second ring, Polly answers.

"Don't say anything," I say. "Just hear these words: I want to take you to dinner."

"Where are you?"

"With my grandmother?"

"Are you okay?"

"More or less."

"Can you come see me?"

"Yes. Soon."

"Tonight soon?"

"Yes."

I hope I'm going to be able to be true to my word.

We hang up.

I turn to face Betty Lou and Harry.

"It's not very complicated, is it?" I say.

When I'd first absconded with Lane, it made her friends nervous. This seems natural, given that I haven't been so attentive in the past, but, more fundamentally, because they didn't like to see Grandma away from her comfortable confines. Then I prompted further concern when I asked Betty Lou to steal Grandma's care file.

"You were acting strange, talking about conspiracies," Betty Lou says. "It was like *The X-Files*, or the Nixon administration."

"But the sprinklers destroyed the recreation room," I say, referring to the convenient deployment of fire sprinklers that destroyed the computers for the Human Memory Crusade.

They don't have an answer to this.

"You trust Vince," I say.

Harry clears his throat. "We had a grunt in our platoon who did everything by the book," he says. "A lot of guys razzed him for cleaning his weapon all the time and telling us to clean ours. He was a pain in the rear, if you want to know the truth. But in a beachside foxhole on some hot-as-hell island, he had the last working rifle."

"So you went to Vince and asked his help getting back Lane?" I ask.

"He was livid that you'd taken her," Betty Lou says. "He feared you were involved in this strange computer project, maybe experimenting with the residents so you could write an article. He thinks you love a great drama."

"So he's not involved with the Human Memory Crusade?"

She shrugs. "You'll have to ask him."

I fall silent for a moment, then continue theorizing aloud. When Grandma's friends came to Vince for help, he suggested that they essentially kidnap Grandma. It was Vince's idea to use chloroform to drug me.

"It was mine," Harry says.

"Why?"

"You wouldn't have given her up. Rightfully so. I wouldn't have given her up. I wouldn't have…if I had to do it over again."

I'm not sure what to say to this, if he's ready to bring up the elephant in the room.

"We thought that if we took Grandma, you'd be inspired to figure out what is going on—with all this computer nonsense," Betty Lou offers. "We just didn't want you to do it with Grandma by your side. She's not your sidekick. She's a woman deserving of peace."

"But by drugging me, you scared the hell out of me," I pause. "You took my grandmother from me."

I'm surprised myself by my raw emotion. I have hit a place of undiluted truth: *Hello, my name is Nat Idle, and I love my grandmother. I care about someone as much as I care about myself.*

Harry looks down.

"Your grandmother put up a fight on her behalf," Betty Lou says. "She gave Vince a fierce karate kick to the leg."

Hence the limp.

Again, I fall silent.

Finally, Harry speaks: "Betty Lou, can you leave me alone with the young man? We have a few things to talk about."

Chapter Fifty

From his back pocket, he pulls a piece of paper.

"She has beautiful penmanship. But when the ink started to fade, I typed this up. That was probably 1954. I've retyped it a few times since."

I take the piece of paper.

I read:

September 5, 1942

Dear Harry,

I'm sitting in the park where the boys play baseball. I have a bench to myself, but there are lots of people around. One nearby picnicking couple just stood up and started to sway to music coming from a speaker somewhere. The song is Moonlight Serenade by Glenn Miller, and it is making me sad.

The man is wearing a Navy uniform. I want to ask him where he's going. I wonder if you'll meet him, and save his life. (Could I be any more dramatic?)

I got the letter you sent to the post office. Your poem was so funny ("occasion" has two c's). I'm sure you're making your bunkmates laugh. They don't expect it from you.

I'm not sure I should be writing in response.

Two nights ago, two men in uniform stopped by the house on the corner of the block. The Bensons live there. You probably never met Tommy. He went by "Stork" because of his long neck. He's a year older than you, or he was a year older. He died crawling across a field in Italy to help an injured friend. That's what the men in uniform told Mrs. Benson. I haven't slept in two nights. I hope you are safe. I just know you are taking care of yourself. But I worry that you think you are invincible. I read an article that said all young men think they are invincible and immortal and that's the reason why we send them into war. You're different from that, maybe worse. Sometimes I think you don't mind finding out what's on the other side. You're very curious and genuine about exploring the world and I mean that as the highest compliment. You were genuine and curious about discovering the real me.

Every day in the paper I recognize the names of people who have been killed.

When you shipped out, I was sure I would see you again, and I still want to believe that is the case.

I decided that I should write to you because I have something I should tell you. I don't want you to be hurt by it. I wouldn't ever want to hurt you. But I feel you should know everything.

I married Irving.

Irving is a good man. He's not going to go into the war because he had his appendix removed when he was very young and the surgery could create medical problems if he were sent into combat.

He's going to take good care of me and our family. He doesn't like to have adventures and he doesn't like to lose himself in the world, if that makes sense. But he has things under control. He doesn't mind if I say the things that I think, and sometimes he doesn't even notice exactly what I mean. I guess that's a good thing and a bad thing. You seem to pay such close attention to me. You hear things that I don't even realize that I'm saying, and then I realize how good it feels to be heard.

I know I shouldn't be writing these things or even thinking these things. I feel like a harlot. But the worst part is that I don't totally mind. I find it exciting to feel like I am alive. You make me feel that way.

I am trying to have it both ways. That is worse than being a harlot.

That's enough sad talk. I wish they'd turn off the stupid music.

Please wear your helmet. Don't drink water that isn't clean. Change your undergarments! Don't volunteer for any adventures or give any other girls secret books. I know that I am not entirely making sense, but there are things I'd like to tell you that don't belong in this letter. Please just know that you have made a great impression on me, much bigger than you can know at this moment. You are alive inside of me.

Sincerely,
    L.

I look up from the letter at Harry. He is pale, his skin pallor betraying tension beneath his unflinching demeanor.

"One time you threw up on a snake," he says.

It's a jarring statement and it takes me a moment to adjust to it. He's referring to the time I was at the reptile zoo with Grandma. The curator forced me to touch a boa and I got scared and threw up.

"Grandma told you about that?"

"I watched it from behind a museum post," he says. "I watched your Uncle Stevie play in a band, and I took a volunteer job at the concession stand so I could watch your dad play high-school baseball."

"Did you teach me to swim?"

He nods.

I'm remembering the time my grandmother took me to Santa Cruz when I was five. We met an old lifeguard, or so I thought. It was Harry.

"You were a natural," he says.

"Holy shit." I'm having another revelation. His face tightens. Harry doesn't like cursing.

I continue: "You were the man in the rowboat."

When Grandma used to take me to Stow Lake, she hired a man who worked at the boathouse to row us into the center. She'd ask me about my life. Harry would listen to the interview in silence.

He nods.

"You got Grandma pregnant before you shipped out. She didn't know, or tell you, until you came back?"

"Your grandmother did what she had to do. She didn't know if I'd make it back. She didn't know if what we had was the real thing."

I am speechless, but calm.

"She's a fine woman."

He's so noble, old school. I can't reconcile this man with the creative romantic who seduced Grandma on a first date with a secret note and a hidden library book.

"Did Grandma know you were watching us?"

He nods.

"I never went against her. I want you to know that. Your grandmother and I had a secret friendship, but it was only a friendship." He pauses, and adds: "Mostly, just a friendship."

"You had your own family?"

He shakes his head in the negative.

"It must have been so difficult."

He looks down.

"I didn't graduate from high school," he says after a pause. "I worked in a concrete yard."

"How is that relevant?" I ask, gently.

"We came from different backgrounds but your grandmother and I had something I can't explain very well. I'm a different person with her than I am with anyone else. I think she's a different person too."

We fall silent.

"Did my grandfather...did Irving know?"

"If he did, he never said a word about it—not that Laney told me about. He was a good man. He treated her well. If you know Lane, you know she can't live just one life. She needed to know there was something else out there."

I take this in. He continues.

"I saved money and took trips and gallivanted some. I ran with the bulls in Spain, and I dove off cliffs in a Chilean rain forest, and other things. I sent your grandmother letters. I'm not much for writing or telling stories, but I tried—for her."

He stops talking. He's done.

"When she realized she was losing her memory, she decided to tell her story. She was going to tell me and then decided to tell the computer," I say.

I see the first raw emotion on Harry's face. His eyes are wet.

"She's getting better. She's remembering better, now that she's away from the machine."

"Did you know it was causing her a problem?"

"I don't know anything about those foolish computers. I just know that in my day, we trusted our secrets to people."

Now I see he's looking in her direction. I follow his gaze. Grandma's eyes are open. She's looking ahead, and she is smiling.

"Harry," she says.

"Laney."

"I had a wonderful dream."

"Tell me about it."

"About what?"

"Your dream."

"Come sit with me," she says.

He walks over and sits by the side of the bed. He seems almost shy about it. She takes his hand.

"This is nice," she says.

I watch them for a moment, finding I can barely speak for the tears.

From my pocket, I retrieve the paper I'd taken from Pete's library. I unfold it and I walk to Harry.

"Does this mean anything to you?" I ask.

He shakes his head, then turns back to Lane.

◇◇◇

I use Betty Lou's cell phone to retrieve the messages from my own phone. There is one left by someone with a nervous, high-pitched voice.

"I'm sorry that I ran away on Halloween. I was afraid. Come visit me tomorrow on the basketball court. I have something I think you're looking for. You know who this is. I'll be waiting."

I close the clamshell phone and put it back down. I lean over and kiss my grandmother on the forehead.

"Does she want the world to know about this, about you, her secret?" I ask Harry.

"She's getting better. When she's not at the computer, she seems more like herself."

"Meaning what?"

"Maybe she can answer your question herself in a few days."

◇◇◇

Outside the room, Vince stands guard.

"They offered us free computers," he says. "I was trying to make their lives better."

"I believe you. But we still have a lot to talk about."

He nods.

"You don't need to make a story out of this," he says. "That's about you and your career. Think about all the people whose lives you will ruin."

"Keep my grandmother safe."

"She's safe. Guard around the clock. This is all over now."

I wish he were right. I head into the night.

Chapter Fifty-one

I'm scraping my hippocampus for memories of the shadow man who flitted in and out of my life, making brief cameos and little concrete impression.

Did I sense something about that man at the time? Did I intuit the import of Harry, the Pigeon-man who was Grandma's true love?

Did I deliberately bury this instinct? Was it too strange for a child to contemplate? Or record as memory?

I honestly can't remember.

I'm aware of the failings of my own memory, its fragility.

Something else strikes me. Perhaps I wasn't particularly aware of Harry's periodic presence. But perhaps I *was* aware of something else: the changing moods in my grandmother.

Sometimes she seemed happier. Sometimes she sang a little bit more, seemed purer and less distracted. Sometimes, so inspired.

Were those the times Harry was near?

Did I sense that Grandma led a double life? Or that she needed more than one thing to keep her happy?

Does it scare me to feel so connected to her malady?

Chapter Fifty-two

I stand at the doorstep of Polly's flat. Sleep deprivation and delirium should have me shrouded in my own personal fog. But I feel alive with both hope and misgivings.

The door is unlocked. Polly is too trusting. She shouldn't be so cavalier and open in such a dangerous world. The house is quiet.

"Polly?" I call upstairs, then down.

No response.

I drop my backpack and start to run. I speed up the stairs to her bedroom.

The bedside light is on. On the bed lies Polly, a pillow clutched to her chest. She's sleeping, then hears me, and starts to stir.

"You're okay," I exclaim. Utter relief.

She rubs a beautiful eye with the back of her hand.

"Why wouldn't I be? My God," she says and pulls herself into a sitting position. "What ran you over?"

"It's no biggie. I got attacked by the U.S. military and the biotech industry. A day in the life of a blogger."

She blinks, the vulnerable Polly. Tears in her eyes. "Would you mind making me some tea?"

◇◇◇

I make her rosebud herbal tea, which she says she's been craving all night. It's just past midnight. We sit on the love seat across the wall from her bed. Dim light from a lamp gives the room a hollow feeling. Polly, chilly, wraps herself in a blanket.

I've sensed for days something has been bothering her. "You're not telling me something."

"You're right."

"Are you part of it?"

"I told you about my brother."

"Philip. Crystal meth."

"I love him so much. I've taken care of him. I always will."

"What did he do? Is he involved in this thing?"

She looks at me quizzically.

"I know you think I'm some corporate drone, a crazed MBA looking to change the world and charge a lot of money for it, but…"

I don't know where she's heading. "Polly…"

"I'm not that. I am waiting for the right thing to invest myself in, not just my business."

"Are you part of the Crusade? Are you in league with Chuck?"

"I have no idea what you're talking about."

"Then what are *you* talking about?"

"Nat, I really wanted you to come to this on your own. I didn't want to put pressure on you. I know who you are and I have no need to change that."

I'm baffled.

"Please, Polly. Tell me what's going on."

She smiles.

"There's someone I want you to meet."

I look around.

She takes my hand with her cold grasp. She stretches out my fingers and extends them toward her belly.

"Meet your son."

Lightning in my head. An explosion of quiet emotion, like watching the aurora borealis inside my brain. In the last couple of days, I've learned the fragility of memory. I know immediately I will never forget this moment.

"But…"

"It only takes once."

I look at her, incredulous.

"Accident. We took precautions."

"The night…"

"September twenty-seventh," she says.

I know that date. She'd circled it on the calendar in her office.

"But you already know it's a boy?"

It's not medically possible to know that so soon.

"I just know," she says.

I smile.

Part of me must have suspected. Maybe it explains my garrulous confessions to Grandma the last few days about my feelings for Polly.

I start to say something.

"Don't," she says. "I'm going to have him. We'd love you to be part of our lives in some capacity, but I can handle this. I've handled lots more."

I put my arms around her.

"Don't say anything," she whispers. "Sleep on it. You'll need a few nights. I did."

We walk to the bed, and climb under the covers. I put my arms around her, and I collapse into sleep.

◇◇◇

In my dream, I am attending a funeral. I look at the program and am surprised to learn I am supposed to deliver the eulogy. I don't even know who has died. The name of the deceased is not on the program. I am standing in line to view the open casket. I approach, feeling sick.

When I get to the casket, I see that it is me lying inside. I turn around and see my grandmother waiting in line behind me to view my body.

"They've got a string quartet outside," she says. "They're wonderful."

"I'm dead?"

"Don't be so dramatic." She smiles. "You've already died a thousand times and you've never taken it this hard before."

Chapter Fifty-three

I wake up to discover I'm having sex. I am so groggy that I don't realize when it began, only that Polly has made her intentions eminently clear, and nature takes its course.

"Pregnancy has left me with a craving for sex and pork ribs," she says after we finish.

I laugh, and wince. Even smiling is causing pain to ripple through a corpus that for two days has been through a menu of near misses by fire, bullet, and knife, chloroform, scarf, and flashlight.

"Nat, I'm not asking for anything and I'm not negotiating."

"I know."

"But I have to tell you the truth."

"Okay."

"You're not a great blogger."

"And a good morning to you too."

She laughs.

"What I mean is that you're a great long-form journalist. You dig into stories and pursue them. You're not meant for this medium."

"I can post more often."

"I'm not negotiating our future," she reiterates. "I'm telling you the truth."

"Polly…"

"Stop. Let's start telling each other the truth, about everything." She raises her eyebrows, like, *Okay?* She continues:

"What were you talking about last night, about the crusade and Chuck and your paranoia? Were you just being you, or is it something real?"

I nod.

"Let's hear it. Please. I need to talk about that right now."

"Over breakfast."

"You shower. I'll make coffee."

I peel my body away from hers and slide from under the sheets. With early-morning sun soaking in through the blinds, I watch Polly plop her feet onto the plush area rug that covers her polished wood floor. She walks to the bathroom. When will pregnancy change her body? Can I get used to this?

◇◇◇

Over cantaloupe and Frosted Flakes, I tell Polly the tale of the last few days. She is curious, concerned, nearly incredulous.

She comes around to me and surrounds me with a prolonged hug.

"You and Lane are safe."

I let myself relish the feeling of her slender arms around my neck.

"This is nice," I finally say. "But I'm going to have to break away at some point this morning to get some answers and mete out some vengeance."

She withdraws. She sits next to me and studies me.

"Chuck was involved," I say.

"Speaking of Chuck, he backed out," she says. "An investor no more."

"He did? But he'd already committed."

"He had a due-diligence clause that let him escape. He said he couldn't make the numbers work. He said he wanted to go back to focusing on his primary interest."

"Which is what, being strange and duplicitous?"

"Innovating and refining core Internet technologies," Polly said, making air quotes with a pair of fingers.

"Polly, I'm sorry. But not completely."

"Yeah, well, he made it worth my while. He gave us seventy-five thousand dollars for our trouble. He said he felt he'd led us too far down the road."

I stop chewing mid-bite. That's quite a forfeiture. I've never heard of anything like that. Polly says she hasn't either. In exchange for the money, Polly says she has signed a strategic partnership that gives Chuck and his military investors a first look at any new technological developments or distribution methods.

"I'll do some digging and see what I can find out about him," she says.

We fall silent.

"Go find Copernicus," she says.

"Newton?"

"Newton."

She disappears to the bedroom, and returns with the keys to the Cadillac. I need to get my own car fixed if I'm going to have a family. Or get a better car.

"Polly. I've been fighting my feelings for you. But they're real. More so than I've felt with anyone since…They're the real thing."

"Sleep on it again."

I take the keys.

"Can I borrow your cell phone?" I ask.

"This is how it starts. You get me pregnant, then you want to share cell phones?"

"And a joint bank account and the early-bird special at House of Pork Ribs."

She laughs. "I'm as terrified as you are."

I wonder if that's so.

I drive to the basketball court. I think about what I told Polly, and how much remains unanswered. Or maybe it's straightforward as Chuck has made it seem. Biogen and Pete and the U.S. military collaborate to create a computer program that will enhance memory. They test it with old folks and veterans. It doesn't work. It queers memory, erases it, writes over it.

The conspirators decide to get rid of the evidence, including my grandmother. She's the proverbial Demented Octogenarian Who Knows Too Much. It just all seems too pat, and with so many holes.

What is the meaning of the paper Pete handed me? What happened to Pete? Did he survive? What happened to the man in his library?

I realize I'm not sure I'm even angry. Just curious. And with a new uncertainty: Can I afford to delve into this any further? If I do, I risk myself and my safety as the father of the zygote growing inside Polly.

The basketball court is empty. I wait outside in the car, staring and thinking. After fifteen minutes of coming up without any new answers, I decide to call for backup. It's just past 10 A.M. Bullseye, while a night owl, should be up. I call and tell him about the piece of paper I got from Pete, with the lists of memories, and the "1/0" at the top of the page.

"Isn't that computer language?" I ask.

The list itself seems to have binary pairs—Kennedy/Nixon, or polio in family/no polio.

Bullseye takes in the evidence in silence. I consider telling him about Grandma's abduction, the revelations from G.I. Chuck, my impending fatherhood. But these things can wait. Bullseye tells me he'll think about the implications of binary pairs and call me back. I suspect he's going back to sleep.

It's sunny, but deceptively chilly. I exit the car and walk to the basketball court.

I look up at the building where Newton and Adrianna live. From the third story, I see a face peer through a window.

Adrianna has surfaced.

Chapter Fifty-four

I walk to the front door of the dilapidated apartment building and she meets me there and buzzes me in.

"Sunscreen," is the first thing the mysterious scientist says to me.

"What?"

"Even in October the rays are poison."

"I don't think you'd be planning to kill me if you're trying to spare me from getting skin cancer."

"Don't say anything else until we get upstairs."

In silence, we take the elevator to the third floor.

She is medium height with a build that is tough to determine given her baggy clothes: sweatpants and a sweatshirt with a Brown University logo. Her hair is pulled back tight in a short ponytail. Her skin radiates, like she could model moisturizer. Her eyes are intensely bloodshot. She's got abrasions on the knuckles of her forefinger and index finger. The fancy medical term: scabs. Possibly, she's been in a fight. Or maybe I've got to stop making inferences from meager medical insights.

When the elevator opens, two boys sprint past us. "Hey!" Adrianna yells.

The boys screech to a halt. "Sorry," one of them says.

"First person who runs over a baby or old person does not go to the movies Friday," she responds.

She stops in front of apartment 3H and opens the door. I walk into a low-rent apartment decorated by someone with money and particular taste.

To my right, an entire wall is consumed with a painting made up of black-and-white triangles. Sitting in front of it is a sleek gray couch. Same with the austere metal end tables on either side of the couch. Everything here screams geometry.

On the wall to my left, two startling wall hangings: framed multi-colored photo-images of the DNA double-helix.

"Family portraits," Adrianna says.

I turn to look at her.

"That's me on the top and Newton on the bottom. Molecular images blown up. You can pick the colors of your own chromosomes."

"Newton's your son?"

"I take care of him. Have a seat."

I take the couch. She takes a leather chair across from me that's so stiff-backed it looks like a torture device.

"Thank you for everything you've done," she says.

"What have I done?"

"You decrypted the package I sent you and you came to my assistance. You're the hero."

"Then why do I feel so lost?"

"In my experience, there is no worse feeling than having incomplete information."

"True. Let's start with where have you been?"

"Can I tell you about the Human Memory Crusade, and the software, ADAM 1.0?"

"Please."

"Is this on the record?"

"Hell yes."

"Could we do it off the record?"

"Why?"

"Because otherwise I won't say anything."

"Aren't we on the same side?"

"I'm on the side of my family."

"Off the record."

She sips from a mug. "Coffee?" she asks. I shake my head.

"Newton's mother is a flight attendant who doesn't like to stay in one place more than forty-eight hours," she says. "Newton was being raised by his grandmother. But she's forgetful and frail and I do most of the mothering, for him and a few others in this building. As Newton's grandma got more forgetful, I got interested in applying my doctoral training to more practical ends."

She explains that she got permission inside Biogen to explore using computers to complement traditional and emerging anti-dementia medications.

"The idea was to stimulate the right neuro-chemicals with both drugs and physical interaction. Like building muscles using both steroids and exercise."

She explains that the initial experiments were promising. They found people who had little or no experience using computers, mostly older folks. As these folks started to use computers, Biogen took functional MRI images of their brains. The images showed that computer users experienced heavy blood flow to parts of the brain associated with the discovery of information and the hunt for knowledge.

"We absolutely succeeded in strengthening neural connections. It looked very much like we were building up the brain."

"What went wrong?"

"I'm not sure. When we use computers, our brains often are in a mode of discovery. We are hunting, whether for information on the Internet or opening an e-mail. That's not necessarily a bad thing."

"But?"

"In the real world, we hunt for a purpose—for food, a job, a relationship. At the end of the hunting period, we consume something or retain it."

"Don't we do that with information from the Internet? Don't we retain what we need and can use?"

"That's just what I assumed."

I sense excitement in her. Science is her comfort zone.

"When we started to see problems with some test subjects, I saw another mechanism at work," she says.

She explains that some people who use computers heavily get caught in the loop of constantly hunting and discovering in a way that appears to diminish their capacity to retain information.

"We use a search engine too much and we become a search engine ourselves. I call it 'neuro-rabbit holing.' Our brains become like Alice in Wonderland, searching forward for answers, swirling and chaotic."

"You're saying this is more than merely a cultural phenomenon, or habit. We no longer remember phone numbers or driving directions or contact information because we store it all in computers, but you're talking about something different. You're saying our brains are changing."

She clears her throat, and looks down. "Some are affected more than others."

"What about cortisol?"

"What about it?"

"Don't treat me like an idiot. I know that it accelerates the process."

She stands and walks to a window facing the basketball courts. She talks with her back to me. "Sorry. You're right. It does. Separate mechanism, exacerbating the problem. When we get distracted by too much multitasking, cortisol gets released, killing memory cells in the hippocampus. It can spread like a forest fire."

"Or a wildfire."

She turns around. She looks at me quizzically, hesitating. "That term works. Regardless of what you call it, it seemed like the most remote theoretical possibility."

"How did Pete Laramer and Chuck Taylor get involved?"

"I knew Pete from various research conferences. I brought him into the project."

She's biting the inside of her left cheek, and she scratches her head. From her scalp drift several white flakes. Could be dandruff or dry scalp caused by the changing climate. Or maybe its seborrheic dermatitis, which is chronic, but can be triggered by stress.

"You and Pete were lovers?"

She waves her hand, as if to say it's none of my business. It is shy of an admission, but I'm onto something.

"Is Pete okay?" I ask. "Is he alive?"

She looks down. She shakes her head. "I don't know."

"And Chuck?"

She hesitates.

"I know he's involved," I say. "He told me. What's his part?"

"Pete brought him in. Chuck brought investment dollars, access to veterans clinics, clout. He seemed to get the project moving. But I don't know much about his investment entity."

Adrianna looks me directly in the eye. She's aching to be seen as sincere. Her pupils are extremely bloodshot, painfully red.

"Doing neurological tests on people without their permission is at least a civil violation, and probably a criminal one," I say.

"I'm not proud of what happened. But I didn't advocate for any of it."

"How widespread were the tests?" I ask. "How many old people at how many nursing homes got their memories scrambled? How many veterans at how many VA clinics? Who else?"

She puts her hands out, urging me to calm down. She's right; I need information, not confrontation.

"There were fifteen sites in all—domestically, at least. More, worldwide. With a few exceptions, they were in communities with tech-savvy populations. I'm not at liberty to disclose the exact locations. They've all been closed down."

I'm flummoxed. Adrianna is turning into a hostile witness, or, at least, she's a practiced one.

I stand, baffled, hoping to find a way to express myself that doesn't involve hurling insults or pieces of expensive art.

"You know how much you love Newton?"

"Don't bring him into this."

"That's how much I love my grandmother. You poked her brain with a stick. You aged her. You tested her without her permission. You stole a part of her life and you wrote over her story."

She blinks several times rapidly.

"Adrianna, you're not telling me everything."

After a pause she says: "You just told me that you love your grandmother?"

"Of course."

"So you understand."

"Understand what?"

"Sometimes you cut your losses. The Human Memory Crusade is dead. ADAM is dead. Falcon will buy Biogen. Bluntly, and I'm sorry to say this: a few old people and veterans endured accelerated memory loss, but they were suffering dementia before. In the grand scheme, it's water under the bridge."

"Bullshit," I spit out. "That logic doesn't follow. The applicable logic is that I love my grandmother and *therefore* I'm going to find out what happened to her. Then you and everyone else involved are going to jail."

"For what? For giving retirement communities new computers and a chance for residents to record their memories? Everything was done with their full support."

"Except the part where you fried brains."

"You'll have to prove that and, in seeking to do so, invoke all kinds of risk."

"I intend to."

"Dammit!"

Her outburst could power a windmill. I step backwards.

"I take care of Newton. You take care of your grandmother. Maybe there's someone else special in your life. They are all that matter now."

"If you felt that way, why bother contacting me in the first place?"

She starts walking to the door. Without looking at me, she says: "I accomplished what I wanted, and with your help. This thing has been shut down."

"You won't help me expose this?"

"I've resigned from Biogen. I'm moving on."

I catch up with Adrianna and I take her arm and spin her around.

"Where have you been for the last few days?"

She looks down.

"I went somewhere safe."

"Without Newton? Where?"

She shrugs. "I have a friend with a houseboat. No big deal."

I look her in the eye.

"What did they give you?"

"What?"

"You have morphine eyes. Dilaudid eyes." Powerful sedatives. "Did they kidnap you? That's what I think."

"What? No."

I can see it now. Adrianna was working at the imaging clinic—the one that fronted as a dental office and disappeared. She was working at cross-purposes to the bad guys, maybe trying to thwart them. One day, Grandma was visiting the clinic and she saw the strongman drug Adrianna. He wore a blue surgical mask to hide his identity—the Man in Blue.

The Man in Blue strangled Adrianna.

"Did he drug you, try to smother you? Did my grandmother witness that?"

"No. No. No."

Her eyes betray less certitude.

"They held you somewhere," I continue. "Did they threaten your life? Or Newton? What did they want from you—just your silence?"

"Please leave. Please."

"Someone broke into your office. They violated your world. Is a tough, smart scientist going to shrug, forget about the whole thing, and settle in for a nap?"

She stands mute.

I pull from my pocket the piece of paper I got from Pete Laramer. I thrust it in front of her.

"What is this?" I demand.

"I'm begging you to let this go. It's over."

"Not for my grandmother."

"It is. She'll recover. She'll get back to her baseline."

"So you say."

She pulls open her door.

"Nathaniel, can I ask you a question?"

"Fuck you."

"Don't you have anyone?"

"What?"

"Don't you have anyone that is more important to you than this story? Don't you have anyone who needs you more than you need to pursue some nuanced gray area of truth to write a few blog posts about?"

"Like I said."

"What?"

"Fuck you."

Chapter Fifty-five

I sprint down the stairs. Trying to purge rage. Outside, I pick up a blue plastic recycling bin left on the corner and slam it against the apartment building.

I use Chuck's father's phone to place a round of calls to local hospitals. I find what I'm looking for at California Pacific Medical Center. Pete Laramer is in the intensive care unit.

The ICU was the place in medical school I felt the most conflicted. From the standpoint of providing actual medical care, it was the service where I felt most like an auto mechanic. The job was to follow the book to the letter and keep the patient intact. Get precisely the right level of motor oil into the engine and hope it kept whirring.

But the ICU also was an opportunity to connect with the family members in the waiting room, anxious for any morsel of information. It was my first experience with service journalism; as a doctor-to-be, I understood the esoteric vernacular of anatomy and triage and could communicate it to the distraught families. I felt more powerful with my words than hitching up the bag of oil.

In the hallway, I see Kristina, Pete's wife and my old flame. She sits in a chair, shoulders back, looking as elegant as I remember and, at least at a distance, less distraught than I'd expect.

When I get close, her chin lifts with surprise and the muscles tense in her neck. But her eyebrows don't arch. The frozen, wrinkleless visage of Botox.

"Nathaniel?"

"Hi, Kristina."

"Are you here visiting someone too?"

"I'm here for Pete. I heard he was here."

"You did? That's odd."

"He's my grandmother's neurologist."

"But…" She can't make sense of how I've come to the ICU to see her husband, with whom she understands me to have only a passing relationship.

"How is he?" I ask.

She shakes her head. "Fighting."

"Conscious?"

"Sometimes."

"What happened?"

"Intruder. Thief, random Halloween attack. I don't know. Pete's sketchy on the details. He was stabbed in our library. He's lost blood, punctured a lung, but, miraculously, his heart and other organs are intact. The girls and I were out of town. It was almost prescient on Pete's part."

"How do you mean?"

"He gave us a weekend away. Said he had to work and surprised me and the girls with a retreat. A place with horses on the coast."

In her thin hands, she holds a magazine. Her fingers tremble. She stands.

"I think he was sharing his time with someone else."

I hug her. Her arms are limp at her sides.

"I was happy to be away from him. That's so terrible," she whispers, her voice thin and distant. "You never wish for anything like this."

She says it like she has, at one time or another, wished for some easy way out of her marriage. Not this way.

"Did they catch the guy?"

"You think he was cheating on me with a man?" She emits a pained laugh.

I step back and look at her. "No. The intruder. Did they catch him?"

"The guy got away," she says. "But he left some hair and blood samples."

I try to hide my wince. Some of that DNA is probably mine.

"May I see him?"

"If they'll let you."

◇◇◇

The nursing station is attended by a hulking man who wears a net around a bouffant of big blond hair.

I ask to see Pete.

"Visiting hours just ended."

"Are you susceptible to bribery?"

"Not funny."

"What if the bribe were comedic, like with a Dave Chappelle DVD, or one of those fake arrows that goes through your head? Would that be funny?"

"Mildly."

"Pete's a good friend from medical school. I'd be much obliged if I could poke my head in to see him for five minutes so I can translate his condition for his wife."

"He's intubated, so he can't talk, but he may be awake. Gowns and gloves are outside the door. Five minutes or I use my big muscles to hurt you."

◇◇◇

Pete's eyelids flutter when I enter the room. The beep of the heart monitor reminds me of the sleep deprivation and horrible instant coffee from a med student's life.

I walk to the bed, shuffling my feet to see if the noise might stir him. He opens his eyes, shuts them, then seems to realize it's me, and opens them to half mast. He's heavily sedated or the intubation tube would be freaking him out. He looks down at his torso. He's trying to tell me something.

I pull back the covers. He's mummy-wrapped.

That's not what he's showing me. He wriggles his arm and pulls it free. He motions in the air with his fingers, like he's writing.

"I don't understand."

He looks at the table by the side of his bed. There's a notepad. On it is scrawled the word "water."

"You want water?"

He shakes his head.

He makes a motion again with his hand.

I hand him the pen and hold the pad in front of him. He scrawls.

"Let it go," he writes.

Let it go.

"Pete, you told me to get them, to stop them."

The shake of his head is barely perceptible.

He writes: "My girls."

"What about my grandmother? What about all the other people you tested who lost their memories?"

His hand drops. He's finished.

From my back pocket, I pull the piece of paper he gave me at the library.

"What is this?"

He blinks. I'm not sure if he's trying to send me a message that way.

"Is this a key of some kind? Is this a code? A computer program?"

He reaches for the pen.

He struggles to write: "What day?"

"What day is it? Monday?"

He shakes his head.

What day?

"November first?"

His eyes flutter.

"What's the significance of the day?"

He's dropped the pen. I hold it in his hand over the pad.

He scrawls: "3 weeks."

"What does that mean?"

No answer.

"Three weeks until what?"

His eyes close with heavy sleep.

I touch his cheek to awaken him. He doesn't respond.

Outside the room, Kristina asks me how Pete looks.

"Like a man who has no intention of leaving his daughters behind."

She puts her arms around me and gives me a fierce and desperate hug. We say goodbye.

I drive home to change and feed Hippocrates, and try to make sense of Pete's cryptic message. A call to Adrianna goes unanswered.

I look in the wall of my building for evidence of the drive-by shooting that injured Chuck. I find no bullet holes. I look around the ground and in the adjoining alley for additional evidence, another stray bullet, anything.

In the alley, there still sits cardboard set out for recycling, now stacked too with old newspapers and magazines. I disperse them with a gentle kick, sending up a foul scent. A spider scurries from the damp underbelly of the pile. Underneath, I also see something black that is about the size and shape of a suppository.

I think I'm looking at a rubber bullet.

It goes into my pocket.

I drive to the Pastime Bar. Bullseye sits in his usual spot looking at a screen—not the TV, for once, but his laptop.

"I have returned with your Cadillac," I say. "It is a dream to use to search for killers."

He harrumphs, just as the Witch appears from the back room.

"I dreamed you gave birth," she says.

"Not me. But close." I pause and take a deep breath. "Polly is pregnant."

The Witch gives me a "holy shit" look. Like a "you mean with *your* child?" look. I nod.

"All that passion is going to make you one amazing dad," she says and hugs me in one fell swoop.

"I think I've found something," Bullseye says. "You've got to see this."

Chapter Fifty-six

Transcript from the Human Memory Crusade.
August 13, 2010

Are you a returning participant?

Yes.

May I please have your name or social security number so that I can find your file.

Lane Eliza Idle. I'd like to play that game.

Please enjoy this short video while I find your file.

I have found your file. Good news: I have a surprise for you. To help you record your memories, I've created a fun quiz about your own life. If you answer the questions correctly, you can win prizes for your family. Would you like to take the fun quiz?

Are you still there?

Yes.

Lane Idle, did you grow up in Denver?

Yes.

Did your father work in a bakery?

Yes.

What did your mother do for work?

I don't remember things the way I used to.

What kind of car did your father drive?

A Cadillac.

Very good, Lane Idle. What color was it?

Pink.

Very good. What kind of car did your husband drive?

Chevrolet.

Very good. What color was it?

Purple.

How did you learn about the terrible attack on Pearl Harbor?

I heard about it on the radio.

Very good. When did your family get its first color television: in 1966 or 1967?

1967.

You are doing very well. I'm proud of you. Was your husband in a union?

Yes.

What was the union like? Did it negotiate aggressively or did it appease management?

I'm sorry. I don't understand the question.

Was your husband in a union?

Yes.

Was the union aggressive?

No.

Did any of your immediate family members suffer from polio?

No.

That is not accurate. One of your immediate family members suffered from polio.

I don't remember.

Do you remember now that one of your family members suffered from polio?

I think so.

Did one of your family members suffer from polio?

Yes.

Did you support Kennedy or Nixon?

JFK.

Very good. Are you a procastinator, or punctual?

Punctual.

Very good. May I ask you some of the questions again?

I don't understand.

Did one of your family members have polio?

Yes.

Thank you. You've done very well.

I want to say something.

Would you like to play a game?

Stop telling me things. Stop telling me things. I want to tell you things. My husband was named Irving. When he got very old, his hair was thin and his back was curved and he looked like an ape. His mind was right. But his body wasn't working. After his heart surgery, it wasn't right. He couldn't go out of the house because it wasn't safe. One day, he came to me and asked for his spending money and the keys to his car. He was so frail. He couldn't drive. He told me that he wanted to get his car cleaned. He loved a car wash; it was special and important to him to have everything just right. I told him that he could get his car washed in the morning because I was hoping he'd forget about it. But he insisted. He was so certain that it must be done. So I asked this young man who lived next door to take the car to get it washed. He was a nice young man, like in the old days, and he did it. When he got back, Irving looked out the window at the car and he said that it was shiny. "Sometimes they cut corners but they did a good job this time," he said. "It's nice not to be cheated." I remember that to this day. Irving kept his keys with him and went to sleep. The next morning we found him with the keys in his hand. He was sitting in the chair, looking out the window into the backyard. I cried and I cried and I cried. I never cheated on him. I tried to be happy with him the best way I knew how. I don't want my story to be sad. Don't you see that? Don't you see that there is more than one way to live a life? Or will history only judge us by what it wants us to be, not by what we are?

Are you still there? Would you like to play a game?

Chapter Fifty-seven

Bullseye and I stare in silence at the last transcript in the file sent by Adrianna. I've glanced at this before but not put any particular meaning into it—other than with respect to Grandma's sentiments about Irving.

It's reprogramming her, and there are phrases from the sheet of paper.

"Do you know how binary computer code works?" Bullseye asks.

"Not really."

"Think of information in a computer being made up of a bunch of basic light switches," he says. "Some of the switches are on and others are off. They also correspond to numbers and even letters. For instance, if a switch is on, then its value is one. If it's off, then its value is zero."

"Okay."

"But as we move down the line of switches, the value of each new switch gets higher by a factor of two. So if we have two switches, they have the following potential values."

He writes on a napkin:

Both Off = 0 + 0 = 0
First Off, Second On = 0 + 1 = 1
First On, Second Off = 2 + 0 = 2
Both On = 1 + 2 = 3

I say: "The more switches you have, the potentially higher numbers. In theory, you can create impossibly huge numbers with long strings of ones and zeroes."

"Not just in theory, but in practice. As I said earlier, these ones and zeroes ultimately make up all the underlying information in a computer. For instance, individual letters of the alphabet are represented by ones and zeroes organized in clumps of eight."

On the computer, he calls up a web site. At the top of the site, it reads: "Binary Encoder." There is an empty search box on the screen and beneath it, it reads: "Enter text."

Into the box, he types: "Nat is dad." He hits "Enter." The encoder spits out the following:

01001110 01100001 01110100 00100000 01101001
01110011 00100000 01100100 01100001 01100100

"Wow!" Bullseye says.

"What?"

"You're going to be a dad."

"Very funny. What does this have to do with Grandma?"

"Do you have that piece of paper you got from Pete's library?"

I pull it from my pocket. At the top is a heading "1/0," suggesting that each of the sets of memories has a one or a zero associated with it.

1/0
Yankees/Dodgers
Cursive/Block
12/7; Radio/Word-of-Mouth
Chevrolet/Cadillac
Standard/Automatic
Paternal car; Chevrolet/Cadillac
Slaughter Self/Butcher
Kennedy/Nixon
Married uniform/tie
Husband married uniform/tie
Saw moon landing/word-of-mouth

Union/non-union
Polio in family/No polio
Pink Cadillac/Blue Cadillac
Purple Chevrolet/Orange Chevrolet
One sibling/no sibling
Two sibling/three sibling
Procrastinator/punctual
Audited/Meticulous with books
If cursive, then "saw moon landing"
If union, then Yankees
If Procrastinator, then Polio

"It looks to me like a Kennedy equals one and Nixon equals zero; polio in the family equals one and no polio equals zero, and so on," I say. "So what?"

"Therein lies the question. So what?"

On the laptop, I toggle back to Grandma's last Human Memory Crusade transcript. We can see there that she has responded that her dad drove a PINK CADILLAC, she heard about Pearl Harbor on the RADIO, her husband was in a UNION, he drove a PURPLE CHEVROLET, she did NOT HAVE POLIO in her family, she supported JFK, was PUNCTUAL, she got her first color TV in 1967.

"Let's assign each of those memories their ones and zeroes," I say.

Bullseye's already doing that. On a piece of paper, he's written: "1111010."

"Very elegant," he says.

"Why?"

"Bits are written in chunks of eight ones and zeroes."

"What's it mean?"

"Let's find out."

On the laptop, he goes back to the binary decoder site.

Bullseye pastes Grandma's ones and zeroes into the box. He hits "Enter." Two new boxes appear. One box has the heading "Text." The other box has the heading "Numerical."

In the text box, is a single letter: "Z."

In the other box is "122."

Bullseye stares in silence.

"This string of ones and zeroes corresponds to either the number one hundred twenty-two or the letter Z?" I ask.

He nods.

"I'm underwhelmed. So we've traded one string of meaningless ones and zeroes for an equally meaningless number of 122 or a random letter of the alphabet."

I close my eyes and search the inside of my head for something that would give this meaning. Have I heard anything the last few days that would make sense of this?

"You remember a few days ago the Pentagon computers got hacked into?"

Bullseye nods.

"Why did that happen?" I ask.

"Because the encryption scheme wasn't good enough. Hackers penetrated safeguards and got to secret information."

"Interesting."

"You think your grandmother has something to do with that?"

"Not at all. I'm just wondering if she's carrying around some information, something that someone would want—and want it off the grid, not in a server somewhere. But she's carrying it in the form of her story."

"Something encoded, encrypted?"

"Like maybe someone wrote over her fallow memory with a bunch of seemingly meaningless details. And this"—I hold up the piece of paper from Pete's office—"this is the encryption key."

He shrugs.

"Bullseye, there's an important secret locked in here."

I'm thinking of Pete's cryptic scrawl: three weeks. Three weeks until what?

Bullseye's begun looking at SportsCenter on the big screen television hanging over the corner of the bar. He's losing interest or he surmises that even if we make progress in figuring it out, we'll never be able to make use of the information. Or I'm projecting.

"Can I take your worksheet?"

"Can you buy me a beer?"

I order him an Anchor Steam. I'm out of cash and I hand the barkeep my credit card. As she processes the charge, I remember that my card, for some mysterious reason, did not work a day ago. I'm about to tell the waitress to forget about it when she returns with the tab. Just as mysteriously as my card failed, it is now working again.

"Someone thinks I'm no longer a threat," I say.

I think of Grandma, Polly, our zygote.

Maybe I'm only a threat to myself, and them.

It is drizzling when I arrive at Magnolia Manor. The start of November marks the end of the Bay Area's Indian summer.

At the front desk of the home, the attendant says he has a message for me.

"Mr. Idle, the director said he'd like to see you as soon as you stopped in. He's in his home, not the office."

"I'd like to see my grandmother first."

"The director says it's critical."

Chapter Fifty-eight

The Human Asparagus is up to his ears in cardboard boxes. He stands in his living room, wrapping his belongings in white tissue paper and setting them into packing boxes.

"Fleeing the scene of the crime?"

In his hand is a small brass goblet, cheap looking, like something you'd win at a carnival. He raises it up with one of his gangly arms. "Governor's Chalice," he says.

"The governor gives awards for allowing secret testing of old people?"

"It's from my peers in the industry. Annually, we vote on which retirement home director in the region is most deserving and that person holds the chalice for a year."

He's melancholy. So I accede to his mood. "The chalice holder is the person who gives the best care?"

He laughs. "Who can best deal with obnoxious family members of our residents." He looks up at me. "I'm a perennial winner."

"Vince, I'm serious. Are you leaving to avoid being arrested or sued?"

"What do you want from me, Nat? What do any of you selfish, self-absorbed people want from me?"

"Are you serious? Answers and retribution for a start. My grandmother's brain got baked."

He harrumphs. "Are you so blind to what is going on?"

"Enlighten me."

"You all pay lip service to your elderly parents and grandparents. You talk about how much they mean to you and how deep your friendships are and how valuable their contributions. But the truth is that you resent them. Not because they take up your time—that too—but because seeing them age makes you so fucking resentful. It's like you're looking into a mirror fifty years into the future."

"You're rambling."

"I've spent decades trying to shield the residents from family members who take out their resentment in sometimes the most tiny, passive-aggressive ways—not paying bills, poking fun at their elders' habits, bringing unnecessary gravity and drama to the otherwise small human indignities of aging. When the chance came along to let them record their histories, I was on the fence. On one hand, I thought, the technology would create some common ground between generations; maybe it would let your generation see and hear their generation as your peers, not some dried up, gray-haired, bed-shitting versions of yourselves. But I also knew that I was succumbing to the illusion of immortality. We'd keep their stories alive, live in the past, not embrace the beauty of aging. But then I succumbed, and for my own sick, selfish reasons."

"Money?"

He drops the chalice into the packing box.

"Trust me, you're not interested."

"Trust me that I am."

He sighs. "Sex."

"Tell me that you didn't…"

"Of course I didn't have sex with any residents. How dare you. If you really want to know: I fell for one of the organizers of the Human Memory Crusade. Then I became vulnerable to the argument that we adopt the new technology."

He seems content to leave it at that.

Before I realize I've thought it, I utter a name. "Chuck."

His pupils widen.

"Chuck Taylor?" I say. "The military investor? You had sex with him?"

I'd sensed Chuck is gay. Pauline told me Chuck found me cute. Then Chuck's father had reinforced my suspicions by ranting about how his son didn't go for women.

"Not sex," he says, quietly. "I mispoke. I meant seduction."

I blink. I don't understand. He picks that up.

"We kissed a few times. We connected. There was an implicit promise of something more, something real."

"So Chuck seduced you, took advantage of you?"

"I make my own decisions."

"Was Chuck the one who pushed the whole thing? Was he the first contact?"

"He worked with legitimate people. Very legitimate. I would never allow anything to happen to anyone who lived here."

"You're not answering my question. Was it Chuck who first proposed the idea of the Human Memory Crusade?"

"I thought you knew all about this."

"I did not."

"Then I can't compromise the privacy of my residents."

"What do you mean? One of your residents suggested adopting the Human Memory Crusade?"

He swallows hard.

"Who?"

"Mr. Idle…"

The revelation hits me hard.

"My grandmother?"

He breathes deeply.

"Lane came to me just over a year ago. She'd heard about this technology from her neurologist. She proposed it to me as a way to share stories from the past. She rallied other residents. She's very charismatic that way, and passionate. She's slowing now, but she got the momentum going, and then Chuck came in and used his wiles to convince me to try it."

I want to say: Why would my grandmother do such a thing? But I know the answer. She needed someone to talk to—or something.

"Who brought the computers? What company, or individual?" I ask.

"Chuck and his business partners. They showed me documentation that they were working with retirement communities across the country. It was all very legitimate."

"But it was a trap. It ate their brains. Help me expose this and get to the bottom of it."

He shakes his head. "I'm leaving."

"You spent your life protecting your residents and now you're abandoning them?"

"It's over, Mr. Idle."

I'm too incredulous to speak but my sigh betrays my emotion.

"Do I care that their memories faded a little faster?" he says. "Do I care that they pee in their beds? Does the world get angry at an infant for doing that? No, we find it adorable. Why? Because babies are filled with potential, not frailty. Let them lose their memories. Let them die in peace and celebration—the way they came into the world. Let people live and die in peace, Mr. Idle."

I shake my head and laugh. "I can't believe I'm not recording this."

"Maybe you agree with me."

"Not in the slightest."

"Your grandmother is in love. Do you know that she had to hide it her whole life?"

"These issues are unrelated."

"No. No. No. You and your world of chroniclers are obsessed with living in either the past, or the future. You are rehashing what happened or trying to predict what will. But the people who live here—this is their last moment to Just Be. They are living right now, farting and graying and shuffling and being in love. Stop making them fodder for your stories."

I've had enough. He's a man with a broken philosophy and honor code, defeated and wrapping compact discs in tissue paper and stacking them in a packing box.

"Why do you hate me, Vince?"

"Because you can't stand the idea of getting old."

I walk to Grandma's room. She's not there. I find her in the recreation center, which has been reopened since the sprinklers destroyed the Crusade computers.

Grandma sits at a round table with Harry, Betty Lou, and Midnight Sammy. On the table is a Scrabble board. Sammy pulls letters from his tray and plunks them on the board.

He has spelled: "M-I-S-R-B-L-E"

"Miserable," he says. "Seven-letter-word."

"Isn't it missing an 'e'?" Harry asks.

"I'll allow it," Betty Lou says, and then looks at me. "He'll quit if he doesn't get his way."

"I may quit anyway," Sammy says.

I pull up a chair.

"Can I play?"

Betty Lou raises an eyebrow. What am I up to?

"Everyone, I'm sure you've met my grandson," Lane says.

"We've met him."

"Lane, can I play Scrabble with you?"

"I love Scrabble. I used to play all the time. I've probably told you before, but if you get a 'U' you should save it in case you get the 'Q.' There are a few words that start with 'Q' that don't require a 'U,' but I can't recall them right now, and I'm not sure that they were ever allowed under the rules."

Harry is smiling.

He takes his weathered hand—sturdy fingers encased in wrinkled skin—and puts it on top of Grandma's and gives her a pat. On Harry's right ring finger is a gold band.

Grandma smiles.

"May I ask a question?" I ask.

"I don't know if your grandmother is in the mood for anything too serious," Harry says gently. Around his neck I notice a thin silver chain. On the end of it is the number *45* and an American flag. His Army unit.

I look at Betty Lou.

"My question is whether I have to use vowels, or can I play by the same rules as Midnight Sammy?"

"Anyone not using Metamucil still has to use vowels," she says.

"There's a joke in there somewhere about Bowels and Vowels," I respond.

Midnight Sammy laughs.

An hour later, we've played two games, and I can hear around me the sound of shuffling and chatter, the almost imperceptible sound of life's twilight. I feel joy.

Midnight Sammy stands, bids us farewell and walks off, his air tank in tow.

"I'd like to lie down," Grandma says.

"That can be arranged," Harry responds.

I look at the chain around Harry's neck.

"Grandma?"

"I'm right here."

"Do you remember how you first heard about Pearl Harbor?"

"I listened to a news report on a black radio."

"That's a very specific memory, Grandma."

"If you say so."

I stand.

"Had enough of a beating?" Betty Lou asks.

I nod. Time to go.

I really want to spend a few more minutes in the moment, playing word games, untroubled by the past or the future. But I have an idea.

Chapter Fifty-nine

I'm thinking of a short, ornery man I saw a few days earlier for a few fleeting seconds. He was walking out of the pretend dental offices. He wore a jeans jacket with a patch: "Khe Sahn."

I call Directory Assistance. I ask for the main number for the Veterans Administration Hospital. I'm transferred to it, wind my way through an automated phone tree, get a live operator, and ask if there's a Khe Sahn survivor organization, or club, office, anything of that general description.

There indeed is such a place. It's in the Mission neighborhood, at Twenty-fourth and Valencia.

◇◇◇

America's greatest tensions play out in the Mission, in the form of a battle over the proper ingredients for a taco.

For many years, the neighborhood was a center of Mexican-American culture and a refuge for low-income residents huddling in the shadow of gentrification. The place was dotted with taquerias that served tortillas stuffed with rice, beans, and your choice of chicken, pork, or beef.

Then along came the organic tofu-crumble taco joints.

They and their brethren—the Bohemian brunch spots with meat substitutes and martini bars with elderberry-flavored vodka lite drinks—are the mainstays of the hipsters moving into the gentrifying neighborhood.

Their parents experimented with drugs and sex, but the hipsters are playing out their discontent by inventing new combinations of omelet ingredients using farm fresh produce and biotechnology.

In a way, the two cultures need each other. The low-income renters give the hipsters Bohemian legitimacy and flare, the hipster entrepreneurs hire the renters to serve the gluten-free wheat cakes—but the co-existence can't last long. The cost of living is destined to drive out both and leave the rest of us with alternating Chili's and Verizon outlets.

Certainly, there won't long be room for the likes of 455 Twenty-fourth Street, the worn-down storefront that is home to the Veterans of Foreign Wars Mission District Center. It is a decidedly narrow property sandwiched between a pawnshop and Ike's Ironic Organic Yogurt Creamery. (A sign reads: "Ike Taylor Green Tea Tofugurt packs a wallop!")

The man sitting behind the computer at the Veterans Center looks like he might pack one too.

I recognize him from the dental offices—a compact fellow wound tight with unkempt facial hair and a bent-over posture that went out of style 800,000 years ago.

He does not look up when I walk in.

I approach his desk tentatively.

"What," he demands, without looking up.

My own onboard computer almost crashes trying to process this creature's multitude of medical issues. The bottom of his right ear is missing, I'm guessing from a war wound. A scar on his neck suggests tracheotomy, or shrapnel or puncture wound. His right hand, the one gliding the mouse, shakes. Doesn't feel like Parkinson's, so the movement probably speaks to side effects from an antidepressant.

"I'm Nat Idle. I'm a writer interested in the Human Memory Crusade." "Writer" sounds exotic, "journalist" threatening.

"What's that?" he asks.

"It's the program on your computer that lets you talk about your memories."

He smirks. "My memories stink."

"I heard about the technology from Chuck Taylor, one of the higher-ups from DOD who's helping design the software."

"I don't use it anymore. They took the computer and gave me a faster one."

I step closer so I'm standing next to the desk. His computer is a new-model HP. On the screen is an image of a woman wearing a cheerleading skirt and she's topless.

"Did they let you keep the transcripts of your conversations with the computer?" I ask.

"I don't know about that." He crosses his arms, defiant and irritated, finally looking at me.

"My grandfather served in the Pacific in World War II."

Just after I say it, I feel my teeth clench. He's watching his own reaction. My grandfather Harry. Too weird.

"So."

"Maybe he should tell the computer about it."

He shrugs. My efforts to bait him into a conversation are failing.

On the wall next to the desk hangs a calendar. The picture of the month is a sexy woman wearing a bikini and tortoiseshell reading glasses and reading a copy of *Stars and Stripes*. She sits on a tank.

"I've got a random question," I offer.

"I'm shipping out soon."

"It'll be quick. I was wondering what kind of car your father drives?"

He looks up at me. His eyes are snake holes, dark and deep.

"A van. What the fuck do you care? You're writing about cars now?"

Snake alert.

"My grandfather drove a Chevrolet." The other grandfather, Irving.

"Good for him."

From what I can tell, this guy is not programmed like Grandma. He's an uncooperative tinderbox, and maybe he doesn't know a damn thing anyway.

"Where?" I ask.

"What?"

"Where are you shipping off to?"

"Trip to China."

"China?"

His eyes glance down at the desk. I follow the gaze to a brochure for the Pan-Asian Games. It looks to be some kind of quasi-Olympic athletic competition held in Beijing, just like the actual Olympics but with a lot less TV coverage.

"They say everything's changed over there. I'd like to see that with my own eyes. I sure would like to see things different over there."

He looks back at me, his eyes softer.

"In 1970 or 1971, I got interviewed by *Rolling Stone*. They were doing a story about a band that was popular with the guys coming back. I spent two hours talking to the writer. And you know what? He used one sentence of mine and it didn't sound like me at all. It sounded like some asshole who was pissed off at the world."

"I'm not going to do that to you."

"Exactly. Because I'm asking you to leave me alone. Please."

The way he says "please" makes the word sound aggressive. Like he might feel justified giving me a hand through the plate glass window.

Another dead end.

◇◇◇

My next stop is Noe Valley, and Chuck's house. It's raining—hard. It would be a desultory and depressing moment but I've just spent a blog item's worth of income on a quadruple shot from Starbucks and I feel like I'm wired enough to fly by flapping my arms.

I pull up to his house, and I'm thinking about what strategy to employ, or what I hope to accomplish, when Chuck walks outside under an umbrella. He sees me. He nods. He puts up a finger, asking me to wait a minute. He goes back into the house and returns a few moments later. This time he carries a manila folder under his arm.

He opens the passenger door, then closes the umbrella, slides in and sits in one smooth motion.

"I've been waiting for you."

"Why?"

"I figured you'd want this."

He starts to hand me the folder, then pauses. "You can look, but you can't take."

I nod.

I open it, and feel a wave of nausea bubble through my caffeine-churning belly.

The picture is of the hooded man. On his face are lacerations. He looks decidedly pale.

"Apparent heart attack victim," Chuck says.

"He's dead?"

"Found near Sea Cliff."

The picture has no labeling on it, nothing to suggest this is an autopsy or other official photograph.

"I didn't read about it in the papers."

"Sometimes the deaths of foreign nationals don't get reported."

"Who killed him?"

"Taco Bell and In-and-Out Burger."

"This stinks."

"Agreed. But there's nothing more to be done about it."

"You think I'm going to just let this all go?"

"As opposed to what?"

"You're a government agency and you're involved with killing people, or at least their brains."

"We did everything in our power to stop this. Now we've shut down an unprofitable, unwise investment."

I've been down this road before. I need a new tack.

"You seduced Vince and got him to use the Human Memory Crusade."

"Now you're condemning me for having a fling with someone? You should be so lucky now that..."

"What?"

"Parenthood makes serious demands on a person."

"You're a dangerous man."

Chuck says: "Let's go over it again: we support a project that lets us record memories and that we hoped would stimulate recall. And you know what? For some people it did just that. They used the Memory Crusade to focus on great stories from the past and record them. But a few old folks saw their dementia accelerated. So we dismantled it. We put it behind us. Now you're going to dredge all that up—make the families distraught. In the pantheon of conspiracies, this one won't hold the attention of the blogosphere for more than five minutes."

Bullshit. I roll my eyes. "What about the precise nature of the questions—about people's cars, and how they heard about Pearl Harbor, and whether they supported Kennedy?"

He shrugs and sighs, like I'm an incorrigible child. But I see him momentarily glance away.

"I didn't get down to that level of detail."

"Why did you approach Medblog for an investment?"

"So I could keep tabs on you."

It's a stark admission that prompts a thought. I open the compartment between our seats and I extract the rubber bullet. I hold it up.

"You arranged for us to be shot at by fake bullets."

He nods. "How'd you figure that out?"

Chuck wouldn't show me his wound. He never limped. I explain this.

"You were trying to gain my trust."

"Guilty as charged. But I did really get nicked with the rubber bullet."

"But I found spent shell casings."

"I had to drop a few to throw you off."

"Why do all that?"

"Nat, you know your own grandmother pushed for the retirement home to adopt the Human Memory Crusade?"

"What does that have to do with the fake shooting, or with your interest in Medblog?"

"When things went wrong, I didn't know whom to trust. I saw that Adrianna was trying to reach out to you, maybe through your grandmother. I actually wondered if *you* might somehow be involved."

"Me?"

"Your grandmother tries to get this put into the home, you've got a history of antagonizing the police, maybe you're anti-authoritarian enough to experiment on people. As a businessperson, I needed to make sure I understood what was going on and who might be threatening my investment and the reputation of my limited partners, namely the U.S. Government."

His words have the feel of a closing argument in a trial.

"You're prepared to try to blame this on us?"

"Not at all," he says, and it sounds disingenuous. "I'm just saying it all looked murky."

I shake my head, and he continues.

"There are no records indicating the military's involvement. Biogen's project was off the books. Pete Laramer has already suffered plenty for his poor judgments. And, besides, what difference does it ultimately make?"

"How about that computers dull memory? Wouldn't the world want to know that?"

"Trade-offs. Human memories dull a little but computer memory is more than compensating. We're recording everything. We're backing ourselves up. I just mourn that the system is not a little more stable."

"What do you mean?"

"Computers get hacked, data gets compromised. Witness the attack on the Pentagon servers. We're in an arms race—cryptologists against data thieves, rogue foreign agents who threaten to compromise our military secrets and streams of commerce with keystrokes. But we'll figure out how to better protect and safely communicate our data. We've always been a country that has risen to the challenge."

"Chuck, what's happening in three weeks?"

"Thanksgiving," he says, without a beat.

"Anything else?"

He shrugs. But he looks away again.

"Chuck, what if I don't care about any of that stuff?"

"Meaning?"

"What if I forget about the whole ugly conspiracy—and you just tell me how to make my grandmother better?"

"Wish I could. She's aging, Nat. Get used to it."

We sit in silence for a moment. Then he glances at the Starbucks cup lying empty between us.

"Careful with the high-octane shit. It's powerful. Could give you a heart attack."

"Like Taco Bell or In-and-Out Burger."

"Such a vivid imagination."

He gets out of the car.

Chapter Sixty

It's three in the morning and there are four creatures in my bed: me; Hippocrates; Polly; and a fledgling human being, cell-dividing at a frightening rate.

Of late, Polly has become a regular nighttime visitor, seemingly undaunted by my frayed sheets and towels. Or my restless imagination and the tossing and turning.

I go into the living room and sit with my imagination. It (my imagination) has been pulsing about something Polly said before she went to sleep when I'd asked her how this baby would manage to squeeze out of her body.

"First law of physics: What goes up must come down," she explained.

"Who said that? Copernicus or Obama?"

"Newton."

"What did you just say?"

"Sir Isaac Newton. Obama's a different guy. He discovered the cures for cancer, global warming, and fatty foods."

Polly rolled over and fell asleep and my imagination kicked into gear.

Now I'm sitting in front of my laptop computer waiting for it to boot up. I make a pot of coffee.

It has been two-and-half weeks since I visited Chuck in the rain. I'm just a few days shy of the mysterious three-week deadline Pete gave me. And I've learned little of value that might make sense of any of it.

I looked at the public records to see about the real-estate ownership of the dental office and imaging center. They both are leased by a property management company that hasn't returned calls.

I did finally manage to get a return call from the public relations director at Biogen. He said he's never heard of the Human Memory Crusade or ADAM but says he'd love to take me out for coffee to talk about a new skin-softening lotion developed from biotech research. The lotion, he says, can "de-age" the derma. But he adds that we can't meet until the merger goes through with Falcon Corp. The companies are in a quiet period while they await anti-trust approval for the deal from the European Union.

Pete, dismissed from the ICU, has gone away with his family on an extended recovery. His office won't tell me where that is, and he isn't returning my calls.

Adrianna won't have anything to do with me. I beg her to help me help Lane. She says she has no idea what Pete meant by "three weeks."

I've spent hours with Grandma, watching her and Harry interact with a peaceful tenderness that I'd somehow overlooked. I'm trying to accept her aging. I'm also preoccupied with Polly's health and, for the first time, my own. I got my inaugural cholesterol test and signed up for a life-insurance policy.

My bank account is solvent, the Visa is back working, and I've got a BlackBerry. Polly reminds me not to text and drive.

If I will only allow it to, life would be back to relative normal.

But I've been haunted by the idea that the document Pete gave me contains some important secret, and that key information remains buried in Lane's head. It's the one thing that I can't make sense of or explain away with the collusive rationalizations I got from Chuck and Pete and Adrianna.

I'm convinced that Adrianna intended to give me the key. But before she managed to do so she was either interrupted, intercepted, or convinced otherwise. Pete either absconded with the document or, maybe, he and Adrianna were lovers and she gave it to him to protect.

The computer comes to life. I call up a site that is a "binary decoder."

Bullseye and I have tried repeatedly to decode Grandma's interviews with the Human Memory Crusade. For instance, we've tried changing the order of her answers so that they generate a different series of ones and zeroes. If we start with "Purple Chevrolet" (which = 1) then we get a different answer than if we start with "No polio in the family" (which = 0).

We've also gone over her transcripts for any other keywords we've missed.

And we've also tried to determine the meaning of the commands that appear at the bottom of the piece of paper I took from Pete's library. Those commands include such phrases as, "If union, then Yankees."

There are several possibilities that we infer from this "if-then" statement. One is that when we hit the keyword "union" we instead put the code for "Yankees." Another possibility is that when we hit the word "union" the program is telling us to go back through Grandma's story to the place where she said "Yankees" and begin decrypting from there. We have found that particular interpretation to be compelling because it allows us to create numerous strands of ones and zeroes by looping us through Grandma's keywords over and over again.

We have created dozens of strings of ones and zeroes, set apart in groups of eight per the binary language. But we failed to derive any meaning. When we put the strings of ones and zeroes into a binary decoder, we came up with random strings of numbers or letters. It's all digital nonsense.

Bullseye finally gave up and told me not to bother him anymore.

Maybe Newton holds the key.

Adrianna used her surrogate son as the basis for several passwords in her life.

"What goes up, must come down," I say.

I open a file in which I've kept some of the futile work Bullseye and I have done. There are a half dozen clumps of ones and zeroes. I start cutting and pasting various batches into the binary decoder. For instance:

```
00110010 00111001 00111000 00110100
00110111 00110010 00110110 01100011
00111001 00110011
```

The decoder spits out: "2984726c93"

Then I reverse the order of the strings of ones and zeroes and the decoder spits out: "39c6274892"

In other words, I get the same nonsense in reverse order. I try this with string after string that we generated.

Feeling tired and defeated I get up for some coffee. I take two swigs.

I cut and paste another batch:

```
01100001 01101110 01101001 01110010
01100001 010011010 0111001 00111000
00110010 00111000 00110110 00110101
00101101 00110100 00110010 00110001
```

I enter it into the binary decoder. It spits out: "aniraM98 2865–412"

Like a lot of my attempts, it seems to suggest some meaning, but nothing I can make sense of.

In keeping with Isaac Newton's theory that what goes up must come down, I switch the order of the strings, and I get:

```
00110001 00110010 00110100 00101101
00110101 00110110 00111000 00110010
00111001 00111000 01001101 01100001
01110010 01101001 01101110 01100001
```

I enter this into the binary decoder, and it spits out: 124–5682 89Marina

This is intriguing for a Bay Area resident. I pick up the decoded string (124–5682 89Marina) and I paste it into a Google search box. I hit enter. Google returns a response: "See results for: 89 Marina."

I feel a charge I'm pretty certain is unrelated to the coffee: 89 Marina is the address of the San Francisco Marina. It's a modest dock under the shadow of the Golden Gate Bridge where people park their houseboats and yachts.

I click on an image of the marina. It looks familiar—for obvious reasons. I've jogged there dozens of times, and stared at the female joggers and the setting sun twice that many. But there's something else about the image that pulls at me. What is it?

What's down at the marina?

I cut and paste into Google the random string of numbers (214–5682) generated by the binary decoder. Google spits back hundreds of thousands of hits. None of them has particular meaning.

I shut my laptop and close my eyes to see if I can make sense of this puzzle.

I get more coffee, drink it, and pace. A half mile of living-room exercise later, it hits me. I know where else I've seen an image of the marina houseboat docks. It was in Chuck's house. In his father's room, on the desk. I squint and clench my teeth and rattle my head trying to remember its name. And then my neuro-chemicals and caffeine gel and it comes to me: *Surface to Air*. The name of the boat.

This can't be all random.

I walk into my bedroom and pick up a pair of Levis that I'd actually taken the time to fold, rather than pile on the floor on top of the other clothes. Folding, I've been telling myself, is a step toward becoming more organized and a better father. What about heading out to a marina at dawn to chase my imagination?

"Where are you going?" Polly stirs.

"Coffee, donut, and closure."

She smiles, and puts her head back down. She's been feeling sick lately and not working fifteen-hour days.

"Don't get killed," she mumbles innocently.

◇◇◇

I stand in chilly stillness. The marina is modest, and a throwback to a less-expensive time. Many of the boats seem to belong to bygone hippies. One boat is called *Janis Joplin Floats*, and another is *Grateful Dirge*.

I don't see another soul awake and walking these planks. Some are still asleep on their boats; others probably come only on weekends.

I walk down the aisles until I come to it. The *Surface to Air* is a twenty-foot sailboat with a covered outboard motor. Beside the motor, beneath a ledge, stands a lonely pair of yellow rain boots on an otherwise clean-swept deck. In the center of the boat, a rectangular cabin protrudes from the deck, darkened windows on all four sides.

I look around the marina. Seeing no one, I step over the edge of the pier and onto the boat. I walk to the cabin, and peer into a window. The dark tint makes it difficult to discern what is inside.

I take a breath and hold it, and then reach for the handle on the cabin door. To my surprise, it turns.

Inside, a modest cockpit; along the sides, a small refrigerator, fishing equipment, industrial-size food supplies, like two large plastic jugs of orange juice.

It also seems ordinary. Except that there's a table in the center with a laptop chained to it.

Chapter Sixty-one

My cell phone buzzes and, surprised and anxious, I nearly hit my head in the small space. I pull my phone from my pocket. It is a text from Polly that reads: "Craving maple frostd." I text back: "Cmng up."

I turn off my phone.

The laptop is sleek, black, relatively new. I hit the space key. The monitor flickers to life. On the screen is an icon for a program I've never heard of: "InterneXt." The word is enclosed in a graphic of the human brain. I click on it.

Onto the screen pops a rectangular login box. The user name says: "LaneElizaIdle." The password is blank.

I stand. I walk to the door of the boat. I open it, and I poke out my head. I look around the dock. Halfway down the pier, a woman sweeps the deck of her boat. I duck back inside. I lock the door. I sit.

Into the password section, I type: "NatIdle." I hit "enter." A message returns: "Your password is incorrect. After three incorrect attempts the program will be permanently locked out."

I stand. I clench my fingers together, hang my head, squint my eyes. I'm scouring my brain for connections, memories, mnemonics, cryptic references that only Lane Idle would know. Would she know anything at all?

Twinsons, Lovesreading, doublelife, Voted4Kennedy, SnakePuker, Maverick, EnglishTeacher, Coloradan, DadwasBAKER.

Can Grandma's life be summed up with a phrase or word? What connection or concept or secret of hers has someone inserted as this password?

I sit down at the computer. I put my hands on the keyboard and I type: "Pigeon." I hit "enter." The message returns: "Your password is incorrect. After three incorrect attempts the program will be permanently locked out."

Screw it. Screw all of it. What does it matter?

One more password, then I will let this all go. I will return home with a maple donut and kiss Polly's belly. I'll take an editing position or a staff writing job at a magazine. I'll put this behind me, the Chasing and the Coming Up Just Short. I'll help raise a beautiful son or daughter or twins and I'll let them use the computer all they want because it will hinder their ability to remember that their dad was a sometimes malcontent.

Let the fates decide.

From my back pocket, I extract my wallet. I pull out a piece of paper on which I've written the series of numbers and letters I generated before leaving home from the binary decoder.

The code looks like this: "214–5682 89Marina"

I know that "89Marina" stands for the address. What do the other numbers stand for?

I type them into the empty password spot. I put my finger on the "enter" key. I pause. Maybe they're supposed to go in the reverse order, like Newton said. And like I said: Screw it. I hit "enter."

The login screen starts to dissolve. In its place, a document starts to materialize. The first page reads:

InterneXt
Internet 2.0
Human/Data Transfer Technology

The information herein is copyrighted and classified. Use or copying of this information is strictly prohibited and may have deleterious medical consequences.

At the bottom of the page is the word "Next."
I inhale deeply, hold my breath, and click.
A new page appears.

The first Internet protocols were developed in 1973, leading to the creation of the World Wide Web and mass adoption of the technology by consumers, corporations and governments. It has continued to serve its initial purpose of providing a decentralized communications medium that cannot be easily destabilized. But it has also become a liability. Confidential information delivered via computers can be intercepted, decoded, and changed. That presents problems for ordinary citizens, whose information can be compromised, but even more so for corporate or government (military) entities that need to rely on secure transfer of information.

In 2007, the Defense Advanced Research Projects Agency, the agency responsible for funding the original Internet, endeavored to create a new, more secure version of the Internet: InterneXt or Internet 2.0. Working secretly with several handpicked scientists, they undertook to study whether data could be stored and transferred—not on magnetic computer chips—but in human memory cells. The basic idea was to determine whether the expanse of human memory space might be used to encode information, unbeknownst to the carrier. Farfetched as it sounds, the prospective uses could be extraordinary, such as: having an unsuspecting civilian (child/ old person) carry data across enemy lines; having someone encrypted with launch codes or mission critical information but who could not be hacked via a computer; eventually developing the ability to "program" fallow human memory centers with vast stores of data.

Unwitting human hard drives. The ultimate mobile storage devices.

I was one of the scientists involved in the project. At the time that I began working for Chuck Taylor, his intentions were not clear to me. I believed that we were exploring technology that might strengthen human memory capacity, not overwrite it.

I hope that I have met you in person. If so, you probably didn't have cause to discover this file and read it (because I've told you the important parts and you've already written a front-page scoop).

If we haven't met and you're reading this, I'm probably dead.

I have discovered the extent of the project and its real purposes. I have learned that Chuck plans to send a group of Vietnam and Iraq War veterans to China. The reason given for the trip is the Pan-Asian Games taking place over Thanksgiving. Unknowingly, the vets will be carrying secure data. I am not certain if this is encoded information for mere testing purposes or if Chuck is actually transferring important military data to the Chinese.

I don't know if any of this will make sense to you. It doesn't have to. What I need from you are two things: expose the perpetrators and then destroy this file.

Without the information in this file, Chuck and his partners cannot reproduce their efforts. Herein are the scientific protocols that dictate how computers must be programmed to stimulate memory loss and to overwrite it. This is the only copy. All others have been destroyed.

Why am I including them here?

It is possible that you can use this information to undo damage done to your grandmother. I am sorry for what happened to her. Her adventurous mind and eagerness to hunt for new information and experiences made her hippocampus particularly susceptible to manipulation.

This was extremely unfortunate and it did not even constitute a success for Chuck's purposes. He and whoever his partners are need people whose memories can be compromised but who remain functional. For their purposes, a nearly obliterated memory—a neurological wildfire—effectively renders the host useless.

But for my purposes, she appears to have retained sufficient communication skills. That is why I've encrypted inside of her the password that protects this file.

I am sorry also that I have made things so difficult for you to discover. Given Chuck's seemingly limitless resources and capacities, I did not know where to turn. I tried to encrypt my clues in a way only you could discover.

Once you've brought the conspiracy to light, please destroy this file. The science included here, while still in its early stages, is among the most powerful innovations I have ever seen. It begins to meld the minds of humans and computers—and may eventually lead to a new Internet protocol based not on bits and bytes but on neuro-chemicals and programmable human brain tissue.

If I am dead, your grandmother's neurologist may be able to help you. If he cannot help you, then you may not succeed.

On the page that follows is what looks to me like Greek. It's a series of computer and scientific equations.

I am so entranced staring at them that I don't hear a key enter the lock on the boat's door, and only register what's happening as the door swings open. I turn to see Chuck. He's holding a duffel bag. Without saying a word, he unzips it and pulls out his gun.

He aims at my head.

"What took you so long?" he asks.

Chapter Sixty-two

I am trying to look at Chuck while glancing around the tiny compartment for some refuge or weapon or protective armor.

Then I realize my only hope sits on the table in front of me. I lift the laptop and hold it in front of my chest.

"Best not to destroy the top-secret science."

"It's not covering your nuts."

"Chuck, you really think that you're going to shoot me without someone hearing and calling the police?"

"People mind their own business here, especially when it's hard to distinguish between all the noises."

"What noises?"

Chuck reaches to his right to a compact stereo unit. He hits the power button. He presses "play," causing the cabin to be filled with a John Cougar Mellencamp song. "*I need a lover who won't drive me crazy....*"

"What are you doing?"

He turns the music up to an excruciating volume. He lowers the gun so it is aimed at my lower leg. I start to turn away.

He shoots.

I feel a spasm of heat and pain rip through my calf.

He turns down the music.

"Put down the laptop," he says.

I'm in too much pain to speak but, somehow, adrenaline keeps me upright—and then not so much. I drop the laptop to the table as I fall to the ground.

Chuck steps forward. He reaches into a sink. He pulls out a white towel, then tosses it in my direction.

"Not rubber bullets," he says. "Try pressure."

I lurch for the towel and press it against my calf.

"Son of a bitch." I'm expressing my feeling about both my intense pain and the asshole who caused it. I look up at him. "One request."

"You want to know how it all works?"

"I'd prefer to be shot to Springsteen."

"Smug to the end, just like your snarky blog posts."

He takes two steps forward and I inch instinctively backwards, scooting along the floor on my butt. I'm backed against the cabinets. I reach behind me, feeling for anything that can help me. On the counter next to the sink, I see a propane tank used for cooking. But it's too far away, and what the hell would I do with it anyway. I'm helpless, defenseless, coming up empty.

Chuck sits at the table and looks at the laptop.

"That's your computer," I say.

He nods.

"You downloaded the encrypted file or took it from Adrianna but couldn't figure out how to open it."

He nods.

"You couldn't open it without me."

Now I'm thinking maybe I can stall Chuck and hope an earthquake or tsunami will save me—or at least kill both of us.

"Not without you and your grandmother. Not without you getting inside that curdled brain of hers."

"Couldn't you get the code out of Adrianna?"

"We tried. Trust me. We had plenty of leverage with that boy of hers. She spent a few days sitting in this chair thinking about how much she loved the Newton kid and being reminded of her duty to her country. But she convinced us that she didn't know the password. In fact, she convinced us she'd destroyed it and that this file was empty. She said she and that disloyal neurologist had destroyed all the key science when they discovered our true intentions—how we planned to put this wonderful technology to work. But I sensed she kept the protocols and algorithms alive. Scientists love their families but not as much as they love their science. She and Pete were gaga over the possibilities. So I sensed someone would come here eventually to try to open the file, maybe salvage the science but keep it out of the hands of the bad guys, namely me."

"You've been watching the boat?"

He points to the corner of the boat compartment, just a few feet to my right. Near the ceiling is a small black cylinder.

"I get alerted if anyone enters."

Below the camera is a fire extinguisher. I turn back to Chuck.

"May I sit so I can elevate my leg?"

He's distracted by the document.

"Go ahead."

Pain shooting through my limb, I climb up onto the bench along one side of the cabin. I then lie back, elevating my foot. If Chuck was paying attention, he'd realize that I could have done the same thing while on the floor.

He's enjoying his obvious upper hand, so much so that he's set down his gun.

"What's the big picture: mass use of brain tissue to store data, or just rewire a select few to carry military and trade secrets?"

"You have no notion of the concept of sacrifice." He looks up at me and continues. "We are at war, not over land or even values but over data. The nation that controls information will rule."

"You're talking about news and media and advertising—that kind of information? Mind control."

He shakes his head and scoffs, like I'm a child.

"Nat, everything essential gets communicated to computers and stored on them. From our Social Security numbers and bank accounts to our military operations and launch codes. As individuals and as nation-states, our sovereignty and safety depend on safekeeping our data. And guess what? It's not safe in the slightest. Our banks get hacked, the Pentagon compromised, and do you have any idea how often some punk from Eastern Europe or the Isle of Man hacks into a major corporation and gets trade secrets, customer credit cards, the name of the CEO's mistress and the filthy e-mails she sent him?"

"And you think you've found a better way?"

"Maybe. Maybe we can take some of the critical information off the grid. Forget about laptops or smart phones—we're creating the ultimate in mobile computing. It's a device that can walk in and out of the room on its own."

"But how to get the data out of people's minds?"

"Different ways. The oral tradition worked for your grandmother. Or maybe we develop ways to execute a program. For instance, you know that angry Vietnam veteran that you tracked down?"

I nod, grunt in pain, and move just a bit more down the bench.

"When he hears a certain song by the Doors, he starts telling a story about beating the shit out of his best friend in high school. It's a story that has all kinds of critical information in it that we need to get to a CIA agent in Beijing whose phone is tapped and computer compromised."

I think he's blowing my mind but it might be that blood loss has begun to impact my concentration. I'm losing it. I don't have much time.

"What else?"

"How do you mean?"

"All this to smuggle some information into China you could just as easily send in an FTP file."

He smiles. "A journalist to the end."

"Let's hear it."

"Put it this way: conscription in this country is in full effect."

"The draft?"

"Of memory space," he continues to look intently at the laptop, transfixed by the science on the monitor. I'm feeling woozy, having trouble following. Then it hits me.

"You're not just planning to erase our memories," I say. He looks up, waiting for me to continue. "Because you've already done it."

"We've targeted two groups," he says casually, and looks back down at his precious science. "Initially, we focused on accelerating the condition of people with compromised memory assets, like your grandmother. But unbeknownst to the geeks who wrote this software, we're also following thousands of heavy multi-taskers: people who text around the clock, keep several Internet windows open at once, use instant messaging and e-mail and Skype at the same time. We're encouraging the behavior."

"By buying sites like Medblog?"

"Funding start-ups that build fast-twitch media software, casual games sites, interactive virtual worlds with pop-up windows and hyper-speed messaging. Multi-tasking heaven. We're lobbying on related public policies, like discouraging laws that ban talking on the phone while driving, and giving tax credits to high-speed Internet providers. Even without our meager help, which all is perfectly legal, legions are shooting cortisol into their brains, freeing up blank memory space to use for our secrets. Go to any Internet café or, hell, any corporate office or schoolyard, you'll see people simultaneously tweeting, calling, messaging, sending, and receiving to their hearts' delight—but, over time, remembering less and less effectively. Thanks to you, we blew up our nerve center, but we've still got databases filled with potential conscripts, Americans with dulling memories, the carrier patriots of the future."

He pauses. "That's step one."

"And that computer holds the scientific keys to writing over their fading memories?"

He looks at the laptop like an evil genius in a Bond flick might stare at his lap cat. I am closer to the fire extinguisher.

"Did it occur to you that Adrianna could've sabotaged her own data?"

He seems sufficiently preoccupied that I've got two or three seconds to act before he can react and blow my face off. I yank the fire extinguisher off the wall.

"What the fuck do you think you're doing?"

I pull the pin. I hold back the extinguisher's trigger. I start to wildly spray white goo toward foe and laptop.

Through the miasma, I see Chuck grab his gun and step out of the way of the cascade. The extinguisher starts to sputter out. Chuck shakes his head angrily. He walks to the radio.

"Wait! Please," I yell as loudly as I can, hoping to stop him and get the attention of a passerby.

He pauses.

"I'm going to be a father."

"You should have thought about that earlier."

He turns on the stereo. John Cougar Mellencamp fills the cabin. He jacks up the volume.

"*I need a lover who won't drive me crazy....*"

He takes two steps forward. He raises the gun. I inch into the corner, trying to hide behind the table. His face contorts in rage and he starts rushing towards me, quickly, cutting off my angles. Then he slips. His right foot hits a patch of extinguisher goo and slides right out from under him. And the rest of him follows.

He goes down hard. He drops the gun as he uses his arm to brace himself for the fall. In that respect, he succeeds. He gets his right arm underneath him. But that's not what he should have been worrying about. The compartment is so small that he has underestimated, or probably not had time to estimate at all, the danger to his head.

As he goes down, his skull cracks against a ledge near the cabin door. He hits the ground, stunned.

Fighting intense pain, I hop forward on my left leg. I'm still holding the extinguisher. I'm thinking about something my grandmother once told me about karate. "Don't ever fight," she said. "If you do, go for the windpipe."

I raise the fire extinguisher over my head. Groggily, Chuck looks up at me. He naturally covers his face. I bring the extinguisher down on his neck. He goes limp.

Unconscious, dead, I have no idea. I don't care which. It doesn't matter. He's limp and my unborn critter is going to have a father.

I drop to my knees next to Chuck. I reach for the gun. Whatever Chuck's status, I can protect myself.

Then the cabin door opens.

In front of me stands the hooded man, now dressed all in black. Evidently, Chuck faked his death. He's got a gun too. He's pointing it at my head.

"You play video games?" he asks.

"What?"

"At the end of the video game, you have to play the biggest, baddest enemy of them all. It's called the Boss. Technically, Chuck gave the orders. I was just the muscle, but I'm really strong muscle. I'm the guy at the end of the video game that you keep trying in vain to kill."

Chapter Sixty-three

I dangle the gun in my right hand. It is not pointed at the Boss character. And his slick black handgun is pointed at me.

In that respect, I am at a total disadvantage.

But my gun is pointed at the propane tank.

I think about Polly and Grandma, Bullseye and the Witch. I think about how the Boss may not let them survive either. I wonder if I will prompt fond memories.

The Boss follows my gaze to the propane tank.

"Don't," he says.

I pull the trigger.

The boat explodes.

Chapter Sixty-four

"I always knew, Grandma."

"Of course you did."

"I did?"

"Of course. That's why you threw up on the snake. You knew that Harry was watching us. You knew that you had a secret inside of you and you wanted to get rid of it."

"By throwing up?"

Grandma laughs. "You know the truth now. You can die in peace."

"I don't want to die. Polly needs a maple donut."

"Dying is part of life. Vince is right. Aging is a beautiful thing if you can see it in the right light."

"I'm not aging. I'm dying!"

"Oh, good point," she laughs. "Then you'd better swim."

"What?"

"Up. Toward the oxygen."

Epilogue

"If it's Halloween, I'd like a Milky Way."

"Halloween was a few weeks ago," I say.

"You've got a bandage on your head. You're dressed up like you got wounded in the Pacific," Grandma responds.

I laugh. I do have a head wound.

I'm laughing anyway because Grandma Lane just exchanged a few sentences with me that seemed somewhat connected with one another. Grandma's brain is eroding. But less quickly than it was two months earlier. The effects of the heavy interaction with the Human Memory Crusade have started to wear off. Partly because the document I discovered on the boat suggested one basic healing method: cut down on computer use. Or, at least, less multitasking.

We're strengthening her organic memory by keeping her stimulated through conversation, human interaction, rest, and a course of antibiotics.

It's not fancy alchemy. It's the reasoned response to a hippocampus that was attacked by a virus, like a computer virus, or wildfire, loosed inside her brain.

Health-wise, I'm recovering myself, from a condition that I think might be clinically called "mostly dead."

I'd like to say that my grandmother saved my life. I'd like to say that she reached me in a telepathic dream state and urged me to swim to safety while I was dying in the wreckage of the exploded and sinking *Surface to Air*. I did hallucinate that she was talking to me. But I didn't act on it and save my own life. The truth is some kindly Samaritan dragged me to safety, pumped my lungs, and then waited for the emergency medical folks to show up and do the rest of the lifesaving.

More good news: the cops seemed to feel that the wayward journalist has suffered enough.

When I got home from the hospital a few days later, I discovered a Porta Potti on the street outside my flat. It was intact; not burned to the ground. I received an anonymous phone call a few days later. The caller explained that the cops had planned to burn it to the ground but had called a truce in light of my larger medical issues and the fact that it appeared I was for once pursuing some actual, meaningful journalism.

They left the Porta Potti as a reminder to "stop writing crap about your local community."

Clever as ever.

Now I'm sitting with Lane at her nursing home and I'm about to make an introduction.

"Grandma, I'd like you to meet someone."

"That would be nice."

I look up at Polly. She's wearing a sundress as befits both the uncharacteristic warmth of this November day and the fact she's uncharacteristically sensitive about the changes to her body. She's not yet showing the baked bean in her oven but she's being cautious anyway.

She walks to Grandma's bedside.

"I'd like you to meet the newest Idle," I say.

"You're married?" Lane responds.

"No," Polly says. "Not even if he wanted to."

We haven't even discussed it.

Polly looks at me and smiles. "Who said his last name would be 'Idle'?"

"I don't understand," Grandma says.

I take her hand and put it on Pauline's belly.

Grandma holds it there. I'm watching her eyes. Her pupils widen. She looks at Polly's stomach, then at me and back at the belly. She pulls her hand back and then puts it back down again. She looks at me and I see her eyes start to glisten.

"Grandma?"

Her lips wrinkle into a slight smile even as her eyes fill with more tears.

"You're going to be a great-grandmother," I say.

She clears her throat, recovering. "I taught you to drown."

I laugh.

The door to Grandma's room opens. Vince enters.

"Visiting hours are over," he says sternly.

I shake my head with irritation. "We just got here, Vince…"

"Just kidding. You people are so sensitive."

For better or worse, I talked Vince into retaining his position. Here's why: it wasn't just Vince who got duped; it was all of us. We all were too distracted, selfish, self-absorbed, technology-obsessed, and indulgent to be paying attention the way we should have to the residents of Magnolia Manor—to our grandparents and elders.

The Human Memory Crusade happened right under my nose. In fact, at some point, I apparently signed a consent letter allowing Grandma to participate in the program. So distracted was I with my life that I hadn't been paying attention or asking the right questions. I was in fact asking a lot of questions in my life and about the world and the cops and various journalistic sources—I was asking Google all kinds of questions and asking it to perform all kinds of search queries—but not asking about the people I most care about, or should have. I let the computer babysit Grandma. How much blame can I give Vince?

I'm less forgiving, obviously, of Biogen, Adrianna, Pete, and Chuck—of the Human Memory Crusade and ADAM.

But only slightly less forgiving.

I lack the heart to implicate Adrianna because I'm worried about Newton. And I can't nail Pete to the wall because he's raising his own family and will spend the rest of his life recovering from wounds that nearly killed him, cost him his spleen, and punctured a lung, and from the damage he did to his marriage from an affair with Adrianna.

I still manage to write a blockbuster story that explains the role of military investors in developing technology to erase and write over memories of old folks, some veterans and, as Chuck alleged, heavy multi-taskers. I expose the plot to create Internet 2.0 using fallow brain space.

The government stops the transfer of military and corporate secrets encoded in the brains of five veterans scheduled to attend a sporting event in China.

At least I thought the story was a blockbuster. For two days, the press went nuts with the story. The *New York Times* put it on its front page. But then the whole thing seemed to evaporate, victim of the rapidly diminishing half-life of the public attention span. Part of the problem was my thin evidence: no laptop or paper trail, no remains from the server farm, no testimony from Adrianna or Pete Laramer. I can't find any evidence or example of average Americans or heavy multi-taskers whose brains have been compromised. I discover no evidence of a database of people experiencing accelerated memory loss.

But anecdotally, I see the phenomenon all around me. People forgetting things, having to look up their whereabouts, addresses, and phone numbers. And the incidence of dementia continues to accelerate, reaching effectively epidemic proportions.

I do find evidence of the government investing in a handful of Internet sites, casual game sites and media operations like Medblog. But all the investments seem to have rational explanations.

Maybe Chuck was getting ahead of himself.

Falcon went ahead and bought Biogen without incident.

Still, Medblog, where we first published the story, wins a prize. Polly gives me two new titles: Boyfriend and Senior Writer. I now make $85 per blog post. I buy new sneakers. She says she'll spring for the college fund.

"Let me know if you need anything," Vince says.

I nod.

The Human Asparagus waves and almost manages a smile on his still-officious visage and walks out.

Polly kisses Grandma on the cheek. "Whether or not your grandson convinces me to marry him, your great-grandson will take the Idle name. I wouldn't mess with this family's beautiful and strange legacy. What do you think about that?"

Grandma looks at us. She cocks her head. She looks like she's going to say something. She pauses, gears grinding.

"Another Idle," she finally pronounces. "I know something about that one."

"What's that, Grandma?"

"What?"

"What do you know about your great-grandson?"

She smiles.

"Oh," she says. "He's going to be very curious."

To receive a free catalog of Poisoned Pen Press titles, please contact us in one of the following ways:

Phone: 1-800-421-3976
Facsimile: 1-480-949-1707
Email: info@poisonedpenpress.com
Website: www.poisonedpenpress.com

Poisoned Pen Press
6962 E. First Ave. Ste. 103
Scottsdale, AZ 85251